Worse Than Murder

A Food Truck Mystery

Inspector Grimes Rhymes with Crimes # 1

Fred Aronson

To J and L and C

(Order determined by coin toss)

###

This book is a work of fiction. Names, characters, places and incidents are either the product of the author's imagination or are used fictitiously. Any resemblance to actual events, locales, organizations, business establishments, or persons, living or dead, is entirely coincidental.

Copyright © 2017 by Fred Aronson

ISBN 978-0-9831401-5-3

Visit the website: www.WorseThanMurder.com

All rights reserved. No part of this book may be reproduced, scanned or distributed in any printed or electronic form without prior permission in writing from the author, except in the case of brief quotations embodied in critical articles and reviews.

PART I

1. Shutter Down

"THAT'S ODD," I SAID TO MY friend and downstairs neighbor Wilbur as we approached Chauncey Chambers' food truck, Chauncey's Chow.

"Yeah, the side shutter's been pulled down," said Wilbur. "Must have just closed."

"And it's only 2:15, for God's sake," I said. "On the edge, but still lunchtime by my watch."

Disturbing. I couldn't speak for Wilbur, but it had been over a week since I've had Chambers' sugary, salty, and spicy sweet potato fries. Comfort food at its best. He uses some rare heirloom sweet potato variety he gets from a farmer friend in Missouri. The fries are coated with peanut oil and oven-roasted. There are hints of smoked paprika. I can't eat enough of them. That's why I get a large order. The jury is still out, but they may even beat Butter Bar's sausage gravy fries. How rich was I to have two top-notch food trucks—Chauncey's Chow and Butter Bar—within walking distance from my apartment? That is, when they're open for business.

"Isn't he here 'till four when he sets up in this part of town?" said Wilbur. "Rodney, what on earth was that noise?"

A loud crash inside the truck sounded like someone had hurled a fifty-pound sack of heirloom sweet potatoes into that rickety shelf of lattice-pastry-topped raspberry-apple-crumb pies I'm always eyeing on the truck's back wall. Then more loud noises with intermittent shouting, then a muffled *plumphh*, then quiet. As I grabbed the handle of the driver's-side door to see what was going on inside, someone jumped behind the wheel and started the engine. The truck and my arm jerked forward a foot or so. I think I shouted *Ow!* Then *Hey! Stop! What's the idea?* A gun behind the window, pointed at my face, shut me up. The gloved finger on the trigger seemed magnified tenfold. I started to wish the window were down. Being struck by bullets *and* flying glass wouldn't exactly make my day. The truck's gears were ground, the right gear found. The truck sped off. I was clever enough to let go of the handle before it did.

Wilbur and I could only look at each other and at the empty lot.

"That wasn't Chambers behind the wheel, was it?" asked Wilbur.

"Not unless he lost about seventy-five pounds in the last couple of days," I said, once I stopped shaking, "and started wearing a ski cap, thick-rimmed glasses, a mustache, and beard. I think we just witnessed a kidnapping."

Wilbur suddenly pictured leaving water running in his bathtub and needed to rush home. That didn't surprise me. He does that often. I went to the police. Told them who I was and what had happened to Chauncey Chambers. I even demonstrated some key evidence: the limited range of motion in my right arm.

"So you're the guy who writes those detective stories with that Inspector Grimes character," said the desk sergeant. "Me and the boys have read a bunch of them. You got quite an imagination, don't you? Sure that actually happened today? This isn't about promoting your series, is it? Sounds like something I remember reading in one of those books."

"I know what I heard, and saw, and felt," I said.

While he spoke, the desk sergeant was dabbing several

layers of a three-part form with white correction fluid. "I stopped by Chauncey's Chow a few days ago for a bowl of chili," he said. "The best around. Chambers' secret ingredient: dried Thai basil. Don't tell anyone I told you, but it makes all the difference."

Only last week, Chauncey had confided in me that his chili's secret ingredient was fresh sweet basil.

The desk sergeant continued. "Anyway, Chambers told me he was about to take his truck on the road. Expected to sell a lot of his famous kielbasa and onions at some county fair. So there's nothing to worry about, my boy, but thanks for coming by."

Two weeks passed. Still no Chauncey's Chow.

2. The Crimson Stigma

THE TALL, STYLISH WOMAN with killer curves entered my apartment like she owned it. She looked as if she had stepped off the cover of some pretentious fashion magazine, sporting a fitted jacket, straight mid-calf skirt, high heels, and silk scarf. She was stunning, yet I took an immediate dislike to her. And I like people. Some people. Remind me not to open my door again to strangers at 12:27 p.m. on a Monday, or at any time, for that matter.

"You're Rodney," she said. "Pen name Randall Reed. Am I right? Author of the *Inspector Grimes Rhymes with Crimes* mystery novels. The Grimes who solves crimes before they happen, who finds clues even where none exist?"

The woman not only knew my name, she stood much too close for comfort. Then it hit me. "And you're Maris Chambers, the third wife of Fern Creek's eccentric comfort-food cook and TV celebrity, Chauncey Chambers." I said that with a bravado I didn't think I had, especially since she was taller than I was and would likely take me in a fight. "Terrific food truck—Chauncey's Chow—though lately I haven't seen hide nor hair of him or his truck." I chose not to mention my wrenched arm or that guy's gun barrel in my face. At least, not yet.

"How do you know who I am?" she said.

"The subtle aroma of sautéed shallots on your clothing, a scent that stays in your kitchen despite your husband's recent absence and your maid's constant efforts to get rid of it. Isn't your husband known for sautéing shallots, when he's home, for the inspiration he says it gives him?"

Was I on a roll, or what? If only Inspector Grimes could have come to life just then to see how I handled her. He'd surely be impressed by my shallots remark. Why admit that I had been watching TV last spring when Chambers introduced this woman as his new wife on one of the shows broadcast from his food truck?

"I need you to find my husband," she said, handing me what appeared to be a ransom note scrawled in reddish-orange ink. "It came two weeks ago. I'm afraid to think what they might do to him."

"I'm an author, not a detective. Call the police."

"No police, no private eyes, no reporters, no publicity. You created Grimes—you must have the skills to find Chauncey."

Something about this situation seemed familiar. As my loyal fans read in *The Crimson Stigma* when it rolled off the press a few years ago, Inspector Grimes is shown a ransom note like that in a back alley of Istanbul by the wife of a wealthy spice merchant. Grimes determined that the 'ink' had been a concentrated solution of saffron threads in rose water, pointing to a culprit in the culinary arts. That might be the case here as well.

"Take a seat," I said, showing her to a cushioned chair. I sat opposite her.

"I don't know who the hell's behind this," she continued, "but they must be stopped. Money's no object." She opened her purse and removed a thick wad of hundred-dollar bills.

When I edged closer to the money, an item in her purse caught my eye. Though only a glimpse, it was a rewarding one. A corner of an envelope bore the distinctive gold emblem signifying the Grand Duplex Suite of the Cunard Line's *Queen Mary 2*. Strange time for a cruise if it was just booked.

I wondered if money *was* the object. As was the case in

Stigma, the wife here stands to inherit millions if her husband is declared dead. But she couldn't collect until he's proven dead—until someone with Grimes' abilities proves him dead. Her refusal to involve the police or a real private investigator was bothersome, like she has something criminal to hide. The woman was waiting for me to act. If I smoked a pipe, I would purposely have fumbled attempts to light it, as Grimes would do to buy time.

I could have simply gone for it, borrowing Grimes' tactic in *Stigma*, and right or wrong, accuse her outright of arranging for her husband's disappearance and his murder. Adding that her highly cunning co-conspirators have now turned against her and done a skillful job keeping her in the dark these last two weeks as to his whereabouts—or, I should say, his remains. That they are not ransoming his life but offering proof of his death. But what evidence did I have that she was complicit in his disappearance? None at all. Except maybe a reservation for one person on the *Queen Mary 2*, if it was a reservation for one. I decided to test the waters.

"I'm afraid your plans for a posh cruise as a pitiful widow are a bit revealing," I told her, adopting Grimes' signature, matter-of-fact tone.

She shot up. "I expect my husband to be returned safe and sound. His TV fans need him returned safe and sound. I must be mad to have come here!"

I stood as she started out the door.

"Incidentally, it's lunchtime," I called after her. "The Butter Bar food truck is right down the street. My treat."

"Now I'm sure I'm mad, or maybe you're the one who's mad," she said from the hallway.

I called a little louder. "Butter Bar. Great macaroni and cheese. I can ask the cook to add sautéed shallots."

But she was gone. What the devil was wrong with me? My, er, Randall Reed's novel-in-progress suffered from lack of inspiration, and sales charts for previous titles had lately been pointing east-southeast. Next month's rent was once again coming due. It'd been six years since I quit my supervisor job at Crawley's Market to write full-time. Now it looked like I might need to go back.

I could have kicked myself for not taking the case. My gut shouted stay away, it wasn't clear that woman could be trusted, yet I could have had a bunch of hundred-dollar bills for merely playing detective. But maybe all was not lost. She wasn't telling the police that her husband vanished, so I could eat crow and accept her money or look into it on my own. Success would bring publicity for my mystery series, and new ideas for current and future novels would be worth a fortune.

I knew precisely where to start. In *The Spurious Kumquat*, Grimes ties the kidnapping/murder of a kumquat grower to the deranged owner of a rival kumquat grove. Maybe I could connect the disappearance of Chauncey Chambers and his food truck, if not to a ruthless third wife, then to a competing food truck, now the town's *only* food truck—namely, Butter Bar.

3. Most Likely to Rant

Can I tell you about Butter Bar?

Aside from the possibility that its cook arranged Chauncey Chambers' kidnapping, then murdered Chambers with the razor-sharp butcher knife the cook uses to slice onions, I'd bet there's no finer food truck than Butter Bar in any nondescript, mid-Atlantic region, two-bit town like Fern Creek, except maybe Chauncey's Chow. (By the way, no one should ever move to a place with only two regular restaurants and fanatically health-conscious ones at that.) I stumbled upon Butter Bar a month ago, about two weeks before Chambers' food truck disappeared.

Butter Bar occupies a small piece of undeveloped land in Fern Creek's business district. If you can call one main street with a smattering of stores three blocks long a business district. It's always in the same place, on Beacon between Warren and

Sinclair, crammed between a low brick building selling Sidney's Handbags and a two-story frame building housing Ye New Antiques. Not much to the setup. There's no motor—Butter Bar has to be towed. A bright yellow-and-red exterior draws in the customers. Four leather-covered barstools are put out each morning, then taken in late afternoon. Inside the truck, a pint-size stainless-steel grill sizzles behind a long Formica counter. So far I've had breakfast or lunch there about a dozen times.

Customers sitting at the counter have no idea what the cook looks like from the front, though he stands just five feet away. He never turns around. Still, it's clear from his back he's someone to be reckoned with. Given his professional football offensive tackle build, I get the feeling he can crush a competitor or a customer with one hand. Chauncey Chambers wouldn't have had a chance.

Comfort food's my obsession, but I have no worries about calories. I never seem to add weight to my 5' 8" frame, which has one big advantage—I can still wear my size medium *Lotsa Bacon* sweat shirt from my high school days. Butter Bar's food is not its only attraction, however. There's the waitress. Her nametag reads *Ginger* ☺. Tough, gruff on the outside despite her pressed pink uniform, she's as good as can be, I bet, on the inside. Even though Chauncey's Chow was Butter Bar's sole competitor, I can see Ginger pleading with the cook to stop wringing Chambers' neck. By the way, Chambers runs his food truck by himself. No waitress.

Ginger's a pro. She never fails to set the cream in front of me the moment she serves me coffee. To keep the cream nice and fresh, it's stored in a small refrigerator under the counter. She puts it away once I use it but brings it back when she pours my second cup. So efficient. I expect she'll try bringing me 'the usual' in due time, but why order the same dish when there's so much to choose from?

Although it *is* hard to pass up Butter Bar's banana buttermilk pancakes. Always on the menu. Two breakfasts ago, I caught a glimpse of the cook sprinkling his hot griddle with wheat germ and strategically placing on it several sets of banana slices, allowing all to sizzle for a few minutes. He then ladled on buttermilk batter, which expanded over and around the bananas into perfect five-inch circles. The pancakes magically rose and bubbled. As their edges began to glisten and lift away from the surface, he flipped each pancake, one after another. I nearly blacked out from anticipation, revived only by the sight of butter softening over the hot, golden-brown stack Ginger placed before me. I made short work of that dish, I assure you. The pancakes, that is.

The morning after the Chambers woman's visit, I hurried the six blocks to Butter Bar from my second-floor apartment in Fern Creek's Van Dyke Estates. I slid onto the second stool on the right, the only open seat. "Hi Ginger. It's me again. Rodney."

Blank stare from Ginger.

"I was a year ahead of you at Fern Creek High. Remember? You were voted Class Secretary, they named me Most Likely to Rant. A mere sixteen years ago."

"That's the third time you've reminded me," she said. "What'll ya have?"

I am nuts about her voice, a delightful combination of scratchy and perky. "It's two times."

I watched as Ginger stuffed a huge pile of napkins into a small napkin holder. It's hard to get through to her, but I will, one way or another.

"Anything serious between you and Cook?"

She looked the hulk of a cook up and down, then laughed.

"I hear Chauncey's Chow is nowhere to be found," I said, watching closely for any kind of reaction. "Doesn't harm your business any."

"Don't know nothing about it. So what'll it be, sport?"

"Happen to know of any vacant apartments nearby, especially across the street? I'd be sorry to leave Van Dyke Estates—you know their motto, *Nobody Hates...Van Dyke Estates*—but I'd like to be closer to you, I mean Butter Bar, I mean all the breakfasts and lunches. It's not like I want to spy on the cook."

Ginger's eyes opened wide, then glanced back at the cook. "You'd be smart to ditch that idea," she said.

That sounded like a warning. Was she concerned about my health—too much of Butter Bar's butter and cream—or was the cook involved with Chambers' disappearance and Ginger was protecting him?

"Keep an eye out for apartments, will you?" I said, choosing not to ask what she meant by *smart*. "I heard your Blowout Breakfast is today's special. What's in it?"

"Waitress-squeezed orange juice..."

I pictured squeezing this waitress squeezing OJ.

"...all-anyone-can-eat buttermilk biscuits, sunnyside-up eggs from our favorite hens out back, maple-smoked Hidden Valley ham, sweet paprika hash-brown potatoes, a fork-split English muffin with grade AAAAA country butter, and a bottomless cup of coffee."

"Sounds good. I had been worried because there are two things I can't eat for breakfast—"

"Made up your mind?" she asked, looking like she had something better to do.

"...lunch and dinner." Okay, I told a crummy old joke, worth a try. But she wouldn't even spare a chuckle. "One more question, though."

"You out to give me a hard time? What'll it be?"

"How does coffee stay in a bottomless cup?"

"Take these if you're so worried," she said and plunked down a bunch of extra napkins in front of me.

The bottomless cup, no problem. The Blowout Breakfast, memorable and satisfying.

"Oh. And one doughnut to go," I said before heading home.

"All we have left is glazed lemon poppy and toasted coconut apple crumb."

"Surprise me."

You already know I write the *Inspector Grimes Rhymes with Crimes* mystery novels using the pen name Randall Reed, and when I'm not eating, or thinking about eating, I'm writing. Lately, though, it's mostly thinking about writing. I've won numerous awards, much too many to count—in my dreams. And get this: I sometimes write in pen and ink on a late-nineteenth century lap desk. It has a slanted velvet surface and compartments for inkwells, dip pen holders, and nibs. I also work on parchment paper, and by candlelight, even in the daytime. Why do that? Because with shades drawn and lamps off, a captivating aura takes hold as my eyes adapt to the warm glow of the flickering flame (although it flickers only if I blow on it, which I have no reason to do, or if the overhead fan is turning). Then there's the slow repetitive process of dipping the pen, placing the point down just so, and stretching ink across the page. I literally touch each word. Not a word can be taken for granted. Not one gains admission solely to up the word count or fill space. That would tend the finished work toward floccinaucinihilipilification, though I try to avoid long words like that. They use too much India ink.

My phone rang. I was sorry I picked it up. It was my publisher.

"Where the deuce is the rest of your manuscript?" she said. "I better have interrupted a fiery writing session."

"Do you realize what you just did?" I asked. "You just interrupted a fiery writing session!"

4. Hatchet Man

I DIPPED MY PEN TO PUSH ME to start writing before it dried, and before she called again. Now, what was the tall, gaunt Inspector Grimes with a distinctive—okay, aquiline—nose up to when I last sat down to work?

"Hello, what?" said Inspector Grimes, finding five words scrawled with red crayon across the mirror in Charles Cooper's London townhouse bathroom. "A message, from Cooper, I believe."

"If so, a rather obscure one, Inspector," said Detective Watley. "*That which cannot be seen.* What could it mean? Not much help, if you ask me."

"Seems that way on the surface, my friend. But I predict Cooper has brought us closer to solving the Spice Murders."

"A gruesome business, that," said Watley, momentarily covering his rugged, square jaw and bushy moustache with one hand as he was wont to do when a case made his flesh crawl. "The kidnapping, ransom, mutilation, and murder of celebrity chefs in London. And poor Cooper, now the latest victim of the Spice Murders, even though a sizable ransom had been paid for his return."

"If what had been dumped on the townhouse steps was, in fact, Cooper. His estranged wife—surprise heir to his substantial fortune—could barely recognize what remained of the body. You seem distracted, Detective. A tuppence for your thoughts."

"I so adored Cooper's steak and kidney pies. The other night at his restaurant in…er…but where to from here, Inspector?"

"The Mangle, Cooper's country estate, tucked away in dense forest in the West Country. According to his valet, Cooper, feeling his life in imminent danger, told the valet that a journal hidden at his estate contains clues to the perpetrator of the Spice Murders."

"Perpetrator?" said Watley. "That elusive and dastardly miscreant, Jon Johns, I suppose."

"These heinous deeds were orchestrated by Johns, I would wager," said Grimes, "but they would have been carried out by Johns' hatchet man, Drago. What we need is proof, which the journal might provide."

"Sorry I…"

I knew I should keep at it, but a dash to the kitchen for the doughnut I got at Butter Bar couldn't hurt. I opened the bag. Surprise. Toasted coconut apple crumb. Back to work in thirty seconds.

"…can't accompany you this time," said Watley. "Prepaid fishing holiday and all that sort of rot. But I know The Mangle. *British Country Life* featured it in a spread recently. Magnificent house, and huge. I trust it will be a fool's errand for you to search it alone, much less to find the journal."

"You may be right, my good man, but I will have help."

"How so?"

"Cooper's last words—*That which cannot be seen.*"

Inspector Grimes felt relieved with Detective Watley off on a fishing holiday. His close friend and colleague was often clumsy and sometimes got in the way. Besides, Grimes cherished some alone time.

The estate had seldom been used of late and its overgrown access road prevented Grimes from reaching the house by car. He trudged on in the dark, his flashlight struggling to follow the remnants of a gravel path. It would be over a half mile through thicket and thorns to the main gate. After a time, Grimes pushed open the massive front door—Cooper's valet had given him the key. His first impression: Bizarre family portraits, including a number painted on wood panels in the 1600s, had a lively effect on what appeared to be an otherwise eerie and dreary house.

With three main floors, an attic, and a cellar, Grimes figured there would be thirty-five rooms to search.

"*That which cannot be seen.* Where shall I start?" Grimes asked a portrait of a young soldier holding a sword pointing down to his right. "Ah, ha. Downstairs to the kitchen, it is," said Grimes.

He began by inspecting every inch of the estate's kitchen, pantry, and staff dining room, finding a hidden compartment in a revolving china cupboard, a false bottom to a pickle barrel, and a trap door under a pie safe leading to a subterranean passage. But to no avail. Several of his other discoveries throughout the house seemed promising, but sadly missed the mark. A marble statue of Aphrodite next to the grand staircase was so well balanced that gentle pressure on her left shoulder caused the piece to tilt sideways, uncovering a concealed drawer filled with gold coins. Coins yes, and gold no less, but still no journal. A fireplace lacking any evidence of soot raised a red flag, but the secret safe room behind it yielded nothing except a seated skeleton holding a soup spoon over a bowl long since devoid of any nourishment. To a small degree, the inspector started to regret Watley's absence, thinking his friend might have inadvertently discovered the journal by knocking over some priceless artifact or stumbling on a turned-up rug to expose yet another trap door.

Next, a visit to the library. An ornate room crammed with thousands of books on row after row of elaborately carved bookshelves.

"A smashing place to hide one's journal," said Grimes, even though that soldier's portrait was out of earshot. "If only Watley were here to plod through all these books while I smoke two pipefuls or three."

The bookshelves were set so close together one could barely glimpse The Mangle's legendary frescoed ceiling from any point in the room. Perhaps it is this glorious ceiling that *cannot be seen*, thought Grimes. On a whim, he cleared several shelves near one corner of the room and climbed his makeshift bookshelf ladder until he had a full view of the ceiling. From all four corners, small stone gargoyles glared at the bookshelves. Three had the same orientation. That of the fourth gargoyle, the one next to Grimes, was unique. A lack of dust at its base proved someone had shifted it, and recently. Did it hold a clue to the whereabouts of the journal? Grimes noticed that this gargoyle's line of sight intersected two books in the library—one on the fifth shelf in the fourth row of bookshelves, the other on the second shelf in the third row of bookshelves. The first book—a rare advance edition of *The Hound of the Baskervilles*, replete with hand-tipped pencil illustrations signed by Sir Arthur Conan Doyle himself—led nowhere. But when Grimes grabbed the other book, a hatch in that bookshelf's base sprung open. He reached in and came out with...nothing. The newly revealed space—dead empty.

Time to press on. *That which cannot be seen*, the inspector reminded himself once again. He continued searching room after room, finding sliding wainscot panels, revolving armoires, and removable floor boards until seeing his reflection in a gilded mirror in the conservatory caused him to immediately stop and act on what he did not see. Grimes only saw his reflection—the mirror glass itself *could not be seen*. He removed the mirror from the wall and slid off its back panel. Cooper's journal. And there written in bright red ink on its middle folio, an incriminating list of names, dates, and amounts. The evidence Grimes sought!

At such a late hour, he was desperate to get some sleep—the list would have to wait. The next morning he dressed and made his way down to the kitchen. It is a pity Watley's not here after all, he thought. There's dangerous business astir and Watley is never without his Webley revolver.

Given the ever-present chill in the house, Grimes' immediate requirements were a wood-burning fire and a hot cup of tea. Passing by the small dusty cabinet in a kitchen alcove where he had left Cooper's journal the night before, he was shocked to see the book now out and open to its center stitching. Grimes knew he had closed and secured it in its tooled leather pouch and hid it beneath the cabinet's false bottom. He lit a silver candelabrum to supplement the dim light.

"How extraordinary." He couldn't help but say it out loud. The middle folio with the evidence had been ripped out. Left in its place, the sign of the Spice Murders—three black raven's feathers cradling several red threads of saffron!

Grimes grabbed a large butcher knife from the kitchen and braced for he knew not what.

I checked my watch. Better stop writing and feed the fish. Why such concern? I had attended a mystery writers' symposium last month and my fish went three whole days without food. That still haunts me. Maybe that's why I now drop in too many flakes. But even if they're forced to skip a meal every once in a while, it's not such a bad life. No predators (except for certain other fish). And the temperature's a constant seventy-two degrees. For them, I guess it's like living in San Diego.

5. Gravy-Induced Hoax

My beeline for a combination late lunch/sleuthing session at Butter Bar stalled when I ran into Wilbur. He was out walking with Harry, also a friend. Harry's my mailman. Wilbur's a…actually, I don't know what he does, or did. He once mentioned something in passing having to do with many years at flight school, though I'm not sure whether it had anything to do with his career or someone else's. It's an aside, but you'll rarely see Wilbur without a tie.

"How would you like to be up there?" I asked Wilbur, glancing toward the sky as a plane flew by. I shouldn't have said that. I should have been more sensitive to the fact that there have been a lot of layoffs recently in that field, and that he was out walking early afternoon, on a Tuesday, holding the classified ads section of the *Fern Creek Gazette*.

Wilbur didn't respond, adjusted his tie, then asked, "What's that in the air?" He sniffed several times before he and Harry continued on. I watched as they walked away. They looked as different as night and day—Wilbur, thin, just under six feet; Harry, stocky, just over five—while they act much the same. I often ask myself why I pal around with them. Except for the occasional gem, their ideas and opinions typically defy logic. Then again, so do mine.

Wilbur said it. There *was* something in the air. Butter Bar onions frying? It couldn't be—Butter Bar's the only food truck left in Fern Creek and still over three blocks away. But around the next corner, the sight of a new food truck jolted me.

Blackeye Pete's. Set up in a large open lot that had been empty for years. Gaudy banners from the truck to nearby lampposts shouted *Grand Opening.* Unlike pleasantly old-fashioned Butter Bar, Blackeye Pete's was motorized and a dreary gray green, quite different from Butter Bar's bright yellows and reds. The name was spray-painted across the front. Crudely drawn dirty-yellow flowers on the roof and sides were a failed attempt to liven it up. Not appealing. I hesitated when the cook motioned me over. He looked tough and lean and mean, with no excess anything. Would he get the best or worst of it in a match against Butter Bar's cook? He seemed friendly, but his voice lacked conviction.

"We're Blackeye Pete's, best comfort food in town," he said, while holding out a tray of chicken salad sandwich samples. "Try one. We opened yesterday. Peter I. Black's the name, but you can call me...Peter I. Black."

I inched closer to decline the samples. "Sorry, can't." I was a Butter Bar and Chauncey's Chow regular. It didn't feel right.

Black's face reddened, frightening me. And when his gum-chewing waitress nametagged Mabel winked at me, saying, "Hi, cutie. What'cha doin' tonight? You have a steady girl, or are you lookin' for one?" I moved back a few steps. But in the end, I couldn't resist the free chicken salad sandwich samples, even from a uninviting place like Blackeye Pete's, which led to my hunkering in to try a full Blackeye Pete's lunch, pulling up my collar so I wouldn't be recognized.

Feelings about Butter Bar loyalty took a backseat. Before I looked at their menu, this Mabel gal served me one of the highest 'mile-high' meat loaf, mashed potatoes, gravy, and green beans platters I had ever seen—it even rivaled Butter Bar's—along with a wicker basket full of hot, buttered buttermilk biscuits. And she passed me two soft cotton napkins, one for using and one for my lap, saying, "There's plenty more where these came from, sweetie, for any gravy mishaps."

I tried some gravy. "Rich and savory."

"That's Pete's signature gravy. He sells it, but here, take home a jar."

I pounced on the meat loaf and when Mabel came by for me to preview the higher than the meat loaf slice of lemon meringue pie she said she saved for me, I couldn't help but wink at her.

"There's a hint of Ginger in the pie," she confided.

I wouldn't swear she included the capital *G*, though after my first glorious forkful, oddly enough, it tasted like Butter Bar's very own lemon meringue. I left Mabel a healthy tip, which she promptly stuffed down her low-cut T-shirt tucked into her short shorts. She's no Ginger, that's for sure. Last time I left a tip on Butter Bar's counter, Ginger scooped it up and dropped it into a donations box for the Orphaned Kittens and Puppies Fund. But then again, there's Blackeye Pete's meat loaf and lemon meringue pie, lemon meringue pie and meat loaf, meat loaf and lemon...

Harry and Wilbur came by my apartment that evening and they were stunned as I filled them in on Maris Chambers' visit and my experience at Blackeye Pete's.

"I called the Chambers woman," I said. "I apologized for acting so cocky and told her if she wants her husband found, Grimes and I are the only ones who could do it, and to meet me at the riverside park benches tomorrow at 9:00 a.m. And to bring lots of cash. I said if today's *Fern Creek Gazette* is upside-down on my lap, that signals the coast is clear. If it's not, then she should walk on by and we'd arrange another meeting."

"Is that tomorrow today's newspaper or today's newspaper tomorrow?" asked Harry.

"Good question, Harry. I think that's why she nixed my

park bench idea and wants to meet at her house instead."

"What's your fee as a hotshot P.I.?" said Wilbur.

"More than I get as an author, and more than it would have been only yesterday," I said. "The disappearance of Chauncey Chambers just got a lot more complicated. Now there's a second food truck in the picture: Blackeye Pete's."

"I can't vouch for Butter Bar's cook," said Wilbur, "but it's hard to believe Ginger would help getting rid of Chambers."

"Ginger? My feelings, for sure," I said. "As for Butter Bar's cook, there's more there than meets the eye. As for Peter I. Black and Mabel, your thoughts are as good as mine."

"Anything concrete to go on?" asked Wilbur.

We were sitting around my kitchen table staring at the jar of Blackeye Pete's gravy at the time.

"Can you freeze gravy?" asked Harry, absentmindedly.

"What do they charge for a jar this size?" asked Wilbur.

We examined the label more closely. Tasty design. It said *Blackeye Pete's Signature Gravy* with a colorful drawing of a gravy pitcher pouring gravy over a mound of hot, buttered mashed potatoes.

"I need this for my gravy label collection," said Harry.

Before Wilbur and I could stop him, Harry had peeled off the label. And what was underneath? What surprised the heck out of us? Another label with the exact same drawing, but this time under the words *Butter Bar Signature Gravy*! I looked from Wilbur to Harry. Wilbur looked from Harry to me. Harry looked from me to Wilbur. We were dumbfounded, thoughts frozen in place.

I tossed and turned all night about this new wrinkle: I had to know if Blackeye Pete's was selling Butter Bar food as its own, like the gravy and lemon meringue pie and who knows what else. And if so, why? If it was only because Peter I. Black lacked competency as a comfort-food cook, why open a food truck, of all things? Wouldn't that say there was a more serious type of illicit business afoot? Like Peter I. Black getting rid of Chauncey Chambers and his food truck and then cashing in on the expected surplus of comfort-food-craving customers?

I started to formulate a plan to expose the possible gravy-induced, comfort-food hoax when Harry called. Early, not yet 7:00 a.m., but he still called. Said he was curious if I was awake. I confessed I had shady signature gravy on my mind and was poised to make a move. "It's full-speed ahead on this," I told him, "as soon as I feed the fish and meet with that Chambers woman."

"Find some way to watch Blackeye Pete's operate from the inside, from the cook's side of the counter," said Harry. "Then, do the same with Butter Bar. Let me think. A wild idea, even for me, but it could work. What if you were some sort of repairman rushing over to fix Black's broken grill, the grill that had conveniently crashed at the height of a Sunday breakfast rush?"

"A repairman, on a Sunday?"

"Well, even though it's Sunday, your repairman character is not off on Sundays. He takes off Mondays and Wednesday afternoons unless there's some emergency for which he charges double. Of course, this entire plan probably means first completing an accredited restaurant appliance repair program at some technical college, then opening up shop, building a clientele, etc. Black would hear about you by word-of-mouth because you'd be the best grill repairman in town. Black would call you that Sunday when his grill goes on the fritz. You'd fix it. Customers would be pounding on the counter for their food. He'd forget you were still standing there, but if he does notice you about to watch him prepare food, or not prepare it, you could start fumbling around working out his bill."

I knew I shouldn't listen to Harry—it goes against my

better judgment—but if I have one character flaw, it's that I listen to Harry. So I decided to jump in and initiate what I'll now call Plan X, really Harry's Plan X.

But first, my meeting with Maris Chambers.

6. $189.56 Plus Tax

Chauncey and Maris Chambers' house wasn't a house—it was a mansion. Sixteen rooms, Colonial Revival, 1887, according to the Fern Creek Historical Society. The meeting was set for 9:00 a.m. I rang the bell at 8:57.

A maid showed me into some type of salon, then left me all alone. No fancy tea service and plate of curried egg salad sandwiches to keep me company.

Maris entered the room wearing a karate outfit. A miniature poodle came in with her. It started humping my leg and wouldn't stop. Maris seemed not to notice. The meeting was brief.

"I'm already late for a lesson," she said. "When you find my husband, you will report to no one but me. Then you will forget we ever met. You have two weeks."

I wondered how that 'two weeks' coincided with her Queen Mary cruise.

"We haven't discussed my fee," I said. My chance to make a bundle was at hand.

"What is it?" she asked.

Being a dreamer and avid Humphrey Bogart fan, I said, "I get fifty bucks a day plus expenses."

"Done!" she said.

I was off and running as Rodney, P.I. But not before I was off and running to Butter Bar for their orange-and-caramel French toast.

The website for the Grill Maintenance Institute at the Fern Creek School of Appliance Repair promises a *Degree Certificate, Suitable for Framing*. The program was not that much of a commitment—two three-hour classes—and, would you believe it, the building was a short eight blocks from my apartment. I wondered how their cafeteria rated, and whether they ever served fried green tomatoes with a spicy buttermilk sauce, one of my favorites.

A security guard greeted me at the main entrance. "Cafeteria's in the basement, one flight down. Go through those doors. Not those doors, you idiot, those doors."

The cafeteria was crowded, as expected. With tray in hand, I zipped through the hot-food line. I'll talk later about the double-crust beef pot pie, but I started to get a bit stressed out on the dessert line. I couldn't decide between coconut cream pie and apple pandowdy when the person beside me whispered, "Double Dutch chocolate pudding today, pass it on." Don't ask how many desserts I ended up with.

I rapped on a door marked *Admissions*, then walked in. After explaining why I was there—I don't remember exactly what I said, something based on Harry's suggestion having to do with either wanting to continue a long family tradition in food truck grill repair or begin a long family tradition in food truck grill repair—they gave me six sharpened pencils and showed me to a small cubicle to take a comprehensive entrance exam. I scanned a few questions:

> **Question 147**: (Fill in the blanks.) On a routine service call, the most commonly found _____s are _____ or _____, except when _____ _____ _____. The experienced repair person would therefore _____ a _____, while an unqualified person would typically _____ the _____ _____.

Question 258: Referring back to question 147, how much should one charge for the repair job?

A) $186.95 plus tax
B) $189.65 plus tax
C) $189.56 plus tax
D) $185.96 plus tax

That did it. I bolted out of there, taking several deep breaths once outside. They were nuts. Why was life so hard? I was back to square one with Plan X, back to the proverbial drawing board.

When I awoke the following morning, I decided to make every breakfast or lunch for the foreseeable future a food truck breakfast or lunch, sometimes at Butter Bar, sometimes Blackeye Pete's. Not out of laziness, or gluttony—purely business. More opportunities for sleuthing, especially since both food truck cooks were prime suspects in Chauncey Chambers' disappearance. It would also save much-needed time for working on my current novel. Or it should, if I didn't waste too many minutes on any given day choosing what to order at which food truck. Would I be to blame? Both featured burgers from coarse-ground chuck, both slipped you a powdered apple cider doughnut when it was least expected. I could simplify matters and stick with Butter Bar if I assumed Blackeye Pete's was selling Butter Bar takeout, but what if I was wrong? What if Blackeye Pete's made their own chicken salad and it was better than Butter Bar's?

So what was next? I could resurrect Plan X to get the behind-the-counter scoop on both food trucks, but I should be prepared to ditch it for a Plan Y if Plan X failed again, once I put together a Plan Y. In any case, I needed to stop this gnawing in my gut, and it wasn't just hunger, though breakfast was less than an hour away. Maybe it was only the mystery writer in me, but I was beginning to get bad vibes about coming between competing food truck cooks with butcher knives, even if one was ripping off the other, or any plan to jump headlong into a kidnapping and murder investigation. At least Inspector Grimes carries a gun. Well, not him. Detective Watley.

I tried to put aside such thoughts and get in a few minutes of writing, but little did I know at the time where those suspicions about food trucks and kidnapping and murder would lead me.

7. Aversion to Corduroy

WHY SO HARD TO REMEMBER where I left Grimes and Watley? And it didn't help that the last bunch of pages I wrote were blown out of order by my workroom ceiling fan.

"Greetings, Detective. It appears you're back early from your fishing holiday," Inspector Grimes noted too casually as he looked up from cleaning his meerschaum pipe. "But why so highly agitated, my good fellow?"

"Ha! I'm not back at all, according to this," shouted a red-faced Detective Watley, tossing his evening newspaper across Grimes' desk. The headlines were shocking:

> *Crushed Beyond Recognition by Steamroller. Remains Peeled Off High Street. Wallet at Scene with Detective Watley Suicide Note. Gruesome Color Photos, Page. 2.*

"You don't seem surprised, Inspector."
"I saw the paper earlier and knew right away after examining the photos that it couldn't be you. You would not be caught dead in those trousers. Aversion to corduroy, green at that, am I correct? And a suicide note after your fishing trip? Despondent over the one

that got away, was I to suppose? This stinks of Jon Johns. First, he needed you out of the way. Tied to a tree in dense woods would do, to be tortured by a huge pack of ravenous weasels. The few chicken feathers still clinging to your trouser legs gave that part of Johns' plan away. At a minimum, it must have been most awkward to have three or four dead chickens hanging from your belt as bait. Then Johns faked your death in town to force me into action."

"I never said they tied me up."

"Bound and gagged, to be more exact. Rope burns on your wrists. Minute fragments of tree bark on your back. Spruce, I gather. And evidently, the north side of the tree, based on evidence of moss on the bark. You are also still slurring your words from dry rag mouth. Lucky for you that badger came around to chew through your bindings."

"Even the badger?"

"A lucky supposition on my part, Detective, which you have unwittingly just confirmed."

"Why so sure Jon Johns was behind this?" asked Watley. "You have other enemies. Especially the diabolical Sir Giles Gilbert."

"Ah, Gilbert," said Grimes. "The man who would poison his own mother a second time, given half the chance."

"Lifelong prison sentence for murder just overturned," said Watley. "Exonerated by 'newfound evidence.' He is out for revenge, on you, Inspector—you almost had him behind bars."

"No, I believe this time it's Johns," said Grimes. "Gilbert despises chicken. But down to business. What would Johns hope to gain from all this?"

"Perhaps he—"

"You are way off the mark, my good man. You are slated to present the Chef of the Year Award tonight at Town Hall, correct? With the news out that you are, sadly, no longer with us, I am the obvious choice to present in your place. Johns is using you to get at me. And do not forget what Johns thinks of celebrity chefs after that incriminating mushroom casserole.

With public access to the auditorium difficult to control, the chef and I will be sitting ducks, er, standing ducks behind the podium. Now, let's see. The mayor will be on my right. His height and breadth will block audience views from that side. The chef will be next to me on my left. I would guess him to be five feet eight inches tall based on a newspaper photo I saw recently. If I remember the upward slope of the seating configuration at Town Hall, the ideal seat for one of Johns' henchmen to occupy would be row F, seat 107. From that spot, he would have an unobstructed view to put one bullet in my head and one in the chef's, in rapid succession. I am off to the theater, dear boy, there is no time to lose. You stay out of sight. We can beat Johns at his own game."

"Quite right, Inspector. I suppose Johns will be using Drago tonight?"

"Not this time, my friend. Someone much more expendable, given there would be little opportunity for the shooter to escape."

That did it for the writing session. There's a limit to how many words even a motivated author can be expected to write each day.

8. Kippers Deboned

WILBUR WAS ENTERING MY apartment building as I was leaving. "Wilbur, how would you prove Blackeye Pete's is selling Butter Bar's food as its own?"

"First off, order the same dish at each food truck, then taste both at the same time—that's a must—because memory of tastes, colors, and smells is fleeting. If there's no difference, Blackeye Pete's dish is most likely Butter Bar takeout. Also, get to know each waitress. The more you know, the more alert you'll be if they slip. Forget looks. Check out their intrigue quotients."

I usually consider Wilbur's advice, although I wasn't sure I followed that part about the waitresses, but let me take this piece by piece. How would I try the same dish from two different food trucks at the same time? I couldn't be in two places at once and the chances of my finding some long-lost genetically identical twin brother to help me out was slim. Takeout's one obvious way, but since food often loses some of its shine as takeout, the possibility that Blackeye Pete's' takeout might begin as Butter Bar takeout—in other words, taken-out takeout—complicates the comparison. And even if I could overcome those obstacles, which menu item should I try?

Then, there were the waitresses, Butter Bar's Ginger and Blackeye Pete's' Mabel. Ginger acts tough, but her nametag has the contradictory smiley face. Mabel plays easy-to-get, but her T-shirt the other day had some kind of exploding hand grenade cartoon. I could try leaving each a lousy tip to see who's more into the waitressing job just for the money. If it's Mabel, that would be telling—she might be more apt to go along with something crooked. I already saw Ginger give her tips away to charity, but who knows if she raids that donations box at day's end. Or I could see which waitress is more into mysteries. That would be an important piece of the puzzle. Those inclined to skirt the law like to pick up hints about what and what not to do. I think those are the kinds of things Wilbur was getting at.

Fern Creek has one of those soft-rubber children's playgrounds. Not that I've jumped on it, but I did spend a good part of a day behind a fence watching them put it together. Like a giant jigsaw puzzle of interlocking red, blue, yellow, and green sections.

Who did I bump into near the entrance this afternoon while heading to Blackeye Pete's? No, not Mabel. Ginger, *sans* nametag when not at work. (So taking French in high school does come in handy. My teacher swore to us that it would, but I didn't believe her.)

Ginger was holding hands with a cute little boy who looked antsy to get inside. She doesn't generally speak to me unless she's taking my order or asking if I'll have a second dessert (does she need to ask?), but this time she seemed forced into it or something. "This is my, um, nephew, Corey," she told me. "Corey, this is Rodger."

"It's Rodney."

Corey's paper bag broke, scattering marbles in every direction. I helped pick them up and before I knew it, I had edged my way into the playground and onto a bench with Ginger. Great chance to learn what she knew about Chauncey Chambers' disappearance and the arrival of Blackeye Pete's, if she'd confide in me. I still hadn't been able to breach some kind of wall between us.

"Have the day off?" I asked. I couldn't tell if she was annoyed I came in and sat next to her, or preoccupied watching

Corey dangle by one hand off the top rung of the monkey bars, but it didn't seem like she heard what I said. "How's Butter Bar doing? Business must have picked up right away without Chauncey Chambers' food truck around."

"Huh...oh, no. Cook expected a sudden windfall, but not much changed. Chambers had been too popular—personality over food, I'd say—and his customers weren't so ready to switch so soon after he disappeared. They may still be holding out hope he'll be back."

"And now there's Blackeye Pete's to compete with," I said.

"Yeah, but somehow we've now begun to do well even though Blackeye Pete's is around, all because our takeout orders have almost tripled recently. Figure that one out."

I started to ask if Butter Bar had been selling a lot of take-home gravy but held off, moving on with a hypothetical shot in the dark: "Did you ever see Cook speaking to a stylish woman with killer curves?"

"Cook doesn't speak to customers."

"Maybe she wasn't a customer," I said. "Did you ever meet Chambers' wife?"

Ginger looked up at the sky. "How would I have met Chambers' wife? But I can't say I'm not thrilled Chambers is out of the picture, at least for now."

"Sounds like you didn't think much of him."

"Not me so much—I'm glad for Cook's sake. Cook hated Chambers after what Chambers did to him."

"I just have to ask."

"Cook doesn't like me talking about it."

"It won't go any further."

"Oh, all right. Chambers sent Cook a signed copy of one of his comfort food cookbooks. When Cook read the inscription he turned red, tossed the book, and stormed off. I dug it out of the trash to see what Chambers had written. It said, *I figured you needed a few pointers. Your pal, Chauncey.* Then Chambers ridiculed Butter Bar on live TV. He accused Cook of copying his recipe for Dutch pea soup—an out-and-out lie—and even flubbing the execution. When Cook heard about that he grabbed a huge salami and twisted and twisted it, yelling that he'd wring that bastard's neck. Chilling to watch."

"And he eventually acted on that, didn't he?"

My last question disappeared into the ether. We sat quietly for several more minutes as talk of Chambers and cooks and competing food trucks faded away, and when I summoned up enough courage to put my arm around her in support of National Waitress' Day next month, she got up to give Corey a box drink.

"Do you like to read?" I asked, the first in a barrage of questions when she returned. Others followed rapidly before she could respond.

"Novels?"

"Mysteries?"

"Authors like Randall Reed?"

"Inspectors?"

"Grimes?"

"*The Case of the Bungled Bugle*?"

"*The Weeping Stone Enigma*?"

"*Murder Most Mundane*?"

"Yes, yes, yes, yes, yes, yes, yes, yes, and yes," she said.

I failed to notice her one extra *yes* at the time. "Have you read more of them than Mabel has?"

"Huh?" She looked at me sideways, then went off again to check on Corey.

"I've got to feed my fish," I called out. "Catch you later." Having grilled Ginger, I might as well strike Mabel while the iron was hot.

I picked up a copy of my novel *The Kipper Caper* at my

apartment and went to Blackeye Pete's. Mabel came over, order pad in hand.

"What'll it be, stud?" asked Mabel. "Or do you got a name?"

"The name's Rodney." I put the book on the counter. She grabbed it and flipped through the pages. She couldn't tell I wrote it. Pen name. No author picture on the book jacket.

"Oh, just so happens, I read that one. And two others. Found all three in a trash heap outside my apartment. You like Randall Reed mysteries?" she asked. "You should come by my place some evening. I'll get rid of my roommate. We'll turn the lights down low, put on some scary whodunit, snuggle up on the couch and see what happens."

"Yeah, sure," I said. "Maybe. Sometime. And I do dig his mysteries. Finished this one last night." I don't like to mislead anyone, but the stakes were high.

"What's your opinion?" she continued. "Did you buy the schoolmaster's alibi? I didn't at first, but then was shocked to find out that Barnaby, not Simons, deboned the kippers. Clever of the author to hold that back from readers until the police arrested Mullins, don't you think? However, while the last scenes were well crafted, it seemed forced that Grimes' accusation took place at the crossroads, rather than in Greer's rear pantry."

That totally unexpected side of Mabel threw me for a loop. There was obviously much more to her than I first thought. "I'll have the turkey club," I said, all the response I could muster.

Peter I. Black had cut the sandwich in fourths. Halfway through the third quarter, Wilbur walked by. I motioned him over, then took him aside. "Wilbur, I've questioned both waitresses. Mabel gets an A+ in Inspector Grimes 101. That's significant. Ginger's giving out mixed signals. She likes mysteries, but her nametag sports that you-know-what."

"Think about it," said Wilbur. "That smiley face might be a devious attempt at deception. I'm on my way to meet Harry. See ya."

When I returned to my seat, Mabel came by and whispered in my ear. "Keep it down, sugar, but next time try Pete's shockingly good macaroni and cheese. He calls it *Just Bacon, 'Roni, Chives & Cheddar*. It takes a while for him to get it, I mean, to prepare, but it's well worth it."

Blackeye Pete's' *Just Bacon, 'Roni, Chives & Cheddar*? What the...? Butter Bar's known for its *Smoked Bacon & Chives Mac & Cheese*, which gets an involuntary, taste-bud-popping *Oh, Momma* from me each time I have it. Even picturing it is enough: Homemade golden egg pasta, melted mild cheddar and heavy cream, cubes of extra-sharp cheddar and hickory-smoked bacon, and bright green snips of chives. Cook then goes the extra mile, topping it all with crisscrossed slices of even more hickory-smoked bacon. I'm sure anyone trying a forkful would be sobbing, *Oh, Momma*.

That did it. A new plan took shape. Tomorrow I would call in for takeout at both places and compare their macaroni and cheese. If Blackeye Pete's' matched Butter Bar's, that would confirm there was much more to Blackeye Pete's than selling comfort food.

9. Delivery Boy Strangler

The first step in the takeout comparison was to find phone numbers for each food truck. Butter Bar's was easy. Their jingle plays over and over in TV ads and I knew it by heart:

> "♪ *Soup in a mug for ya? Burger on a bun?*
> *Dial 8-6-7-3-4-7-1.* ♪"

Blackeye Pete's' phone number, a little more difficult to find—no TV ads. But there it was on page 7 of the spanking new Fern Creek telephone directory I found leaning against my apartment door as soon as I made it home.

...
Blackeye Pearl's
Blackeye Peg's
Blackeye Pete's 867-3472
Blackeye Phil's
...

Next I needed to pick surrogates to call in each order. Someone for each food truck. My voice might be recognized. I could get Harry to call Butter Bar, maybe Wilbur to call Blackeye Pete's, or should it be the other way around? And I thought they should also disguise their voices for extra security. Harry could pretend to be Wilbur and vice versa. I'd work all that out later.

The third step would be to train the surrogates on what to say. For example, Harry's or Wilbur's telephone script might be something like, "Hello. Is this [*fill in the name of the food truck*]? Nice day we're having. Oh. There's no real hidden reason I'm calling, but while I'm on the phone, how about an order of [*fill in the exact name of the dish*] to go? For pickup at [*fill in a time*] o'clock. The name's [*Harry would use Wilbur; Wilbur, Harry*]."

Next, I had to decide where to rendezvous. I chose the centrally located game tables at Checkerboard Park on Crenshaw.

And lunchtime tomorrow would give Harry and Wilbur time to practice their scripts and impersonations. With all that settled, the waiting started to get me down. A sandwich for dinner would have helped fill the void. Something overstuffed. Too bad Butter Bar and Blackeye Pete's weren't open for dinner.

At 10:00 a.m., Harry and Wilbur slouched on my couch munching crackers and nervously practicing their lines.

"Hello there. This is…is this…what number did I call? Have I reached Butter Bar?" Harry pretended to be Wilbur, but mostly managed to spit cracker crumbs across my coffee table as he spoke. All eyes went to the table thanks to Harry.

"Classic Eames molded plywood coffee table," said Wilbur. "I've said it before and I'll say it again, excellent choice for this spot, Rodney."

"What else would go there?" I bluffed. It was a cast-off from my Aunt Agnes, and I had no idea what made it *Eames*.

At 12:37, the calls went through without a hitch. One p.m., they would pick up takeout. One fifteen p.m., they would meet me at Checkerboard Park with the macaroni and cheese. "One last thing," I said, handing each of my illustrious special operations team members a khaki green cloth bag. "Check it out."

Wilbur reached in. "A walkie-talkie?" he said.

"Army surplus," I said. "Too old to be traced. Any trouble along the way, call me. I'm counting on each of you. The health of comfort food in Fern Creek hangs in the balance, not to mention my career as a mystery writer slash private investigator, if I can show some nefarious connection to Chauncey Chambers disappearance. Let's boogie."

We headed out after I shifted my Eames coffee table a drop to the left so it didn't leave permanent impressions in my rug. Harry made for Butter Bar, Wilbur went to Blackeye Pete's. Ten minutes later, I was giddy, belting out lyrics for what could be, should be, a country & western top 40: "Sittin' by a checkerboard, waitin' on my mac and cheese."

"Quit that awful racket," said someone who must have just sat down at the checkerboard table behind me, "or I'll quit it for ya."

I turned around. The guy had a ski cap, thick-rimmed glasses, a seemingly false mustache, and either a real or fake beard. A Chauncey Chambers kidnapper look-alike if I ever saw one! "Says who?" I said, as I contemplated my next move.

"Says this," said the man, holding up a switchblade. He began stabbing wooden checkers with his knife point while glaring at me like I was still doing something wrong, even though I had stopped singing.

Meanwhile, a woman hidden behind sunglasses and scarf had grabbed the checkerboard table to my left. She sat a minute or two longer, fiddled with some purchases, glanced at her watch, stood up, and walked rapidly away.

"Hey, you forgot your ticking package under the table," I yelled at her to no effect.

A short distance in front of me, a maintenance worker, wearing an ill-fitting Parks Department uniform and dust mask, was holding a pole with an extra-long spike at the end. Out picking up litter, he headed toward some crumpled paper bags near my shoes, spike-first.

It felt like a three-pronged attack. If Chauncey Chambers' kidnapper and two of his gang were out to scare me, they were doing a good job. I checked my pockets. No weapons. Not even a stick of gum.

Then a walkie-talkie call came in. It was Harry. Thank God for Harry. "Hello, *Police Officer* Harry," I said, emphasizing the caller's faux-occupation as loud as I could. "So you'll be here in thirty seconds with an itchy trigger finger?"

"Police officer? Thirty seconds? Trigger finger? Sorry. Don't get the joke," said Harry. "Listen, Rodney. I hailed a taxi—"

"You were supposed to *walk* the six blocks to Butter Bar," I whispered, while keeping at least one eye on the two men. They had stopped stabbing and stalking. Intimidated by 'Police Officer' Harry's imminent arrival I supposed. The package had even stopped ticking.

"But listen," Harry said. "I got out after three blocks and am now waiting to grab a second taxi the rest of the way. Clever, right? Saw this done in a film. No one cabbie has the full picture. Thought you'd be relieved to know."

If I was relieved, it was because the two men had run off in different directions, after the switchblade guy grabbed the woman's package. A citation for Police Officer Harry? But then there was citizen Harry.

"Harry, you're not exactly on your way to a heist," I said. However, Harry wasn't that far afield. Grimes and Watley did something similar in *The Scorpion Strikes Thrice*, though with camels, not taxis.

Then the second walkie-talkie call came in. Wilbur.

"I'm almost at Blackeye Pete's but a cop stopped me. He's standing here wanting to know why I'm holding a military-grade walkie-talkie."

"Wilbur, say you're not doing anything with it because it's an antique and doesn't even work."

"Roger, Randall. I mean Roger, Rodney, and out."

Nothing like having a team you can rely on.

Wilbur called back a few minutes later. "The baby's in the cradle. ETA: five minutes, forty seconds."

"Hold the food with both hands, please."

Harry called. "Four minutes, fifty seconds away. Over."

"Slow down a bit. You'll get here ahead of Wilbur."

I finally spotted Harry approaching from my left, Wilbur from Harry's left. I couldn't be more psyched. Drum roll please. Is Blackeye Pete's *Just Bacon, 'Roni, Chives & Cheddar* really Butter Bar's *Smoked Bacon & Chives Mac & Cheese*? Harry started to run, holding his takeout order in outstretched arms. Wilbur did the same. Harry then eased up, fearful he'd arrive before Wilbur and jeopardize the integrity of the contest. Wilbur followed suit. Both slowed to a crawl. They now seemed reluctant to reach me and came to a dead stop about ten feet away.

"You see, it was way past our lunchtimes," said Harry with a sheepish grin.

"It all began with an innocent taste or two or three," said Wilbur.

Both takeout containers had been picked clean. Harry and Wilbur had eaten the orders on the way over. *Grrrr.* I wanted to smash them over the head with my walkie-talkie, then use that same walkie-talkie to call Harry at 2:00 a.m. and Wilbur at 2:05 a.m. every night for four weeks. Well, all wasn't for naught. At least I now had the title for Randall Reed's next mystery novel: *The Delivery Boy Strangler*.

10. Comfort Food Flimflam

MIDAFTERNOON AND I STILL hadn't had lunch thanks to my two terrific friends, so I headed to Blackeye Pete's. As I approached, Peter I. Black waved hello. All four stools were empty. Before I could take the second stool from the left, Black himself rushed out and dusted it off. Either he suspected I suspect him and was trying to con me into a false sense of security, or I'd been wrong about Blackeye Pete's all along. Nothing against Ginger, but I don't get that type of service at Butter Bar.

"What'll ya have?" asked Mabel. "Rodney, right?"

"One and the same. How about grilled American cheese, thick-cut bacon, and tomato, on seeded rye? I'm so hungry I could eat a horse."

"Then you need the other food truck."

Despite loyalty to Butter Bar I let that slide and checked my watch. If I was served quickly, then Black was doing the cooking, even if he didn't start out that way when he first came to town. If not, then it's one more tally for Butter Bar takeout.

"I'm already here," I said. "Any chance the cook can make it snappy?"

"All orders are made to order, said Mabel. "Expect to wait."

That took on new significance given my suspicions that Blackeye Pete's was still perpetrating a comfort-food flimflam. When Mabel called out my order, I couldn't see what Black did next—he had his back to me—but it seemed by his elbow and hand motions that he arranged, cut, then sizzled something. So either he was adept at combining pantomime with recorded cooking sounds, or making my sandwich himself—in other words, not getting it as Butter Bar takeout.

"Sorry, Rodney," said Mabel, "I need to check whether this is working properly."

With my order still in the works, she pulled down the accordion shutter that closes off the truck each night. Was she blocking my view of Black on purpose? That happened other times I've eaten at Blackeye Pete's. And like those times, the shutter worked okay, except it needed oil. Quite a screeching sound.

I knew what Harry would say. If the shutter were broken and if I were a roll-down shutter repair person asked to fix it, I could see what Black was actually up to. No way I'd go there again.

After quite some time, Mabel raised the shutter and handed me my grilled cheese sandwich.

That shutter business was one more piece of evidence to be considered. Possibly damning evidence. Something that needed further scrutiny. So what would Inspector Grimes do next if he were me, or what would I do if I were he? Or what if I hired Grimes to help me figure this out? (Although he worked for London's Metropolitan Police Bureau, so I wasn't sure he'd be allowed to moonlight, and, also, he wasn't a real person.)

I found a nearby phone booth and called Wilbur. Sure, both he and Harry screw up from time to time, but I'm not so fast to ditch friends. "Come with me to Blackeye Pete's tonight around eleven."

"They'll be closed," said Wilbur.

"Precisely. Bring your flashlight. It's time we did some serious snooping around."

"What about my walkie-talkie?"

"Don't bring it."

A sunny fall day with a mild breeze—much too nice to go home and write. I drifted over to the park along the river bank. A mime mimicked people as they walked by. If I somehow befriended that mime, I could use him to silently observe Butter Bar's and Blackeye Pete's' operations. He would report back to me in pantomime, unless he was trapped in a box with no way out. I decided to keep that idea on the back burner. It was a good one.

Too bad a third food truck hadn't opened in town, one that hired Ginger away from Butter Bar. I could go all out investigating Butter Bar and Blackeye Pete's with a clear conscience, not having to worry about Ginger losing her job if it turned out Butter Bar's cook got rid of Chambers. Though, if I told Inspector Grimes about my third food truck fantasy, he'd be glad to show me the flaws in my thinking: *How do you know that third food truck isn't the one responsible for Chambers' disappearance? You'd have to investigate three trucks, rather than two. Would you then hope for a fourth?* Some good points by Grimes. Still...

I brushed off one of the park benches and sat for a while. As a rubber ball bounced off the back of one of my shoes, three boys ran up looking for it. "Bet each of you can't name a different food truck in town."

"Blackeye Pete's," said the first boy, smartly.

"Butter Bar," said the second boy, smugly.

"Um," said the third boy, sadly.

I reached under the bench, picked up the ball off a crack in the cement, and tossed it back to them.

"My big brother Danny gave me two whole dollars yesterday," added the second boy. "He says he's getting rich delivering takeout food for Butter Bar."

"That so? I'd like to speak with this brother of yours," I said. "Where's he hang out when he's not at Butter Bar?"

"Oh, here and there," said the boy. "Mostly there."

The boys ran off laughing. So Danny was getting rich delivering takeout? Either something was not on the up-and-up, or I may have found a new career choice.

I walked the few blocks to Butter Bar, hoping to catch Danny in delivery mode, but no such luck, at least not yet. Though I think Ginger was warming up to me. I thought I saw her nod to me as I came near, while handing an ample slice of apple pie à la mode to some lucky fellow. I could be that fellow someday. She started to wipe off the counter.

"These are for you," I said, offering her a small bouquet I had picked up at Fern Creek Flowers on the way. "They're Hawaiian blue ginger." She seemed to soften a bit after hearing the name and couldn't help but give up a hint of a smile. "Are you doing anything tonight?" I asked.

"Soaking my feet. How about you?"

As I searched a lifetime of memories and experiences for a clever response, while doubting there could even be one to such a statement, a young man on a motor scooter buzzed up to Butter Bar's open side door. Cook handed him three bags of food and closed the door. That was my cue to block the scooter.

"You Danny?" I asked, already assuming that he was.

"Out of the way, chump," said Danny. "I got hot food to deliver."

I clearly had the upper hand. He didn't look like he worked out. Besides, he wore glasses. I grabbed the keys from the ignition. "Tell me what orders you have there and I'll give these back."

"Hey, give me those," said Danny. "I'll lose my job if I don't deliver these pronto. Damn you. Okay. You win." Danny consulted the slips. "A rare burger with Asi...Asiago cheese. Cauliflower soup with the words *extra croutons* underlined. Um...Buffalo wings, um...heat level 10."

I tossed him the keys and jogged, not ran, the few blocks to Blackeye Pete's. A man was finishing a rare cheeseburger.

"What kind of cheese?" I asked. Mabel was eyeing me as I stood behind him.

"Asiago," he answered.

"Cauliflower soup okay?" I asked the woman next to him.

"Not enough croutons," she said to me. "Any more croutons?" she asked Mabel.

"You'd have to wait a while," said Mabel.

"How are your Buffalo wings?" I asked the third customer. A woman. "Hot enough?"

"Buffalo wings? I'm having a sausage and peppers omelet."

"Nah. It must be buffalo wings," I said. "It's got to be. Is the heat level at 10, 9 at least?"

"Does this look like buffalo wings?" she asked. "I hate buffalo wings."

Try as I did, her sausage and peppers omelet didn't look anything like buffalo wings.

11. Lambs to the Slaughter

FEELING PARTLY SATISFIED and partly baffled, private investigator-wise, I went home, fed the fish, opened my lap desk, and attacked...inched up to my novel-in-progress. Yesterday, or the day before, I had written *In a nondescript fourth-floor* at the top of a new page, then broke for lunch, dinner, TV, shower, and bedtime. Where was I going with that? Oh, yeah.

In a nondescript fourth-floor walk-up in a gloomy section of the London Docklands, Jon Johns heated a pot of pork sausages and beans over an illegal propane burner. His meals and accommodations were extremely modest for a man who had amassed a small fortune from a life of violent crime. Hundreds of thousands of pounds sterling were now safely tucked away in bank accounts under three different aliases. Why live like this, one might ask?

"Comforts are of little concern to me," Johns would answer. "I care not for anyone, or anything, except perhaps my razor-sharp butcher knife. And I admit I have only one driving obsession—being free to pray on the filthy rich, brutality strongly encouraged—once I have embarrassed, then destroyed, that internationally known fraud of a crime fighter, the highly overrated Inspector Grimes of London's Metropolitan Police Bureau."

Johns scanned the *Times* while waiting for his supper to cool. "What's this?" he said out loud, even though there was no one else around. "A masquerade ball for the cream of London society in one week hence. Quite an impressive guest list. Quite an array of jewelry for the taking. A nice opportunity to put the screws on Grimes' reputation so soon after he foiled my Town Hall plan to kill him and that chef."

Johns left his flat and walked to a telephone booth a short distance away. His inflated ego getting the best of him, he couldn't resist giving Grimes some form of advance notice about his upcoming caper. He dialed the inspector's home number, which happened to be listed for anyone to find.

"Watley, answer the phone," said Grimes, trying a second time to light his pipe. His favorite meerschaum clogged once too often.

Detective Watley picked up the receiver, listened for a moment, then put it down. He looked puzzled. "That's odd. There were five words spoken, then two letters, then a hang up," said the detective. "Black, red, orange and blue. J.J."

"Well, what do you make of it, my good man?" asked Grimes, primed to offer his own opinion.

"Nothing at all, Inspector. Black, then three colors, or four if black can be called a color."

"Some argue it is the absence of color. For me it denotes the lack of reflected light, but that's a discussion for another time. You do realize Jon Johns himself made that call, don't you?"

"Hell's bells. J.J. is Jon Johns? Why, yes, I should have known."

"Let us decode his message then, shall we? I am

sure you have already realized that rearranging existing letters gets us nowhere."

"Why, er, of course. That's obvious," said Watley. "Perhaps we should count letters then. The four main words yield, let's see, 5364. Part of an address perhaps, or a storage locker number."

"I am afraid you are way off base," said Grimes. "Much of what Johns does is the opposite of what one might expect, so I suggest instead that we start by looking at opposites. Black then becomes white. Red represents green. But what about orange and blue?"

"Beats me," said the detective.

"Since orange and blue are already opposites, that means the presence of the word 'and' in his message is key."

"Combined, don't orange and blue make brown?" offered Watley, trying to regain some credibility. "I recall that from art sessions in First School. I found out the hard way. Miss Primrose was not at all fond of my muddy paintings."

"Brown. Well done, Detective. You're right as rain this time and coming along nicely. So we now have white, green and brown to work with, and from there the exercise becomes rather trivial. There's Lady Amanda White, with her Colchester Diamond. Duchess Cecilia Green wears the Carlisle Sapphire. And the Honorable Hermione Brown is quick to flaunt her Castleton Emerald. All lambs to the slaughter for the likes of Johns, assuming those three women will be together soon at some venue. Hand me the *Times*, please. Yes, here's the notice. A masquerade ball."

"Egad! We need to warn those ladies straightaway."

"Not necessary, my friend. We have sufficient

time to put Johns off before the event. Post the following in tomorrow's morning edition and Bob's your uncle: White, Green, Brown, will keep their jewels this round. I.G."

I put down the dip pen to answer the door. Harry filled the peephole. I assumed he stopped by after his mail run to apologize again for the macaroni and cheese fiasco, but he didn't do much apologizing.

12. Really Bacon Grease

"I HEAR YOU AND WILBUR have a caper tonight," said Harry. "Wilbur's psyched. He's already waiting by his door, dressed all in black with a pull-down wool cap and greased-up face."

"Doesn't he realize we have to walk three blocks under a bunch of streetlights to get there?"

"I warned him about that," said Harry, "but Wilbur's Wilbur. By the way, how's it going with your one and only client?"

"Maris Chambers? Well, I'm bringing in the big bucks, given my fee and all."

"Easy money, huh? Do little to nothing for her, collect, collect, collect."

I needed Harry to take me to task like that. To stir up my investigative fires. While my confrontation with Butter Bar's delivery guy Danny brought me closer to unlocking the Butter Bar/Blackeye Pete's takeout issue, coming up with the next steps in solving Chauncey Chambers' disappearance was easier said than done. I could at least pay Maris Chambers another visit. Act like I'm hot on the kidnapper's trail. Exude confidence in my returning Chauncey safe and sound, as I polish off a stack of smoked salmon and dill sandwiches that she's bound to serve me on a sterling silver platter. Comfort food it wouldn't be, but when hobnobbing in Rome...

Maris' maid answered my phone call. She consulted her mistress, then told me it was fine to come right over, but when I got there I learned that Maris had blown off our meeting and gone out. Which, I assumed, also meant no smoked salmon sandwiches.

"Can I ask your name?" I said to the maid.

"Violet. And I'm sorry that Mrs. Chambers stood you up like she did. Doesn't treat me so well, either. She's nothing like Mr. Chambers' first wife, even his second. They had grace. They've both been calling, very concerned about him. Praying he's okay. So am I."

I sensed an opening.

"Mrs. Chambers has to be under a lot of stress, with her husband and his food truck missing for so long," I said.

"You wouldn't know it the way she acts," said Violet. "She hasn't changed her ways. Still out shopping and socializing. Still can't get her hands on enough of his money. She had been bugging Mr. Chambers to buy her this snazzy red convertible. He wouldn't have it. You should have heard the arguing last month about it. Though he's not around to stop her now, is he? She's out shopping even as we speak."

"Where to?" I asked.

"Some foreign car dealer. No surprise. But I've said too much. I need this job. You better leave."

"One more thing about Mrs. Chambers. The two other food trucks in town—Butter Bar and Blackeye Pete's. Any dealings with either of those cooks?"

"I said I've said too much."

Harry hadn't convinced Wilbur to ditch his commando outfit, nor could I, so when Wilbur and I headed to Blackeye Pete's a few minutes to eleven, we were lucky the streets were mostly deserted. We did pass two guys, but they were dressed the same as Wilbur, so I was the one who stood out. We reached the food truck ten minutes later and, for the second time in one day, though not a record by any means, I wished I hadn't asked

Wilbur to help me. Not only did he keep shining his flashlight in my eyes each time they had grown accustomed to the dark, he brought his walkie-talkie and while we were circling the truck in opposite directions, he kept trying to call me, even as he was passing me, and even though I told him I had left mine home.

The door of the food truck—locked. Side service area—shuttered. As expected. "Wilbur, there's a hatch on the top of the truck. Black keeps it open sometimes during the day. Let me boost you up."

"It's unlocked," he yelled back moments later before dropping in. He opened the door and we started to search the truck.

I examined the burners and grates of the gas cooktop. "No residue. They're clean as a whistle. What does that say?"

Wilbur tasted the contents of each squeeze bottle. "Ugh, this one's marked *Bacon Grease* and it really is bacon grease."

I sampled some leftover egg salad in the near-empty frig. "Needs more salt."

"What about these?" asked Wilbur, holding two handfuls of discarded PinkyPink bubble gum wrappers.

"Not surprising. Who in Fern Creek doesn't chew PinkyPink?"

"I don't. Harry doesn't. He and I both prefer Gumm Gum's gum. PinkyPink doesn't hold a candle to Gumm Gum and I'll tell you why."

"Not now, Wilbur. Let's see what else we can find."

Other than the heavy book I stood on to reach one of the higher shelves, nothing else seemed out of the ordinary.

"That a cookbook?" asked Wilbur. "I could use a tip or two."

"Let's see. It's a textbook: *Color Chemistry - Syntheses, Properties & Applications of Dyes & Pigments*. And this label inside the cover says *Property of PinkyPink Product Development Laboratories*."

"That's weird. What do you make of it?"

"Could mean nothing, could mean everything," I said. "Seems too odd not to matter."

"Can we go home now?" asked Wilbur. "Aren't we done here?"

"Except for planting this," I said, reaching into my back pocket and removing a small, army surplus listening device. "I got it and its companion receiver when I bought the walkie-talkies. We can monitor Black's and Mabel's private conversations over the next forty-eight hours. That's how long the battery in this transmitter is supposed to last. Now, where to hide it?"

"How about behind one of those vented ceiling panels?" asked Wilbur.

"Perfect, Wilbur. After I install it, you'll let me out the door, lock it, and climb up through the roof hatch. Then we're out of here."

As he and I started for home, I turned around at the edge of the lot. "Wilbur, I'm thinking. Check out the truck from this distance and tell me what you see."

"Must I? It's the Blackeye Pete's food truck."

"Does this truck look familiar?"

"They're pretty much all the same shape and construction, aren't they? Except for Butter Bar."

Wilbur followed me as I returned to the truck, picked up a flat rock, and scraped away the dull green top layer of paint on one small section of side panel, a place that wouldn't easily be noticed.

"Just as I thought. Shine your flashlight here, Wilbur. Now what do you see?"

"Bright orange paint under the green. Why?"

"And what color was Chauncey Chambers' food truck?"

"Bright...orange."

13. By Hook or Crook

I TURNED ON THE RECEIVER at 6:00 a.m. the following morning. Nothing but clattering and clanking sounds out of Blackeye Pete's until 6:13, when I hit pay dirt:

"Can't believe we have to...watch out, that's gonna fall...that we have to get up so damn early and waste the day trapped in this rotten breadbox." (*That's definitely Black's voice.*) "And we also have to deal with that jerk who's always coming around. The guy who knows Butter Bar's food much too well, then gets the same exact stuff when he eats with us. At some point soon he's sure to figure out what's going on."

"Who, Rodney?" (*Obviously Mabel.*) "Yeah, he could blow our cover. But I can't see how we can stop him from eating both here and at Butter Bar without raising a red flag." (*I thought she liked me. Thought she'd defend me.*)

"I think it's best to keep him within striking distance, though. And we should use the fact that he likes you." (*Black again.*)

"Ya think?"

"I'm sure of it. Who wouldn't? You'll try making him an offer any hungry man can't refuse: If he dumps Butter Bar and sticks with us, he gets twice the food here for half the price. If that doesn't work, I'll get him to stay clear of both food trucks for the time being, someway, somehow, by hook or by crook."

"Crook? Ha, ha. That's not like you." (*Mabel. Sounded like a sarcastic laugh.*)

"Then, when all this is over, I'll take him out of the picture permanently, even if only for the fun of it."

"You'll end up back in jail, but hey, we had some good times there, didn't we? Me, the strict librarian, taking you to task in the storeroom for bringing your books back late." (*I pictured Mabel putting her arms around Black's neck and pulling him close.*) "Not a bad job, at the prison. I should've kept it. I would have, but they let you out. Ah, give the poor guy a break. Rodney means well." (*Mabel does care about me.*)

"You'll do whatever I tell ya to do. And then there're those dumb friends he pals around with, like that short, stocky guy. What's his name? Harry?"

"Our mailman."

"Yeah. And there's some other idiot. He came by when Rodney was here the other afternoon. Tall, lean, awkward. A Walter, or Wilbur. He and Harry could also give us trouble. But dealing with those three fools is just noise. You know I have much more lucrative fish to fry, and once that's done, there's no more need for Blackeye Pete's."

"You so sure it'll work out the way you think it's gonna work out?"

"I told you, things are already falling into place. I still have to...hold on, I could use some coffee. Lemme light the stove."

Damn! The receiver went dead after lots of static. And just when Black began talking about some larger plan of his. I must have bought a faulty transmitter.

Wilbur called about an hour later. "How's your spyware working? You still listening now? Thanks to me, I bet the voices are so much clearer than you ever expected. Are they? Aren't they?"

If Wilbur had been with me, I would have given him the evil eye. "And why the hell would that be?"

"Before I climbed out of the truck, I did you one better. I took the transmitter from the ceiling panel where you had left it and hid it under one of the stove grates, which they don't seem to use. That's much closer to where Black and Mabel would be standing."

I imagined Wilbur with a triumphant smile on his face. I could have asked him what he thought would happen if they did light the stove, but at that point, why bother? "Wilbur, ask that cop buddy of yours if they have anything on a Peter I. Black. It seems he's spent time in jail. And see if Harry has any friends in the motor vehicle department. I need to know how Black got Chauncey Chambers' food truck, maybe even how much he paid for it. There should be some record of the transfer since Blackeye Pete's has a different license plate than Chauncey's Chow."

The discovery about Blackeye Pete's' paint job and Black's background and veiled threats about me and my friends were a lot to handle right away. I needed some distance from Blackeye Pete's, some time to consider what to do next. After all, I was new at this game. I was sure even Grimes hesitated when confronted by some surprise developments early in his career, although he was probably in grade school at the time. And while Blackeye Pete's' Peter I. Black was apparently no angel, I still knew little or nothing about Butter Bar's cook. That had to change.

14. Girl Without Crusts

I SLIPPED ONTO BUTTER BAR'S second stool. Cook had been scraping the grill. Not that I could see it. As usual, he was in the way. Then I heard him frying away like a madman. It smelled like sausage and peppers. Even passersby were hesitating with desire. I nodded to the other three customers already in place.

"Know if Cook's ever been in a police lineup?" I whispered to the old lady on my right.

I passed a note to the man on my far left in an attempt to chip away at any denial out of Cook concerning a celebrity cook's disappearance: *Did you see Cook speaking to a stranger some weeks ago about this time?*

"Know if Cook has beady eyes?" I whispered to the young woman on my left.

No one cared (or dared) to answer. Were they protecting the cook? Could they all be in on it, part of the cook's gang? Grimes would say that's highly unlikely, that I'm showcasing the *amateur* side of amateur sleuth, starting to see mystery and intrigue in everything around me, but I wasn't sure I'd agree. This group of customers appeared to be a shifty bunch. That bulge in the man's jacket pocket must be a gun. The lady on my right looked like she got that way after spending years in the slammer, probably in solitary, and that woman on my left, I suspected, was Cook's former moll trying to regain the top position from...no, it couldn't be Ginger.

I tried a more direct approach. "Excuse me," I called to the cook. Then even louder: "Excuse me. Can I see your butcher knife? I'm curious which brand you prefer." Cook didn't turn around, but it sounded like he furiously started to chop potatoes, then he slowly looked up to the food truck ceiling. Either he worried about some pooled grease drops coming unstuck or I had touched a nerve and might be on to something big.

My sweet Ginger sauntered over with her order pad and pencil stub. And when I say *stub*, I mean a stub of a stub. It looked like no more than the pencil point itself. Feeling sorry for her or afraid she'd run out of lead, probably both, I ordered straight away, even before she asked.

"Top of the morning, miss. My, you look lovely today. Wish I had my camera. If it's not too much trouble, a jumbo corn muffin, fork split in half, not cut, buttered on the insides, grilled on the grill. Some eggs over greasy, a ton of home fries, and coffee, too. And three or four strips of bacon while Cook's at it, not too well done, plus plenty of warm maple syrup for a not-so-short stack of...wait, better nix the blueberry pancakes this morning." Out of the corner of my eye, I noticed a delivery truck had pulled up curbside. Several cartons were already blocking the sidewalk. All the fixings for a charbroiled hamburger platter, Butter Bar's special *Twin Burger Deluxe*. I didn't want to pass that up. Might that mean a modest breakfast? Yes. With an early return for lunch? Double yes.

"So that's all? What about the side of pancakes?" Ginger asked.

"I better stick with what I've ordered. Any chance I can reserve a stool at noon?"

I planned to arrive at Butter Bar at twenty to twelve. From half a block away, I could see one seat had been taken by a man in a uniform. With a quarter block to go, the old lady from this morning came out of nowhere and grabbed the second stool. A father (I guessed) and his daughter (I guessed) approached Butter Bar from the right. They looked hungry and I still had to cross the street. Those last seats were taken up in a flash. I was the fifth to arrive, but where to wait? No single line—you had to pick a person to stand behind. Who would Grimes choose based on observation and deduction? Could I match his skills? It would be a test of mine. I strained to hear each order.

Father: "Tell the waitress what you want, sweetie."

Daughter: "I'll have a...I'll have a..." And turning to her father, "What was it I wanted, Daddy? Oh yeah, I'll have a hot chocolate and a chicken salad sandwich on toast with no crusts."

Ginger: "Cook won't cut the crusts. Your dad can cut 'em off. And what'll you have?"

Father: "Hot chocolate, chicken salad on toast."

(Same as his daughter. Now that's a model dad!)

Ginger: "Crusts?"

Father: "No, thank you."

Ginger: "Cook won't do that."

Old lady: "The Southern fried chicken basket, double battered, not well drained, with plenty of your signature gravy on the French fries. And throw in a couple of hot chili peppers. The hotter the better."

Uniformed man: "Triple-decker club please, traditional order reversed. With crusts."

Who did I stand behind and why? The child might leave half, but the father would take time to gobble what remains. No doubt a second helping of fries and gravy was on tap for the old lady. The man in uniform had a big mouth, perfect for a triple-decker. I won't say who I chose. Professional (s)eater's trade secret. Okay, I will. I stood behind the old lady, a simple matter of observation and deduction. Grimes would have been proud. Given what and how she eats, the lady was likely to drop dead before any of the others finished their lunch, thus relinquishing her stool to me.

At last. Plump, juicy, medium-rare twin burgers bursting out of oversize sesame-seeded buns; heaps of crisp, golden steak-cut fries; creamy, carrot-flecked, red and green coleslaw on a lettuce leaf (nicely wilted, as one with experience ordering a burger deluxe would expect); and a pile of pickle chips.

Ginger brought me the ketchup bottle. After thirty hard smacks and slaps on its bottom, not even one drop of the red stuff. I sensed a low rumbling. Empty coffee cups and plates on wobbly wooden shelves started to shake. Cook rotated a full hundred and eighty degrees. I lowered my eyes, involuntarily, out of fear—a lost opportunity to catch what he looks like. But I still made out two huge hands coming toward me. Who would feed the fish after Cook wringed my neck? One hand grabbed and turned the ketchup bottle upside down by its neck, while the other gave its bottom a small tap. One can guess what happened.

Still shaking, yet satisfied, as I headed home—those twin burgers were much more than just all right—I saw Harry in the distance rushing toward me, his mailbag wobbling from side to side, then stopping to scoop up some letters that must have bounced out.

"Did you hear about…ouch, what happened to you?" Harry asked once he reached me, still out of breath. "Looks like you've been shot."

I glanced at the big, red stain on my jacket. "Ketchup."

"Hear what happened to Wilbur?" asked Harry.

"What? Did he lose one of his ties?"

"In a way of speaking. He got assaulted. And he's a mess. I left him sitting outside your building, too frightened to move."

I ran the few remaining blocks. "Wilbur, what the devil? Why are you clutching your neck?"

It took a while for Wilbur to get out the words. "I was several…a few blocks from home," he said, "and had…had a strange feeling I was being followed. The sky grew dark and the thunder in the distance didn't help my nerves one bit. I've seen—"

"That's peculiar. The weather seemed fine by Butter Bar."

"Yeah, well," said Wilbur. "I've seen enough movies to know that when someone's following you, you walk a ways, then quickly turn around...ow, it hurts...turn around to see the person duck into a doorway. He did that. Then you walk a block or two before stopping to see if you can see the guy who's following you reflected in a store window. He was. Then you get mixed up in a crowd as some department store opens and you get swept inside, only to run out a side entrance. No way I could do that—no department stores around. Since I was nearly home, I started to run to get here before he gets me. I almost made it. I had put my key in the outside door when the guy grabbed me from behind with a choke hold, twisted my neck and choked me for a while, then spun me around..." Wilbur stopped to catch his breath, feeling his neck again.

"And?"

"The guy said, *I'm gunning for your friend Rodney, but you'll do fine. Tell that loser*...I told him you're not a loser. He said, *Shut your trap. Tell him to forget Chauncey Chambers, or you'll both get more than this*. Then he snipped off my tie right below the knot with some heavy-duty scissors. The kind you use to cut sheet metal. Scratched my chest in the process. See, it's still bleeding. A little."

"Yikes! Can you describe him?" I asked.

"I didn't get a good look, except to notice he was well-dressed, wore some sort of hat with a prominent crease, and had an engaging smile, even while he threatened me. That was demonic. And then he was gone in a flash."

"I should call the police."

"The guy also said, *Don't dare call the police, or I'll be snipping something worse*."

I tend not to back off when my friends are threatened, at least I'd like to think Grimes would think I don't. "Okay, then, Wilbur. No police. I can deal with this myself. Not to worry."

"Then why am I still worried?"

15. Tin Snips, Perhaps?

I WANTED TO CHECK ON WILBUR so I rang his doorbell the next morning.

"Go away, whoever you are."

"It's Rodney. Open up."

"How do I know you're you, and not...him?"

"If I were him, I'd be well-dressed, wearing a hat with a crease, and have an engaging smile, which I'm not and don't."

Wilbur let me in. "Where's Inspector Grimes when we need him?" asked Wilbur. "He'd have pegged my mugger by now and figured out who hired him."

Wilbur was right. To start, the Inspector would have cataloged the choke-hold bruise on Wilbur's neck and calculated the angle that Wilbur's tie was snipped—neither of which I'd done, I was embarrassed to admit. Then he would have somehow used that information to link the attacker directly to one of the food truck cooks, or, sorry to say, even my own client, Maris Chambers.

As I left Wilbur's apartment, I wondered which food truck Grimes would focus on at this point. I could easily picture Butter Bar's cook dispatching Chauncey Chambers for humiliating him on live TV—I should check if Cook's hands are registered as lethal weapons. However, the orange paint under Blackeye Pete's' green paint and the few words Black let slip about some upcoming fish fry spoke volumes. While Butter Bar's cook's gun-wielding, ex-convict gang hogs the few available stools to protect their boss from who knows what, the antics with Blackeye Pete's up-and-down shutter were much too curious for comfort.

I tossed a nickel. Heads. I would concentrate on Blackeye Pete's for the next day or two. Though stopping first for breakfast at Butter Bar wasn't the worst idea I've had, and I needed a chance to somehow explain away my pending absence to Ginger—something impressive like "I'm going to be out of town receiving yet another English literature honorary degree." But when that stack of Butter Bar's caramelized-apple pancakes appeared before me, I felt like a traitor and couldn't look Ginger in the eye. Although that may have been because she hadn't shown up for work. Some Gladys person had taken her place, without a smiley face on her nametag, I might add, and denied she knew anything about, and I quote, "any Ginger dame."

Who was Gladys? Where was Ginger? Could Ginger have gotten wind that I'm a Butter Bar turncoat, that I have been eating at Blackeye Pete's a lot lately, and she was too upset to come in? Or much worse than that. That Butter Bar's cook had a hand in Chauncey Chambers' disappearance, that he sees me getting close with Ginger and got rid of her before I persuaded her to spill the beans? God knows what a chemical analysis of blood residue on Cook's butcher knife would reveal. Where could I wrangle samples of Ginger's DNA?

"Ah, go take a walk," said Gladys. "I hear they're shooting some star-studded detective flick outside an abandoned building between Warren and Monroe. Should be something to see."

I left Butter Bar and headed first to the riverside park benches. Couldn't sit still for more than five minutes. I got up and sidled past the ever-present mime, knees buckling a few times, but oblivious to any resulting laughter in my direction. I was falling into a deep funk worrying about Ginger and began to wander aimlessly down Warren, then stopped in front of Rainbow Cleaners. I entered and waited near the counter until it was my turn.

"Your receipt, please."
"I don't have one."
"Are you picking up?"
"Nope."
"Dropping off?"
"No."

I left the store in more of a daze than before and slogged on, eventually making my way to the abandoned five-story building at Warren and Monroe. But Gladys had it wrong—no actors, no film crew. Just me and a street sweeper.

Word of advice. Don't stop and look up if you ever hear a strange voice saying, "Yoo-hoo, up here," followed by a piercing two-note whistle. I did and was almost pulverized by a falling flowerpot. The street sweeper had shoved me aside with his broom.

"Hey, buddy," said the street sweeper, "you must have nine lives. Lucky for you I noticed some bearded guy accidentally knock that flowerpot off a fourth floor window ledge. It teetered, or tottered, on the edge, then fell. Barely missed you."

Accidentally? The flowerpot, or what was left of it, had been weighted down with tons of lead pellets and had held one black rose, coincidentally a symbol of death, as Grimes would be quick to point out. It was clearly not an accident. Just like it was no accident when a hapless haberdasher, witness to a kidnapping, met a similar, gruesome, flowerpot-inspired end in my novel *The Trembling Trench Coat*.

Gladys had baited the hook and that bearded guy had almost done me in. Butter Bar's cook hired Gladys for the day, but who was she really working for? And what about that guy? I thought about rushing up to the fourth floor after him, then thought about it some more. Grimes would have gone right in, though he'd have Watley and Watley would have his revolver. If only I had Wilbur, and Wilbur had...no, no, I refused to picture

Wilbur with a gun.

On the other hand, why should I care about any of this if Ginger were already lost to me forever?

I twisted my ankle on one of the lead pellets, glanced at that fourth-floor window, then hobbled on, discretion being the better part of valor. Passing The Tie Shoppe, a curious sight in the window, not that I had much energy to be curious: A Siamese cat curled up in a basket of cummerbunds. The salesman stepped outside and said, with a slightly British accent, "Good morning, sir. Caught needing a tie? May I ask the occasion? Formal or informal?"

"I don't need one," I said, starting to walk off, "but come to think of it, a friend of mine lost a tie in a horrific snipping incident—"

"So sorry to hear that."

"...so I'm thinking I might replace it."

"Splendid. Please come inside."

I left soon after I entered. Did you ever go to buy a tie? From afar, there's a sea of ties on display. You're sure there will be too many to choose from. Yet, up close, not one strikes your fancy. Still, I'll try again at some point.

I needed to change focus, something not Ginger. Dodson's Hardware. Some type of gizmo had come loose from my upstairs neighbor's doohickey and she begged me to help repair it before her company arrived. I approached the counter. A man looked up from his sports pages. Without even hearing the problem, he told me what to buy.

"If I were you, I'd go with either a three-jaw chuck or a topside creeper. Get both, to be safe. They're expensive, that's to be sure, but not to worry, you'll end up using them all the time. And you wouldn't believe what for."

Sensing gross insincerity or something even worse, I beat a hasty retreat.

He called after me. "A nut driver perhaps? Or tin snips?

Last one in stock. Just sold a pair."

I did an immediate about-face and went back inside. Rodney, P.I. was back in action.

"Oh, changed your mind? The nut driver's on sale."

"Who bought those tin snips?" I asked, holding out a ten-dollar bill. Grimes usually starts with a ten-pound note, so given the exchange rate, if this guy accepted ten dollars, I would be one up on the inspector.

"Don't recall his name," he said, grabbing my ten. "Well-dressed, though, wearing a hat with a crease, and he had an engaging smile. Sells butcher knives. Wanted me to stock them."

Back at my apartment, I couldn't stop thinking how the snipper had threatened Wilbur to get at me. But I needed to get some writing done. After feeding the fish, I coated my dip pen with too much India ink and leaned it against the candlestick while I went to feed the fish (odd that they didn't seem hungry), then I returned to my workroom to try to write.

Jon Johns entered the restaurant's airtight walk-in cooler and...

I hadn't been working for more than thirty seconds when my doorbell rang. I checked the peephole. Mabel? Strange. I didn't tell her my address. Turns out she had a professionally bound document about an inch thick, printed with *Rodney* in gold leaf on the cover. She sauntered in and flopped down on my couch, sweeping a pile of detective magazines and an empty jumbo bag of kettle chips off the seat cushion next to her, while saying, "Come to baby."

I stood my ground, as Grimes did in *The Balinese Bluff*.

"Suit yourself, hon," she said, holding out the document. "Listen. There's no need to read all the fine print. It's a simple agreement between you and Blackeye Pete's that all future meals will be equal to or surpass the ones you've been having lately. Most of all, it gives you a double portion of any order at half the regular menu price."

I knew there was a dangerous side to this, given Black's and Mabel's conversation, but signing the agreement still seemed like a no-brainer. I could continue playing detective and eat better at the same time, like Rex Stout's Nero Wolfe. Best to chance it and string them along. "Where do I sign?" I asked.

"And all that in return for a small promise on your part," she continued.

"Damn, my pen's out of ink. Have one I can borrow?"

"An insignificant promise...that Butter Bar is off limits...to you...forever. Forever!"

Up until that point she knew that I knew that I had nothing to lose by signing, but those last words of hers called for shock and hesitation on my part. Like I would give up Ginger's smiley face nametag or Butter Bar's twenty-four-hour, slow-cooked brisket with curly sweet potato fries (assuming for the moment I couldn't always get Butter Bar's food at Blackeye Pete's). "Forever? That's a lot to ask, though I'll concede, it's some deal," I said.

Mabel tossed the document onto my Eames coffee table. "Well, you think it over, babe. And let me assure you that contrary to popular opinion, *forever* is not as long as most people make it out to be." She blew me a kiss as she left.

I went back to Butter Bar the next morning, hoping for some word, any word, about Ginger. No sign of Gladys, or any waitress. Then joy of joys, Ginger popped up from beneath the counter holding a batch of napkins. What a relief to see her still alive and kicking, even if she might be kicking me later on.

"I missed you yesterday," I said. "I was worried. It's not like you to be out. I thought the worst. Came that close to checking the hospitals. I needed to know that everything's all right with you before I leave town."

"Can't a gal take a day off? God knows they're few and far between. Cook hired this Gladys person for the day. What'll ya have? What's it gonna be? What can I get ya? What's your poison?"

"I'll start with a large prune juice here at Butter Bar, then a double order of the Rock'em Sock'em Breakfast at Blackeye Pete's at half the regular price." Whoops!

16. Poke, Shoot, then Whip

GINGER'S ICY GLARE BANISHED me to Blackeye Pete's for the next few days. After some up-and-down shutter business, meals were much the same. No, better, even though I hadn't yet signed the agreement. Yesterday morning, a remarkable plum-glazed ham and Belgian waffle plate, and today, on a chilly afternoon, a garlicky white bean soup drowning one giant butter-fried crouton.

Peter I. Black scowled each time he first set eyes on me, but that could have been my imagination. Mabel didn't mention the agreement. I leaned over to her and whispered, "Where did Black learn to cook?"

"No formal training," said Mabel. "But the way he operates, he doesn't need any."

"I'm curious if he ever uses saffron and rose water. I hear it's all the rage."

"Funny you ask. He bought some of each a while ago, but I never saw him cook with them."

"So why the saffron and rose water?" I asked.

"I think he got them for someone else," said Mabel.

Black shot a glance at Mabel. I felt Mabel absorb it.

"Why are your prices higher than Butter Bar's?" I asked.

"You gets what you pays for."

"How long will Blackeye Pete's stay in town?"

"Three days, two hours, and one minute. Not a second longer, unless you sign the agreement and stay clear of that other food truck."

Butter Bar's cook was still suspect. I needed a good excuse to stall. "But there are gravy stains on the signature page."

"Don't worry about that. That's Pete's signature gravy. I gave you a jar."

A new customer arrived and took the stool next to me. Turned out to be a writer, Westerns to be exact, and he also uses pen and India ink, he says, like they did in the Old West. He introduced himself as C. B. Brantley, as he tipped his Stetson and tapped his oversize silver belt buckle.

"What's the C. B. stand for?" I asked.

"Cow Boy."

"Easy to remember," I said, wondering if he knew we're well east of the Mississippi. "That's quite a hat you got there. Quite a crease."

"I get it redone from time to time in town at Morgan's."

"When's that necessary?" I asked.

"After a scuffle."

"Ever see a snipper at Morgan's? Hat's also got a prominent crease."

"Don't think so, but it sounds like I'd have noticed such a fella if I saw him."

"Nice six-shooters image on your belt buckle."

"I have a real pair at home," he said. "Twin beauties, pearl handles. Ever need a hand with some no-good varmints here in Fern Creek, sure as shootin', you just call on old C. B."

"Will do. So it's pen and ink, huh? You ever use Freeman's Super Duper Black? It's my go-to ink."

"Does a duck shed water? But it's getting harder and harder to rustle up some. I'm on my last quarter bottle."

Nearly out of that ink myself, that struck a chord. I made several excuses, promised I'd show him my best nibs next time, and rushed off to Hudson's Stationers on Beacon and Wright, but the sign in the window turned me off: *Closed for Reasons*

We Can't Disclose. And their window display featured a bottle of the exact ink I needed, and in the more economical 4.2 fluid ounce size. So near and yet so far. I noted their emergency phone number and went to the phone booth on the corner. An answering service answered.

"What's the emergency?"

"I've only a few pages worth of ink left."

"That does sound serious."

I think they're paid to be empathetic, although I'd prefer that response to the opposite, something like, "Can't this wait until tomorrow?" I left a message for Hudson's, but based on past experience, I won't hold my breath until someone gets back to me. And if I'm lucky, I won't think of anything good to write beyond the number of words in my remaining five or ten nibfuls of Freeman's Super Duper Black.

I went home, lit the candle, dipped my pen, and picked up where I left off.

Jon Johns entered the restaurant's airtight walk-in cooler and let out such a resounding and cunning laugh it reverberated from the asparagus to the zucchini. He had invested a full week of his time befriending the restaurant's owner until he secured the cook's job at Detective Watley's favorite breakfast place. Of course, that's not to say that the previous cook's unfortunate and sickening 'accident' didn't help some. "Sure, I could have found an easier way to eliminate Watley, a fundamental part of my crusade to destroy Grimes," Johns told some plucked chickens sleeping on the walk-in shelves, "but shards of glass in Watley's prune juice has a delightfully sharp edge to it."

Johns' plan covered much more than getting rid of Watley. He explained further, this time to a bin of

gutted rabbits. "Given our proximity to Avon Circle, overrun and soiled by the obscenely affluent, many of whom are regular customers here, other enticing opportunities present themselves. Imagine two or three of them inadvertently ingesting some delayed-action knockout potion in their morning prune juice, rendering them easy prey for Drago to beat, hang, then rob. Or perhaps he should knife them first, then bash, then strangle them. Or poke, shoot, then whip them. But I swore not to do this again, micromanage Drago's actions, though it is my only vice."

That was just about it for my ink supply. Barely a partial dip left. Not nearly enough to add six important words to the 'To Do' list I keep by my lap desk:

Don't forget to **fee** th f sh.

And no call back from Hudson's. Maybe they tried to reach me but couldn't get through. I checked for a dial tone. Damn. There, loud and clear.

The phone rang. Wilbur, not Hudson's.
"I found a half bottle of some generic India ink you can have," he said. "It's not Freeman's Super Duper Black, but it might do until you could get over to Hudson's. Also, my cop friend called me back. He told me there's no police record for the guy I asked about, or at least they couldn't find anything yet. He needed a few more days to make sure. Says their system's not always that reliable. Oh, and Harry heard from his contact at Motor Vehicles. Black got his food truck for one dollar. The seller's signature on the transfer papers was scribbled. He said it looked something like Shambors, but it could be Chambers."

"Thank Harry for me if you see him before I do."

"Those things aside," said Wilbur, "I have a great new idea for you."

Glad to see Wilbur taking some initiative. It's a long shot, but he might even make a good sidekick some day. Though at present, he's vowed never to leave our building while the snipper's on the loose.

"We're still not one hundred percent sure that Blackeye Pete's is serving Butter Bar takeout, right?" said Wilbur.

"I'm ninety-seven percent sure," I said.

"Well, then there's still that three percent. Wasn't your Inspector Grimes in a similar spot in *The Wanton Cream Puff*? At a bake shop, not a food truck, but what he did there might work for you here. You would stand by the grill at Butter Bar while I order a certain dish at Blackeye Pete's. I bet Butter Bar's cook starts on a takeout order for the same stuff."

"That could work," I said, "*if* I had a certificate in grill repair. However—"

"I knew running away from that school would come back to haunt you," said Wilbur. "But maybe you could find a different school to study grill repair, or swallow your pride and go back to the first one. You'd still have to take that placement exam, but if they're serving...what's that again?"

"Double-crust beef pot pie."

"If they're serving that for lunch again, it may be worth it. And next time wear a tie to impress the admissions office. I can lend you one of mine. I have a whole closet full, minus one, of course, thanks to the snipper. My favorite. Come down, there's a bunch to choose from."

"Not now, Wilbur. Maybe later."

"Come now."

I reluctantly went one flight down to Wilbur's apartment. He opened his bedroom closet. There were indeed two dozen ties hanging neatly on some racks, but they were all alike—small red triangles on a gaudy blue background, exactly like the one the snipper snipped.

"Which one would you like to try on?"

17. The Platinum Plan

"I APPRECIATE ALL THIS," I TOLD Wilbur, "I really do, but I'm now thinking I should back off trying to blow the whistle on Blackeye Pete's for selling Butter Bar's food. It seems Black has something much more sinful to hide, and maybe it's best not to rock the takeout boat until I'm able to discover what it is. So try this idea on for size. I already bounced it off Harry. He was all for it. We want to find out what Black is up to. Well, I'm going to tail him. Note his every step."

"You mean like taking plaster casts of his footprints, even on the sidewalk?"

"I'd need your help if I'm to pull that part off," I said. "Anyway, I'll follow him home, then stake out his apartment all night, slumped down in the passenger seat of some nondescript rental car. Dark glasses, hat brim pulled down low, trench coat collar turned up, large thermos of hot coffee and a stack of ham sandwiches at hand. Then I'll dog him again the next morning."

"Send word if you need me," said Wilbur, "like if you're running out of sandwiches, but only if the snipper's been caught."

Anxious to get going, I left Wilbur and went straight to Carson's Car Rental. "I need a car that will blend in with the buildings and foliage in front of a particular cook's apartment house."

"Check out space 117, outside to your right."

The car was perfect. A murky midnight blue and already camouflaged. Scratched simulated wood paneling on the sides with some imaginative graffiti, and it must have been in some kind of accident recently, maybe even that morning, because it still had several broken-off tree branches across the hood and a bunch of green leaves stuck in the windshield wipers.

"Are you taking the insurance?" asked the agent when I returned to pay.

"Does it cover a burst of bullets?"

"You'll want the Platinum Plan."

Blackeye Pete's closes at 1630 hours military time. The car and I and Harry's binoculars were in place at 1615, across the street in the shadow of a laundry truck. The last two customers, the little girl without crusts and her father, were finishing their lemonades and getting up to leave. Why weren't they at Butter Bar? What were they doing at Blackeye Pete's?

I still wasn't sure about the cook's name. Maybe it's not Peter I. Black. Maybe that's why the cops couldn't find a record. I slipped into a nearby phone booth and dialed 867-3472. Two out-of-focus Mabels in my left and right binocular lenses picked up the phone. "The jig is up," I said, talking over lots of static. "Give us the cook's real name and we'll go easy on you." But I panicked and headed back to my car before she answered, leaving the phone dangling off the hook. I should have asked Wilbur or Harry to make the call. Mabel could have recognized my voice.

Peter I. Black, if that was his name, pulled down the steel shutter, stepped out the door, waved goodbye to Mabel, and started walking left on Collins. I pulled out and followed half a block behind, cursing the car for making all kinds of loud rattling noises. It even backfired twice, but Black probably thought it was gunshots. He turned left on Beacon, then right on Wentworth. I had to keep pulling over to the side to stay behind him. When he turned right on Wright, I was screwed. Wright went one-way in the other direction. I parked by a hydrant, then ran down Wright in time to see him turn right on Collins. I kept my distance until he came back to Blackeye Pete's. After switching off an inside light, he started again down Collins, then left on Beacon and several blocks down Wentworth until he entered a four-story red brick building. Precisely two minutes and thirty-five seconds later, lights went on in a third-floor apartment. Very suspicious.

I went back for my car, threw the parking ticket into the glove compartment and was soon settled in for what might be a long night in front of Black's building. I started to unscrew my coffee thermos top when Harry, happening by, peeked through the passenger-side window and signaled me to roll it down, while starting to remove some of the tree branches across the car hood.

"Harry, stop! You're gonna blow my cover. And pretend you don't know me," I said.

"Excuse me, stranger, perhaps you didn't notice, but you have tree branches across your hood."

"Act like they're not there."

"How do I do that?"

"Imagine the hood to be branch-free."

"That's easy for you to say."

"Visualize polishing the hell out of the hood until you can see yourself in it, then admire a job well done."

Harry stared at the hood while making imperceptible circular motions with his hands. "It's not working," he said. "I can still see the branches."

I needed to change the subject. "Harry, did you ever deliver mail to that building?"

"128 Wentworth? It's not on my regular route, but yes, I have, once or twice during snowstorms."

"How would you describe the mail box configuration?"

"They're on one wall of the entranceway and I think they may have been marked with names, or was it apartment numbers? Yeah, one or the other. And the tile floor was icy and slippery."

"You're absolutely sure about that? You're not mixing up this building with some others?"

"Positive."

Harry went on his way. As Inspector Grimes would say, some key pieces of the puzzle were now falling into place, but several were still out of reach. Why would Black leave his food truck at the end of the day, then return minutes later? Simply to shut a light, or to destroy some key evidence once Mabel had left? Why would he then not only go home, but go directly home? And must I believe that switching on a light as he entered his apartment has nothing at all to do with the disappearance of Chauncey Chambers?

Harry said the apartment entranceway had a tile floor. How might that be significant? Tile is the material of choice for a restaurant floor. Easy to rinse provided there's good drainage, easy to keep clean. Maybe that extends to food trucks as well. Now if *both* Butter Bar and Blackeye Pete's have tile floors—Blackeye Pete's does, I stood on it—maybe both cooks are in cahoots with Maris Chambers.

Two ham sandwiches down, one to go. I should have known three wouldn't be enough. Even so, I had to stay put until Black made his next key move. I checked my watch every once in a while: 17:48:36, 18:21:04, 19:12:23.

At 20:34:45, Black came out a side door, tossed a plastic bag into a garbage can, then went back in.

Nine and a half hours later Black came out the front door and walked up Wentworth toward his food truck. What on earth did he do in his apartment for those last nine and a half hours?

Nine and a half. Half past nine. Some sort of clue?

"Still closed," said a frustrated Inspector Grimes

as Detective Watley tried in vain to pick the lock on a repair shop door in the dreary basement of 228 Wentwell. "Concentrate, man, time is of the essence. Oh, stand back. Let me try my hand."

Watley's weak attempt at protest ended after a resounding Grimes-induced *click*. Grimes opened the door to reveal a large, musty room filled with old clocks of all shapes and sizes. "You take this side, I'll take that one," snapped Grimes, "and we must hurry. Look for clocks with hands pointing to half past nine or thereabouts."

The two lawmen checked high and low. There were no such clocks to be found.

"Just as I surmised," said a jubilant Grimes. "Sixty-six clocks present. Not one shows anything close to 9:30."

"I fail to see any connection to the Spice Murders or any other case we're working on," Watley noted.

"Correct you are, my good man. This has nothing to do with any of them. It was merely a mathematical exercise to fill our free time. My hypothesis: Given a repair shop with less than sixty-seven old clocks in various states of disrepair, some running fast, others slow, some not at all, *none* will exhibit a time within five minutes either side of 9:30. It's my belief that a minimum of a hundred thirty-two old clocks would be necessary to assure at least one such result, a theory I will test at our earliest opportunity."

"I may call in sick that day," said poor Watley.

18. Unrequited Love

I CALLED WILBUR AND ASKED him to stop by. "It's time to take it up a notch, my friend. You still have your commando duds and grease paint?"

"Two sets," said Wilbur. "But whatever it is, leave me out of it. The snipper's still out there."

"I'm going in tomorrow night and need your help."

"I said leave me...going in? Where to? Butter Bar this time?"

"Yeah, I bought a new transmitter and want to hide it under one of their working stove grates."

"Not a good...you're kidding, right?"

"Our target is the Chambers mansion. Maybe something in Chauncey's possessions points to his captors. Maybe something there connects Maris Chambers to the kidnapping. Harry's driving getaway. He'll pick us up ten to eight. Says to tell you you need to get back on the horse."

"Well, I do have all that grease paint. Okay, I'm in. One last time. But what about that Chambers woman?"

"Charity event to support housemaids of film and TV celebrities, sports figures, and hedge fund managers. Here. Check out the *Gazette*, page 6, second paragraph."

Wilbur ran down to his apartment to get his reading glasses, returning about ten minutes later. "Let's see. Blah, blah, blah...*from eight to nine tomorrow...hosted by Maris Chambers.*"

"Her maid will be with her. Shouldn't be anyone home."

"Vicious guard dogs?"

"We'll find out, won't we?"

Harry called. He was out replenishing his supply of Dog-B-Gone and I asked him to get me a can.

"How's the Chauncey Chambers investigation going?" asked Harry.

"It starts and it stalls. Maybe by tomorrow night..."

"And Butter Bar versus Blackeye Pete's?"

"So far, not enough to go on."

"Go at it from a different angle," said Harry. "Go back to Ginger. Ask her out. Woo her into a tizzy. Grill her about both food trucks when she doesn't suspect it."

I took Harry's advice, mostly because I missed Ginger, so after a more than ample Butter Bar lunch of traditional Dutch pea soup, boiled smokehouse bacon with thin-sliced celery root on pumpernickel, and blueberry crumble pie, and after leaving a more than adequate tip, I asked her, "How's about taking in a movie this evening? The feature goes on at half past nine."

Surprise of surprises, she said, "I guess."

I must be getting through to her. Though I'm not sure why. I called Wilbur to kick around one crafty next approach or another, but he couldn't talk. Said he needed to finish a crossword puzzle if he remembered where he left it that morning.

I was running early so I took the long way around to Ginger's. The more direct route would have taken me past Adel's Doughnut Dugout with their *Hot Right Now* neon sign flashing. Not that I would have passed Adel's—their pumpkin pie doughnuts are too hard to resist. That missed doughnut opportunity was hard to put aside, but at the same time, maybe I avoided some kind of disaster on the shorter route, like stubbing my toe on a section of broken parking meter pole and lurching into the windshield of a Dodge Caravan.

I called for Ginger at a quarter to nine and handed her a large box of assorted chocolates.

"Should we take it with us?" she asked, after pecking me hello on my cheek, a nice first for her.

"You'd have to sneak it in under your sweater," I said, offering to tape it to her waist.

"I'd ask you in," she said nervously, "but my sis...my roommate's icing her toes from a terrible mushroom soup mishap."

That revelation did not go unnoticed. I wished I had one of those miniature handheld recording devices to capture it. I could play it over and over again, and see what Wilbur and Harry make of what she started to say about her roommate, then corrected herself.

"By the way, what's your sis...your roommate's name?" I asked.

"By the way, what movie are we seeing?"

Kiss My Grits, a heart-wrenching saga of unrequited love for Southern home cooking in the backwoods of Louisiana, was playing at The Odeon. I've seen it three times. I motioned Ginger into the back row. A long forty minutes into the film, time to make my move. The next scene was the one I had been waiting for, a close-up of a hog jowl and black-eyed peas dinner bubbling in a cast-iron pot, but Ginger had dozed off. I could have taken advantage and kissed her on the cheek several times, but instead nudged her awake—career over caresses. As she once again focused on the screen, I leaned over and whispered softly in her ear, hoping to trick her into blurting out what she knows about Blackeye Pete's: "Black-eyed peas...Blackeye Pete's...black-eyed peas."

I listened for what she would let slip, checked her pupils, took her hand, felt her pulse, took her hand again. But no revelations, no reaction short of a questioning sideways glance. She was a tough nut to crack. And it cost me over thirty-five dollars, with the tickets, soda (she can sure drink a lot), bonbons, gumdrops, and caramel popcorn. I guess a kiss or two would have made it worth it, but even then, I could have bought six bottles of Freeman's Super Duper Black for that amount of money. That ink would last me several years if I wrote for eight full hours a day, although I can't see that ever happening. Maybe two hours, or four if I'm willing to stretch the truth. And now we still had to sit through the remaining hour and fifteen minutes of the film. I excused myself and went out to the lobby to call Wilbur, unconcerned about interrupting his crossword puzzle.

"Wilbur, she's button-lipped."

"Hold a sec. What's a number, four letters, beginning with 'f'? I think there's also an 'r'."

"Are you working in permanent marker?"

"As always."

Hard to pass up messing with Wilbur. "F.o.r.e."

"But..."

"But nothing. Write it in. Now you owe me a favor. Call Harry and ask him if he's ever delivered mail to number 88 Clausen Street, apartment 8. Ginger's shielding the identity of some mystery woman who's living with her."

Harry got back to me on the stroke of midnight. "It's not my route," he said. "Edgar would be your man, but he's on the straight and narrow. He goes by the book, respects a person's privacy and all that nonsense. Though he's prone to bouts of cold feet, so on a day when he calls in sick..."

I called Wilbur and filled him in on what Harry told me. I braced for Wilbur's thoughts on what I should do next.

"I doubt you can act on this," he said. "Too much involved. But for the record, you should recruit Edgar's replacement to deliver a Registered Mail letter addressed to

Second Occupant Only, then find a former police sketch artist to hang around the scene. When Ginger's sis…uh, roommate, signs for it, he'll do a drawing of her face. We'll see who she is. Might be enlightening."

I put Wilbur's idea on hold. I had a much better approach.

I stopped by Blackeye Pete's first thing the next morning. "I'm thinking of having lunch here today," I told Mabel. "Just checking. Any soup left from yesterday?"

"Cream of asparagus, cream of chicken, cream of broccoli, cream of carrot, cream of cream."

"Cream of anything else?"

"No."

"You're absolutely sure? Need I ask the cook myself?"

"He's not here. Had some meeting this morning. We're not open yet."

"Cream of anything else?" I asked again, but this time the *I'll accept no nonsense* way Grimes would have asked.

"Cream of mushroom," she finally admitted, looking down at her feet and wincing.

I got a bowl to go, then tried a spoonful. Nothing to wince about. It tasted fine. Pretty good, actually. But it was now clear as a bell—Mabel lives with Ginger.

19. Ticket to Paradise

Peter I. Black sat facing the president of the PinkyPink Gum Corporation. *Keep your cool*, thought Black.

"Look, I know you think you got a raw deal," said the president from behind his bright pink bowtie.

Cool went out the window. "Think? What do you mean, think?" said Peter I. Black. "This lousy company screwed me out of my job, my pension, well, everything. It forced me out for no good reason, then sat back while some politicians trying to make a name for themselves got me sent to jail on trumped-up charges."

"That happened before I came on board, but in our defense, from what I heard, at the time it seemed that—"

"Listen," said Black. "I had to buy a food truck to try to make ends meet, and they don't come cheap. I knew little about food trucks, though lately, I've been doing all right. I don't even know why I agreed to meet you. I vowed I'd never set foot in this dump again. And I had to stay closed this morning to be here. You should have come to me."

The president wasn't sure he could trust Black, but with a big PinkyPink media event coming up, ironically, he needed Blackeye Pete's, mostly for its location. Several board members keep pouncing on him for what they've been calling a general lack of decisiveness. And now a critical deadline approached. He had yet to secure an event site. Doing so might get them off his back.

"Perhaps the company fired you in haste without any

hard evidence, so let us make it up to you," said the president, trying his best to be contrite. "We're planning to sponsor a unique and exciting competition a couple of weeks from now. State and local dignitaries will participate in our first annual PinkyPink bubble gum bubble-blowing contest. We need lots of space near the center of town to accommodate a bandstand, tents, chairs, all kinds of media equipment. We'd also like to have a popular eatery here in Fern Creek serve as host and your food truck, Blackeye Pete's, situated on that large piece of land, would be ideal."

Black tried to remain defiant.

"It's exactly what we're looking for," said the president. "There's been much buzz around the factory lately about Blackeye Pete's. Some of our managers, who sneak two-hour lunch hours—they don't know I know—eat there. A few of our other employees do so as well, though they are hard-pressed to get back to work on time. I do hear it's a long wait for the food—"

"Hey. It's not like we send out for it ourselves," said Black. "Everything's made from scratch. That takes time."

"...though at the event you'd be serving only coffee and doughnuts. But they do love your home-style cooking. Comfort food at its best. They say it reminds them so much of Butter Bar's. I know their food. Did you ever try Butter Bar's *Smoked Bacon & Chives Mac & Cheese*? Sorry. I guess you wouldn't want to give them the right time of day. To be up front with you, we first considered using Butter Bar, but their setup isn't good for us. Not enough space. Blackeye Pete's' participation will help assure huge crowds for our contest, and I'm sure you could use the publicity. I hear you have tough competition with, let's say, that other food truck. And the best part is, you'll be paid a tidy sum, half in advance."

Black first raised one eyebrow, then the other, then tested the waters. "Fork over that half today. Now."

"That's a bit sudden...but okay, why not?" The president smiled a false smile as he wrote a check and pushed it across his desk. Anything to resolve his dilemma. "What say you to this amount?"

One glance and Peter I. Black told the president, "Fine. I'm willing to let bygones be bygones. I'm in." Black grabbed the check, stuffed it in his shirt pocket, and left.

Peter I. Black lowered his binoculars and handed them to Mabel. "Tell me what you see," he said, pointing to the valley below.

"You already told me what it is. It's the PinkyPink bubble gum factory."

"Look again."

"Still see that crummy factory."

"Try 'cash cow,' our ticket to paradise," said Black. "Once this and that other deal is over I should clear a cool hundred grand. We can ditch this goddamn food truck once and for all. What the hell. We'll ditch it in a ditch. I paid almost nothing for it."

"Yeah, though you *did* something for it," said Mabel. "But what do I get for going along with all this?"

"How'd you like to be Mrs. Peter I. Black?"

Mabel answered, with a seductive smile, "With that kind of money, do you think I'd say no?"

"I'll take that as a yes," said Black, his hands now around Mabel's waist.

Blackeye Pete's' mail delivery that afternoon included a bright red envelope that cried out *Open me first if you dare*. Harry handed the entire stack to Mabel and left without giving his customary, poorly veiled, daily hint about desperately needing a free cup of coffee to keep him going.

"That's curious," said Mabel, passing the mail to Black.

"It's not like Harry to rush off like that. It's usually all I can do to get rid of him."

"Trouble, big trouble," cried Black, looking up from the sheet of paper he was holding. "And just when things were going our way. Read this and weep."

Mabel read the note out loud: *"$10,000 keeps me mum, or you'll feel the heat(s). Get Butter Bar takeout at Blackeye Pete's."*

"It's blackmail!" said Black. "If this gets out, our food truck cover will be ruined and PinkyPink'll drop us."

"Maybe it's a bluff, without proof," Mabel suggested.

Black reached into the envelope and pulled out a Blackeye Pete's Signature Gravy label still partially stuck to a Butter Bar Signature Gravy label. "It's no bluff. Besides, if it's Butter Bar's delivery boy Danny who wrote the note, what more proof does he need than to know he's always picking up takeout from Butter Bar and sneaking it here to our back window? So far, it seems we've been paying him well enough to keep his mouth shut, but who knows what he's thinking now. We have to find a way to stall the guy until after the contest, whoever he is. Danny, or some other creep."

"We can say we need time to come up with the dough," said Mabel.

"No, I have a better way, but we need Butter Bar to cooperate. And they will when their takeout business dries up. I hear they're still not picking up Chauncey's Chow customers, and of course, now we're around. You'll have to talk to your roommate. What's her name? Ginger? Though, could she be on to us? Could she make trouble?"

"Ginger? Nah. She's a dud. Harmless. She thinks we're close, like sisters. I've been stringing her along. She'll do whatever I say."

20. Dog-B-Gone

WILBUR AND I MET HARRY outside our building at ten to eight. Anyone passing by would have seen two characters dressed all in black, gloves, cap and all, getting into Harry's car, an old clunker with a bench seat.

"Get in back, Wilbur."

Wilbur squeezed into the front with me and Harry.

"What's that you're chewing?" I asked Wilbur. "Gumm Gum?"

"It's PinkyPink bubble gum, this time," said Wilbur. "It's a new flavor, *Papaya Porkchop*. Harry gave me some. You didn't like the taste, right, Harry? Here, try one. See what you think. Though I forgot, Harry told me not to talk to anyone about it. Sorry, Harry. I'm supposed to keep this confidential, so Rodney, make sure to tell anyone you tell not to tell anyone."

Never a dull moment when Wilbur's around. I put the gum in my pants pocket for later, or never.

Harry dimmed the headlights as he dropped us off at the Chambers mansion at 8:00 p.m., then parked a hundred yards up the street. Lights were on in one ground floor room and two second-story rooms. The rest of the house was dark.

"Now that's what I'd call a high gate," said Wilbur. "I'm not sure we can scale it. Hand me the acetylene torch. I'll cut through in three places."

"We haven't got a torch. Do you see me carrying a torch?"

"Then plastic explosives will do fine, except for the noise."

"No explosives. Why not see if it's open?"

The gate wasn't locked. We ducked into shadows along a row of evergreens to reach the building. Landscape lighting made use of the driveway and slate path to the front door out of the question.

"How do we expect to get in?" asked Wilbur.

"You mean, how *you're* going to get in. Follow me." We went around back. "Yes. Just as I thought." I pointed to a hinged metal opening in the rear wall, about a foot and a half by two feet, about two feet off the ground. "Think you can fit through that?"

"What is it?"

"It used to be the coal chute, for deliveries. Most houses this old have one, or at least had one. Lucky for us, this one still does. And chances are, it's a poorly secured way into the cellar."

When we forced the cover, some old boards nailed across the opening from the inside were easily knocked out of the way.

"In you go, Wilbur. Find the rear service entrance and let me in."

He shimmied in and I tried to ignore sounds of the resulting crash. I forgot to warn him that the cellar floor might be considerably below ground level.

I met Wilbur at the service entrance. I could hear him turning keys and removing a chain lock. I could also hear lots of loud yapping, then growling. The door opened. Maris' miniature poodle had locked his teeth onto Wilbur's pant leg and wouldn't let go. Time for my can of Dog-B-Gone to work its magic. I tried. No effect.

"Spray it again," pleaded Wilbur. "My ankle's gonna be next."

The sight of him trying to shake that little dog off his leg would have ordinarily been comical—well, it was comical—but we were losing precious time. Maris Chambers would be gone for little more than an hour.

"Forget the spray," I said. "It doesn't work. He even seems to like it. Let's get upstairs."

The damn dog would not let go. Wilbur had no choice but to drag it along.

"What are we looking for?" asked Wilbur as we reached the main level.

"Clues to Chauncey Chambers' whereabouts? Something implicating Maris? Exactly what, I'm not sure, but we'll know it if we see it. You and the dog take the upstairs. Have him bark if you need me."

While Wilbur bumped and banged his fluffy friend up the central staircase, I surveyed the ground floor layout: parlor, music room, library, dining room, kitchen, office. The office? My first stop. Wilbur showed up about a minute or two later.

"How'd you ditch the dog?"

"I stuck my foot in a closet and squeezed it off by closing the door. But I came to tell you there's a trunk in one of the bedrooms you should see."

"Let's start here in the office," I said. "I'll check the drawers, you look through this pile of papers on the desk."

"What a mess. Looks like someone got here before us."

"Found something," I said, after a time. "Maris' checkbook. So what's here? Carbon copies for Fern Creek Gas and Electric, plumber, *Gazette* subscription, the maid's weekly salary. Wow. I should take that job myself. Here's something. There are checks she made out to herself. Checks she would cash. Big amounts. Seems to be three for $2,000 each, dated...lemme see...every Thursday over the last three weeks. Could be ransom money. Then there's one for $1,200 from about four weeks ago. Anything on the desk? Anything in the trash can?"

"Nothing really," said Wilbur, "except maybe for this—a

takeout menu from Butter Bar. A bunch of things are circled."

"Maris must have used it three or four different times. Inks look different. No way to tell if the orders were placed before or after her husband and his food truck went missing. Let's keep at it."

"Too bad Butter Bar isn't open at night," said Wilbur. "I could go for their—"

"Hold on," I said, flipping through a folder marked *Real Estate*. "Did you know Chauncey Chambers owns land near the river? And three parcels in the middle of...yikes, look at the time. You better show me that trunk now. The third Mrs. Chambers could be back in twenty minutes."

We were greeted by a muffled yapping and scratching as we entered one of the smaller bedrooms. A steamer trunk stood next to the bed, open and stuffed to overflowing.

"I'd say that Maris Chambers has her sights set on an elegant cruise, wouldn't you, Wilbur? Long, sequined evening gowns, faux furs, this velvet gown marked *Hold for Elizabethan Ball*."

Wilbur picked up a manila envelope from the bed and handed it to me.

"Now this is something," I said. "Her copy of the contract for the *Queen Mary 2* cruise. Signed soon after her husband went missing, no less. And here's some more recent correspondence with the cruise line. They wrote, *It's come to our attention that your husband is a celebrity chef. We are pleased to offer both of you free passage in return for several cooking demonstrations by him on board.* Then there's a second letter from them noting their *regrets to hear that Mr. Chambers has a previous engagement and is unable to accept our offer*. I'll assume that's based on her negative response to their first letter."

Wilbur backed up and knocked over a stack of shoeboxes. The dog in the closet stopped his racket, then started in again.

"Set those back up, Wilbur, before she returns home."

"Fancy shoes in this one, fancy shoes in that one, something else in this one."

Wilbur gave me the box. I recognized the threads of saffron wrapped in rice paper, and confirmed the smell of rose water in a small bottle.

"That's odd," said Wilbur. "Why hide saffron and rose water and a fountain pen in a shoebox on the bedroom floor?"

"Not so odd, my friend, when you need to conceal the fact that you sent a ransom note to yourself. The one she showed me when she came to my apartment. But I still think she's paying someone $2,000 a week...crap, it's 9:15. Let's get out of here."

We made it through the coal chute, patched it up as best we could, and were out the front gate and into Harry's car as a taxi pulled up with Maris Chambers and her maid.

"A tall order, but it went well," I told Harry.

"Except..." said Wilbur.

"Except what?" asked Harry.

"We forgot to let the dog out of the closet."

Carl's Cloak-a-Truck on Hansberry is supposed to open at 8:00 a.m., so I got there at 7:00 to poke around, especially through a pile of discarded truck parts on the far side of the premises. At 8:25 an unshaven dude in denim showed up. "You Carl?" I asked.

He looked me up and down, cigarette dangling from his lips. "Got a truck you want painted? Only place in town."

"Yeah, yeah, I know all that. Listen. You painted a truck about a month ago. Some questions need answers."

"You a cop? I don't know nothing."

"Do I look like one?" I showed him an old newspaper clipping with a lousy picture of me running the sausage counter at Crawley's Market, then held up a twenty.

"Maybe I do know something."

"That bright orange food truck you painted a dreary green."

Carl thought for a moment. "Hey, I didn't pick the color."

"Who brought you the truck?"

"Don't know. It was in my yard when I got here to open up. They had slipped an envelope through my office mail slot. With the keys and a note."

Carl stopped short. I had to add a twenty.

"The note said to paint it green. That they don't care what it looks like except that I should get rid of all identifying marks, and that someone named White would come by to pick it up in two days. And I should let him take it, no questions asked. And he did. I paint trucks. That's what I do."

"Forget something?" I said.

"Whaddya mean?"

"The $1,200 cash."

"When someone pays me twice the going rate, I get going. I didn't break no laws."

"What'd this White look like?"

"Medium height, lean and mean."

I glanced at the junk pile. "So you didn't mind removing the *Chauncey's Chow* sign. When almost everyone in Fern Creek thought he left town to take his truck on the road. Didn't that bother you? Didn't you think something was not legit?"

"Like I said, when it's twice the going rate."

"And what about those painted flowers all over the truck?"

"Ha, ha. My stepdaughter did that. She was hanging around itching for something to do. Who are you, again?"

This detective work hiked my appetite to the hilt. I now had a powerful vision—an order of Butter Bar's breakfast sausage and egg sliders, eaten at Blackeye Pete's. (I didn't used to be so cynical.) I seemed more excited about breakfast than I had been in a long time, and I'm always excited about breakfast. And by having a Butter Bar breakfast at Blackeye Pete's, I can keep a closer eye on Peter I. Black. Best of both worlds. So I returned home to feed the fish, then hurried out.

A ten-minute walk brought me to—no freakin' way, I couldn't have been seeing clearly. Surreal. A vacant lot with only a few empty soda bottles scattered here and there, the no-deposit kind, which are rare nowadays. No Blackeye Pete's, no Peter I. Black, not even a Mabel in sight. Was I just hit with a brick? How does Grimes deal with the unexpected? Would he feel as disoriented as I felt? I headed to Butter Bar straight away. I needed to see it safe and sound in its usual place. Besides, I had told Ginger recently I'd be back for their baked cinnamon and pear oatmeal. Why not make good on that promise? I staggered the few blocks. No Butter Bar either. No cook. And no Ginger. Not that I expected Ginger to still be standing there at that point.

A disturbing calm took hold. Butter Bar and Blackeye Pete's had both vanished!

PART II

21. Radio Silence

HELP ME, INSPECTOR GRIMES. Help me find Butter Bar and Blackeye Pete's. Even if you have to bring Detective Watley along. He can hang out with Wilbur. Birds of a feather…

Fern Creek's small. Where else could the food trucks be? They're not allowed on the streets. So I've now lost touch with two suspect cooks, one much more suspect than the other, just when I'm close to cracking the Chambers case. And there's no more comfort food for me in Fern Creek, unless I make it myself, and that's not going to happen anytime soon. There's no more of Butter Bar's spicy paprika egg salad on pumpernickel rye, Blackeye Pete's/Butter Bar's BBQ pork dumplings, Butter Bar's wild strawberry jelly doughnuts, or Blackeye Pete's/Butter Bar's caramelized banana cream pie. And last but not least, no more—dare I think it?—no more Ginger.

I somehow made it back to my apartment. After mechanically consuming several bowls of dry Cheerios, I needed to put aside this major setback and lose myself in my work.

Inspector Grimes' office chair had vanished into thin air—there one moment, gone the next. His file cabinet dematerialized, his wastebasket, unaccounted for. Both housecats disappeared without a trace. The housekeeper was AWOL. As for Watley, his shoes stood

empty in the middle of the floor, his newspaper's classified section missing, his corduroy vest devoid of...

I managed those few words, crossed them out, started again, then gave up. How on earth to rally? How to rise up and spring into action like Grimes would do? I picked up the phone and called Harry, who called Edgar, who called Edgar's replacement, who called me back. "Did you deliver mail this morning to 88 Clausen, apartment 8?"

"Yes. What a lovely older couple. New tenants. He must have been a retired seafaring man, given the scrimshaw collection he insisted on showing me. She lamented ending a long career as understudy to a concert accordionist. She offered me several glasses of homemade lemonade, which were much too tart yet much too sweet."

Older couple? I hung up and made a beeline for Ginger's apartment. The doorbell was broken, so I knocked instead. A man and woman answered. I introduced myself. "Bert, from Best Darn Buzzers." (Could I think fast, or what?) "I take it you're having a problem with your doorbell."

"We didn't request a service call."

"Then it must have been the previous occupants. Two women, I believe. Did they leave a forwarding address? I'll deal with them directly."

"But the doorbell is...here."

"But they initiated the call, didn't they? So where can I reach them?"

"Well, we met only one of the women and she grumbled something about not wanting to shift everything to East Harlan on such short notice."

East Harlan is east of Harlan and north of Southeast Harlan, about seventy-five miles from Fern Creek. I hear it's mostly a huge industrial park and waste dump, not exactly the top of anyone's *can't wait to visit* list.

"I'm heading out to East Harlan by bus," I told Wilbur the next morning. "There's some food truck monkey business and I'm going to get to the bottom of it. I need you to feed my fish for the next few days." Then, recalling Inspector Grimes' savvy tactic in *The Telltale Trombone*, I added, "Let's keep in touch. We might have to maintain radio silence, but if so, I'll find some other way to stay connected."

"Bring 'em back alive," said Wilbur.

Did you ever take the express bus from Fern Creek to East Harlan? There's typically a big commotion when it's time to choose the lunch stop. Half the passengers insist on Raymond's Rest, the rest prefer Patsy's Patties across the road. I dared to suggest Sally's Sandwiches—I touted their corned beef on club with tart and tangy apple and raisin slaw—although I reluctantly admitted to the other passengers that Sally's would be about thirty minutes out of our way. But the bus driver likes Chuck's Stop, not far from Patsy's, so that's where we ended up. As we filed in, Chuck, perched on a high wooden stool outside the front door, pitched the cooks' specials of the day.

"Extra flaky chicken pot pie, a few servings left," he told me, almost in confidence, while handing me a blank slip of colored paper and a crayon. "Write down your name and lunch order, then hand it directly to one of the line cooks inside," said Chuck, winking.

"Chuck, you have an unobstructed view of the road," I said. "Any chance you saw a bright yellow food truck with bright red trim being towed toward East Harlan the other day?"

"Doesn't ring a bell."

"How about a motorized food truck painted a dreary green with dirty-yellow flowers?"

"Doesn't strike a note."

I still have lots to learn from Grimes about not backing

off. The inspector would have presented Chuck with a photo album 'lineup' of five or six food trucks, including Butter Bar and Blackeye Pete's. He would then use Watley's muscle to jog Chuck's memory, although I'm not sure Watley could have done that in front of all the bus passengers. Not that they would have jumped to get involved, but the bus driver may have felt obligated to take some action in Chuck's defense, especially while remembering Chuck's chicken pot pie from past trips. There's nothing like a flaky crust to establish loyalty. Even I may have come to Chuck's defense after having had his chicken pot pie.

Luck of the draw, the paper and crayon Chuck gave me were both yellow. I scribbled *Rodney: Chicken pot pie* and handed it to a line cook, then glanced around for an open seat.

"I can't read what you've written," he complained. He showed it to the other cook, who looked befuddled.

"It's that the yellow crayon doesn't show well against the yellow paper," I suggested. "Try to slant it. Maybe the fluorescents will catch the waxy letters."

The two cooks tilted the slip toward the ceiling and tried to view it all kinds of other ways but still couldn't read my order. I pictured one of the few remaining chicken pot pies slipping through my fingers. "Why don't I tell you what I want?" I said.

"Not allowed," said one cook.

"Against Chuck's rules, and he's the boss," said the other. "He insists his way is more efficient. We tack up each order directly from the customer so there are no mistakes and take it down when it's done."

"What if you held the paper near the stove?" I said. "Maybe some of the wax would melt and be easier to notice."

But the first cook held the paper too close to a flame. It went up in a puff of smoke, with some of the melted wax burning his fingers. I stood there dumbfounded, not sure what to do next. Should I beg Chuck for another slip of paper, a darker one this time? Or muscle him like Watley would have done?

"We're leaving in three. Be there or stay here," announced the bus driver a minute or two later. In desperation, I bought a jumbo bag of BBQ trail mix and several pieces of PinkyPink bubble gum and ran out the door, passing Chuck as he was saying something to himself like, "Come to think of it, there *was* a yellow and red..."

That's all I heard.

We pulled into East Harlan close to two in the afternoon. I couldn't speak for the other passengers, but I was near starving. The Dandy Diner next to the bus depot looked inviting so I made that my first stop. Two other customers were there at the time, a father and daughter in one of the far booths. It looked like the girl without crusts. If it were her, I could have asked them if they saw any of the Fern Creek food trucks while they were here in East Harlan, since they always seemed to be eating, but it couldn't have been her. Wouldn't she be back home about to get out of school at that time? Of course, her father could have taken her out early on some pretext, like for an orthodontist appointment that didn't exist, but if that were the case, she would have had her school books with her. Regrettably, I couldn't tell whether there were school books on the seat next to her or if her father had put them on the seat next to him. They might even have been in their car. I could have gone outside and peeked through the windows—the one car out front must have been theirs—but if I didn't see any school books, the issue wouldn't necessarily be closed. What if her school books were in the trunk? The other day, Harry said he would show me how to pop open someone's car trunk without ruining the lock, but he put me off.

With no waitress in sight, either a cook or a sumo

wrestler in kitchen whites, anyone's guess, came out of the kitchen to take my order. "Too late for today's special," he grunted.

"Nice establishment you got here."

"No good trying to butter me up, butterball. Like I said, you missed it. And I ain't changin' the rules, especially for a squirt like you."

"What was it today?"

"My *Smoked Bacon & Nothing Else Mac & Cheese.*"

"No chives?"

"We ran out yesterday."

After a not too shabby *Twin Burger Deluxe*, which, coincidentally, had been one of Butter Bar's specialties, the cook directed me next door to the Excelsior, as he said, the best, the worst, the only hotel this part of town.

"Like a room with a view?" asked the desk clerk. "Have to warn you, though. It's a few dollars more."

"Go for it," I said.

Once in my room, I'd call the Excelsior the worst. The 'view' from the two rear windows—East Harlan's industrial dump, miles and miles of it, stretching to the horizon. I picked up the phone and gave Wilbur's number to the switchboard operator, at first jumbling it to maintain some degree of secrecy, then giving her the correct number when the first call didn't work. Wilbur grilled me about the room.

"How're the walls?"

"They're so thin, I can hear dust settling on the bedspread next door."

"How're the rugs?"

"They're so worn, you can see through to the room below."

Wilbur hung up before I could tell him why I called.

Could I tough it out here for a few days? There was one

redeeming aspect—the front windows overlooked Dandy Diner. So the binoculars and tripod I agonized about bringing with me might be useful after all. I trained both on the diner's front door and watched for several hours, mainly to check for a delivery of chives for the cook's macaroni and cheese, then I went over to sample their Southern fried chicken.

Still no waitress.

"How about some biscuits with our signature sausage gravy?" the cook asked.

"Gravy?"

"We also sell it."

"Sure, I'll try some," I told him. "Oh. Any place in town I can get a frame for my certificate in grill repair?"

"Interesting," said the cook. "It so happens, I'm having a major problem with our grill."

I stopped at the hotel's front desk on the way back to my room. "I'm in 53. One of the windows looking out toward your town's wonderful dump is stuck. I can't shut it."

"Otto, go up and help this guy."

Otto grabbed his toolbox and followed me upstairs. The room key wouldn't turn to the right. I tried several times until sensing the door was already unlocked. Not a good sign. We both entered.

"Ouch. What happened here? Someone's been through my stuff." I assured Otto that I'm not that messy, not that he seemed to care.

"I see nothing. I know nothing," he said, then banged the window into place and left.

Anything missing? I had little of value in the room to begin with, except for Harry's binoculars, and they were still on the tripod. More to the point, was this miserable hotel safe? It didn't seem so. The three dresser drawers had been pulled out, turned over, and stacked in the closet. My extra belt cinched the neck of my turtleneck sweater which had been stuffed with towels. A favorite shirt was torn down the middle with each half tied into a knot and flung into opposite corners of the room. Not exactly evidence of a compassionate crook. Toiletries were now in the toilet, though in some ways, that sounded right. The mattress had been turned upside down and the pillows moved to the other end of the bed. Large red *x*'s were scrawled across the pillowcases.

But the real focus was something familiar on the desk by one of the front windows—a plastic vase held half a dozen stems with green leaves and greenish-white berry clusters. I once was collecting the same type of leaves and berries at Boy Scout camp until a counselor covered his hand with a rag and batted them away. Hello, poison sumac. I tried hard not to recall the painful rashes almost leading to respiratory failure. But who would place such a dangerous plant in my room? A small, white envelope poked out from between the stems, easily removed with the tweezers I retrieved from the toilet. And a card inside, with a message not as easily dealt with:

*I know where you're from. I know
why you're here. BACK OFF!*

Who even knew I was staying at the Excelsior? The Dandy Diner cook sent me over. Had he set me up? I doubted the girl without crusts would have done so, if that was her, but it could have been her father. Could Maris Chambers' tentacles reach this far, or Butter Bar's cook, or Peter I. Black? I flipped on the chain lock, wedged a chair under the door knob, retreated to the desk, and stared out at Dandy Diner. Antsy, I needed a diversion. I regretted having left my dip pen and ink back home. If I had them with me in East Harlan, I know I would have written up a storm. Especially since some new lines had just come to me. That rarely happens, but when it does, look out. So I needed Wilbur or Harry to send me some supplies, but here's a sample of what I would have written if I had those supplies:

Inspector Grimes noticed his East Harlow hotel room door ajar when he and Detective Watley returned from dinner. "Scrape marks show someone forced the door open while we were at the restaurant," said Grimes. The two men entered cautiously, with Watley's trusted Webley revolver poised for action.

"Thieves in our midst," said Watley, looking around, "yet nothing's missing."

"Not quite, my friend," Inspector Grimes countered. "Precisely five items are missing: My crepe de Chine silk dressing gown, one royal wedding commemorative chutney spoon, an amethyst tie tack, a rare burl wood glove box, and mother-of-pearl opera glasses. Jon Johns' enforcer, Drago, was in our room moments ago."

"Bloody hell. Drago here in this very room, in this very town. But...how did you...?"

"Open your eyes and your mind, man." The inspector put pencil to paper:

Dressing gown
Royal wedding spoon
Amethyst tie tack
Glove box
Opera glasses

"Drago! Bravo, Inspector."

"Child's play, my dear Watley. But there is much to be learned from a child at play. Johns enjoys toying with us, using Drago to taunt us like this, but we now know we were right to track Johns to East Harlow. We must double our guard, no, triple it, given that Johns and Drago now know we're here. And we'll find Johns or my name's not…"

22. Phoenix Rising

A CONVERSATION WITH INSPECTOR Grimes might have gone like this:

    Inspector Grimes: So, my friend, it is conjecture on your part that the Butter Bar and Dandy Diner cooks might be one and the same.
    Rodney: I've never seen Butter Bar's cook's face close up, though both men look identical from the back. But why even ask? If he brought Butter Bar to East Harlan, he'd be operating Butter Bar, not Dandy Diner.
    Grimes: Where would *you* organize two food vans in an industrial town like East Harlan?
    Rodney: Why would *I* want to set up two food trucks in East Harlan? I have enough on my plate back home, except at breakfast, lunch, and dinner times as of late.
    Grimes: I have gathered from Wilbur and Harry that you fancy Ginger.
    Rodney (blushing): That I do, especially when she's wearing her smiley face nametag.
    Grimes: Of all the cases I have solved in our *Inspector Grimes Rhymes with Crimes* mystery novels, which is your favorite?
    Rodney: I'm pleased with all of them, but it will be the one I've yet to write about. There's room for you to shine even brighter.
    Grimes: I have never felt you showed me in the best

possible light. Blast. You never even described my exceptionally good looks and prowess as a pianist.

Rodney: I didn't know you played the piano.

If those villainous food trucks, cooks, and waitresses were somewhere in East Harlan, I'd root them out and force them back to Fern Creek to face the music, or my name isn't Rodger, I mean, Rodney. (I'd take charge of Ginger's return to Fern Creek personally.) Without a doubt, Chauncey Chambers' plight deserved immediate attention, even though I've always preferred Butter Bar over Chauncey's Chow, and I've already said what solving Chambers' disappearance can do for my career as a mystery writer. I could also picture being crowned a local hero for assuring the continued health of comfort food in Fern Creek, be it buttered, battered, or baked, when at least one of the food trucks—hopefully the one that has a waitress named Ginger—was back in place.

The hotel staff left a large map of East Harlan in the bedside table drawer and I divided it into four regions with a thin black marker: north East Harlan, east East Harlan, south East Harlan, and west East Harlan, then partitioned each region into twelve zones, and each zone into ten sectors. That's a total of four hundred and eighty sectors. Each needed to be searched with a fine-tooth comb. The town is 2.75 miles long, 1.25 miles wide. That's 95,832,000 square feet, or 199,650 square feet per sector. Daunting. Although in square yards, that's only 22,183 a sector, which seemed much more doable. And I knew my hotel room, including the bathroom and closet, was food-truck free, so already, twenty-four square yards didn't need to be searched, or better yet, two hundred sixteen square feet were already accounted for. Not a bad head start.

I heard rustling in the hallway, followed by a muffled cough and retreating footsteps. When I peeked out, a thin white bakery box that had been leaning against the door fell into the room. I untied the string and opened the lid. A handwritten note in pencil, *A marzipan welcome from the East Harlan Chamber of Commerce*, covered a layer of miniature skull and crossbones marzipan pieces. Nice touch, especially with Halloween around the corner, but they didn't know there are only two foods I hate: marzipan and marzipan.

More rustling in the hallway, followed by some faint shoe scuffing and a suppressed sneeze. I peeked out again and took in a sturdy mailer with Wilbur's return address. I wondered how the writing supplies I requested could have arrived so quickly. They didn't. Wilbur had sent me the unsigned gravy-stained agreement between me and Blackeye Pete's. I called Wilbur, having given the switchboard operator numbers in the correct order to save time.

"Wilbur, why send the agreement?"

"Mabel said Blackeye Pete's wouldn't skip town if you signed the agreement. If you sign now, maybe they won't leave."

"But they already left. I gotta go, Wilbur. We'll talk later."

Actually, the agreement might come in handy, so I shoved it in a side table drawer, picked up the box of marzipan, and headed out to ditch the marzipan at the front desk. If I did something nice for the hotel staff, they might do something nice for me. Too bad no one saw me leave it. No staff manning the desk.

I entered Dandy Diner—sector B7d, same as my hotel—ground zero for my investigation.

"What'll it be?" said the cook, handing me a smudged list of breakfast items on a small chalkboard.

"Ooached gs."

"*Poached eggs!*"

"Ba...? What's that one? Basil?"

"*Bacon!* Just tell me what you want," said the cook, grabbing back the chalkboard.

"Eggs poached soft. Crisp bacon. Seeded rye toast. Cream

in my coffee. Where's your waitress? She's never around."

"Not true. She's here somewhere. Maybe in the back."

Did he mean the kitchen or outside around back? I went behind the diner while the cook prepared my order. No waitress. Just one small kitchen window high up on the back wall. An empty orange crate brought me to window height, then lots of spit on a rag removed a circle of grime—several years' worth, I bet. A fruitless effort, however. Even more grease coated the inside.

Back on my stool, I tabled finding the waitress for the time being and asked the cook, "Are you still having problems with your grill? I've had a cancellation."

The cook held up two gorgeous strips of bacon. "Seems okay today, but I'll keep you in mind."

There was a huge commotion outside my hotel. Half a dozen police cars had their red lights swirling. A dense crowd pressed forward. I began to force my way to the front door when I had to reverse direction—several policemen were pushing back the crowd as six EMS workers rolled three victims on stretchers out the door to waiting ambulances. Yellow police tape stretched across the entrance, and a young woman holding a microphone and displaying press credentials pulled me aside, her cameraman filming me over her shoulder.

"Would you expect something like this to happen in East Harlan?" she asked me.

"It's truly shocking," I answered, still not knowing what had happened, but realizing what makes good TV news clips. "I'm now thinking of moving my entire extended family the hell out of—can I say *hell* on TV?—taking them the heck out of East Harlan and relocating to a much safer town like Fern Creek, where there's ample public parking and plenty of good clean—"

The reporter had moved on. They had stopped filming me midsentence. But maybe what I implied about East Harlan was true. Maybe my presence here was fraught with danger. I could use some backup. Wilbur? Nah. Harry? Nah.

A lady standing next to me clued me in. "Awful. Three hotel staff, writhing in agony. Dreadful expressions on their faces. I hope they'll be okay. There's rumors about some type of skull and crossbones confection. EMS suspects poison, but they feel sure they caught it in time."

Thoughts about tainted marzipan started to fade by late afternoon. I still hadn't told anyone the marzipan had first been a gift for me, especially since there was no serious harm done in the end. I heard the three staff members would be okay, and even assumed they would appreciate a few days off on full pay. Maybe I did them a favor. Cancel that last statement—a convenient stretch. I admit I should have mentioned it to the authorities, but feared that would delay my work in East Harlan. God knows there were much bigger issues resting squarely on my shoulders. Besides, I had made some progress. The part of sector B7d that includes my hotel and Dandy Diner had already been ruled out, as had sector C6i and most of D8j—a small piece of D8j was still a question mark.

I came close in sector A12f that evening. A newly stuccoed and painted garage mid-block between Carson and Comstock seemed suspicious, the perfect size to stash one of the food trucks, and it was already day's end when they would have closed shop. The owner sat by the side of his house, his right hand reaching into a cardboard box. I approached him carefully, never taking my eyes off that hand, then came on strong, like Grimes did in *The Fluttering Femme Fatale*. "What do you think you're doing?"

He seemed surprised by the way I asked, but answered nevertheless. "Sorting screws, good stranger."

Ah ha. The food truck secreted in his garage needed repair! I now had to play it cagey and gain his confidence, so I

115

toned it down a bit. "Which screws go into that old leather fire-bucket?"

"Common right-hand threaded screws."

"And what about into that paper cup?"

"Rare left-hand threaded screws."

That seemed on the up and up, but why give him the benefit of the doubt. "What do you take me for?" I said, then kicked the paper cup. Two rare screws tumbled out. "C'mon. What's your game?"

"Don't know what you mean."

I'm no Rambo, but if I had to, I could probably twist his arm hard enough to make him talk. "What're you trying to hide? Out with it. What's in the garage?"

"My car."

"Oh, yeah." I dragged him by the collar over to the small window in the garage door, glanced in, then went quietly on my way.

The following morning, an impatient crowd gathered in front of a small bakery waiting for it to open. A woman wearing short shorts looked familiar from behind so I tapped her on the shoulder.

"Mabel, is that you?"

The woman turned halfway around, her face hidden behind large sunglasses and a scarf. "What'll it be? What can I get ya? I mean, who's this Mabel dame?"

When the doors opened, she turned back and slipped into the store with the first part of the group. I waited on a raucous line to get in—the store had filled to capacity. Once inside, no Mabel woman. Customers came in through the front, bought what they bought, and went out the back.

Later that afternoon, I received an anonymous tip that brought me to a hot dog stand on the corner of Wilkens and Watkins. As instructed, I made certain no one followed me, then

I identified myself to the owner by ordering two hot dogs, the first with mustard over sauerkraut, the second with sauerkraut over mustard, said exactly like that. I ate the first one from left to right, the second from right to left, then ordered a third dog, plain, which I could eat any way I liked. I held out three singles and a handful of change and waited for the owner's signal. If the coast was clear, he would take exactly $3.75, which is what he did. I then had to walk away as if nothing ever happened. Which is what I did.

Okay, I hadn't received an anonymous tip. I get hungry at lunchtime. I gave in to temptation. Go ahead, tell my doctor. The three hot dogs were well worth it.

I thought I saw that Mabel woman again across a different street and yelled out, "Hey Mabel. How's about a movie tonight?" As luck would have it, *Kiss My Grits* was playing in East Harlan and this time I might get lucky. "I'm staying at the Excelsior. I could pick you up at nine."

But when the woman yelled back, "Bug off, creep, or I'll call the cops," I slinked away and phoned Wilbur.

"How're the fish? Do they miss me?"

"Two certainly do. The others, I'm not sure how to tell."

"Wilbur, it seemed to be going well here, but it's not. There's no sign of either food truck. I saw Mabel but didn't see her. And I miss Ginger and wonder if she misses me. I'm likely to be in this town forever." I explained how many sectors I'd already ruled out (not many) and how many still needed to be searched (a great many).

"Yeah. I hear what you're saying," said Wilbur. "And what if the hint about them going to East Harlan is all wet?"

"But what if it isn't? Can I, can we, afford to take that chance?"

I think I heard Wilbur shrug his shoulders before handing the phone to Harry, who had a suggestion. "Canvass people you pass on the street at random and ask them where they buy their lunch. Disregard the places you know, like Dandy Diner. Then plot those points on your East Harlan map. There are few eateries in town, you said so yourself."

"That diner's the only spot I know, other than the hot dog stand."

"Food trucks are usually mobile and gravitate to places with lots of customers," said Harry, "and while that can change from day to day, maybe some pattern will emerge. If you can identify where they've been, maybe you can figure out where one or both will show up next."

I had never known Harry to be so perceptive, and articulate. His ideas are usually far afield, but this one had promise. Out of the nine people I stopped on the street, I had nine different points of reference. And it took just nine minutes.

"Simpson and Main."
"Front Street and Oak Drive."
"Parsons and Royal."
"Logan off Pine."
"Rogers Avenue and Handley Road."
"Wilkens and Watkins."
"Washington and Jefferson."
"Homer and Marge."
"Popeye and Olive."

The hotel's street map of East Harlan refused to accept any more information. Black marker sector lines going every which way covered most of it. Instead, I used white stickers to plot those nine points on an aerial projection I got at the East Harlan Chamber of Commerce, a professional grade map sanctioned by the Northern Amalgamated Union of Surveying Employees of America (NAUSEA). I now had nine dots spread across the new map with no idea what to do next. I needed to speak to Harry, who I guessed would still be at Wilbur's.

"Fax me a copy of that map section," Harry said. "I'll review it right away. And stand by for my response."

I found a fax machine in a gun shop across the street, which looked like a good place to kill time.

"See this slug," said the proprietor. "If it can blow a man's head off at fifty paces, which I've seen done, can you guess what it would do to a cat?"

"No...I can't." I stood there in silence until Harry's response came back by fax a long ten minutes later. I turned it this way and that to try to make some sense out of it, then called him from the greeting cards shop next door.

"Harry, what's the deal with that, er, interesting chart you created?"

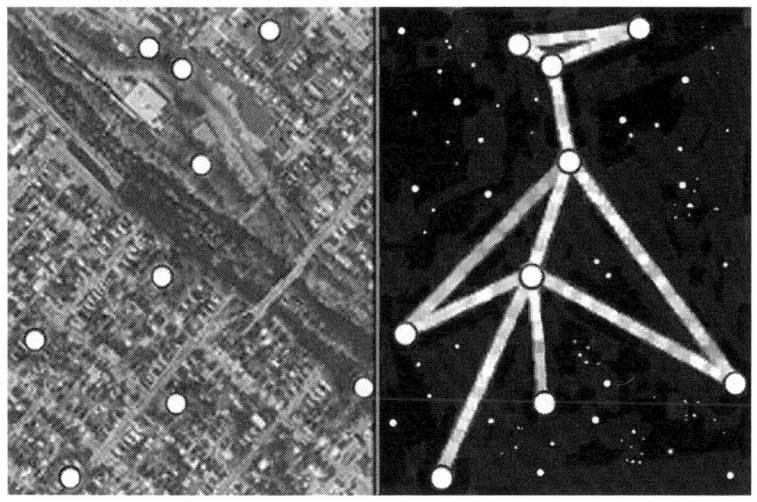

"The Phoenix has risen!" said Harry. "The dot pattern you sent me is a near match for the Phoenix constellation in the southern sky. It's a great omen if I ever saw one. Like the mythological bird, this tells me you will be consumed by fire—"

"Harry, you're scaring the hell out of me."

"...but then you'll emerge from the flames reborn and victorious."

"I don't think I'm willing to chance it, but what does all that have to do with the food trucks?"

"It says you're sure to find them."

I sometimes have high hopes for Harry, but then sink back down to reality. I took another look at my map. Wasn't one of those reference points, Wilkens and Watkins, the site of my rendezvous with that hot dog vendor? I walked over there to ask him about it.

"What do you make of these spots?" I asked, showing him the nine points I had plotted.

"Those are all places I've dragged my cart this past week."

"Another two hot dogs with the works, please."

23. Super Duper Red

A NEW DAY, A NEW PLAN. Art was never my best subject in school, but after a couple of minutes in my hotel room, I came up with a pretty good drawing of Blackeye Pete's. I went outside to show it around, waving the sketch at a boxer in training jogging down the street (he didn't have the courtesy to stop), a mailman struggling with a heavy sack (exhausted stare), a gang of teenage boys rolling by on skateboards (humiliating snickers), and a woman carrying takeout. The woman took the sketch and nodded, an encouraging pinch of recognition. She rotated it left and right, nodded again, turned it upside down, handed it back to me, pursed her lips, and walked off. Another dead end, food truck-wise, but not a total loss. Her plastic bag touted *Kenny's Pancake Palace* and it was time for a fashionably late breakfast.

It happened to be Kenny's 'Grand Opening.' Kenny took over a defunct Japanese hibachi restaurant and kept the setup, so you sit around a tabletop communal grill and, believe it or not, make your own pancakes. The grill can seat ten, though there were only five others when I arrived. While waiting to be served, I passed around my sketch. Maybe someone caught a glimpse of Blackeye Pete's in town, or even had their (really Butter Bar's) open-faced hot turkey and mushroom gravy platter, cranberry sauce on request. But the sketch came back around to me without a peep from any of them.

Despite that, however, the six of us became a cohesive group. After the waitress brought each of us a pitcher of ready-to-pour pancake batter—whole wheat or buttermilk—we had a lively discussion comparing spatula styles, we chuckled when one's own pancakes flowed into a neighbor's on the grill, and we lamented how some restaurants serve so-called 'table syrup' instead of the Vermont maple syrup now before us. After dozens of golden-brown pancakes and many cups of coffee, the talk, as one would have expected, turned to Eames coffee tables and I said I shift mine every other day on odd numbered days so there are no impressions left in my rug.

"How do you handle, say, July 31st and August 1st?" asked the sharpest person in the group.

"Well, that's a good…oh, look at the time. I have to run." I rose to leave. "But before I do, a hypothetical: *If* there were such a food truck in town," I said, holding up the sketch one last time, "where would you expect it to be?"

"One place it should be," said a gray-haired man in the group. "Nowhere, that's where. There's a town ordinance under consideration that would ban those swanky lunch wagons. Protects our fine bricks-and-mortar eateries, like Dandy Diner and now this place. Some, like me, are plum for the ordinance, others vehemently against."

Maybe that was why the food trucks had been so hard to find. They might be keeping a low profile so as not to draw too much attention, given what appears to be the subject of a serious political battle in town.

I returned to my hotel room to make sure they'd left the extra bath towel I requested, then went out again. The elevator door opened with a ding the moment I rang for it. What could be more satisfying? When it stopped at the floor below mine, a well-dressed man got in, tipping his hat as he did so.

"John Johnson, cutlery salesman," he said, introducing himself with an engaging smile. "Sharpest butcher knives east of the Mississippi." Upon reaching the lobby, he took me aside and said, "I'm checking out now, but meet me at the town park under the big oak tree at midnight. I have some information about marzipan I think you'll find awfully interesting."

The phone in the booth outside the hotel was ringing off the hook. No one standing around. Probably the operator. The previous user must have shortchanged the phone company and skipped town. It stopped ringing, then started up again. Not the operator—they wouldn't bother calling back. Maybe a bomb threat or a ransom demand and they dialed the wrong number. Both were intriguing notions. Might make an interesting conversation. I couldn't take the suspense and picked it up. Wilbur. I should have known. He thought it more secure to contact me this new way. I told him about John Johnson.

"Jon Johns' *son!*"

I pictured Wilbur's eyes ablaze. He's read all my Inspector Grimes books, but one. "No, John *Johnson.*"

"That frightened me there for a sec," said Wilbur. "I'm still frightened about it. Hat? Engaging smile? That guy sounds like the guy who mugged me."

"I thought you might think that. I'm meeting Johnson tonight in the town park. If he is your snipper, then you can rest easy today. You're safe at home in Fern Creek."

"Bringing a weapon?"

"All I have is what's left of the Dog-B-Gone. The label warns, *Will cause temporary blindness in humans.* I'll squirt him, disarm him, and force him to spill who he's working for."

"Awesome plan," said Wilbur. "But I wouldn't wear a tie if I were you. Anyway, here's why I called. Something too good to be true. Harry's beyond excited. He says both food trucks are now back in Fern Creek in their regular spots. Like they never left."

"Don't mess with me, Wilbur."

"I'm not. Harry says both cooks are serving our favorite dishes left and right, and Ginger and Mabel are asking where you are. Well, at least Mabel is. And Mabel says she has something special for you she's sure you'll want. Harry says he had beer batter fish and chips at Butter Bar, then a super-rich vanilla malted at Blackeye Pete's. Though when I pressed Harry about it, he admitted he's not sure if all that actually happened or was only a dream during a catnap on the job, and he now wonders if he may be mistaken about the whole thing."

"That makes a world of sense," I told Wilbur, then hung up. I desperately needed some replacement friends. Although what if Harry was correct at first and is mistaken about being mistaken? Did that older couple in Ginger's apartment purposely mislead me to get me out of town? I don't buy their scrimshaw and concert accordionist stories. How do I know the scrimshaw collection he showed Edgar's replacement belonged to him? It might have been rented for the occasion. And she, an accordionist? Come on, now. I wasn't born yesterday, nor was Edgar's replacement, who should have asked her to play something to prove it. Next time I'll ask her myself, even if I have to sit through thirty renditions of *Ach, Du Lieber Augustin* until she gets it right. I never should have trusted what they told me. I bet my time spent here in East Harlan was all for naught. A wild-goose chase.

I needed to get some writing done to preserve an iota of sanity. Luckily, I had received some supplies from Wilbur, or it might have been from Harry. No return address this time. I went up to my room, collected dip pen, paper, and ink, and walked to a small park near the hotel. Some nice benches circled an artificial duck pond. (The ducks were real, the pond manmade.) I should have thought of this earlier. I get to kill two ducks with one stone. I can write and check out this new sector, B7f, at the same time. As soon as I sat down on a bench, a rubber ball bounced off the back of one of my shoes and two boys came running up. I flipped it back to them, then showed them my Blackeye Pete's sketch. Worth a try.

"Have you seen this food truck in town?" I said.

"Sure did," said the first boy. "Gimme a dollar and I'll tell ya where."

"No, gimme fifty cents and *I'll* tell ya," said the second boy.

"Hey, no fair, that's a gyp," said the first boy, and without a moment's hesitation, he pounced on the second boy and began to thrash him about with his fists. I had a feeling they were out to con me. No way I was getting in the middle of that business. I left them in a cloud of dust and moved to a different bench, vowing to sit there until a few words came to mind. By the way, in sector B7f, there were no food trucks in sight.

Those words never came. What else did I have on my mind?

Fast forward to right before midnight when I entered the town park. Glad I brought a flashlight—all the lights along the path were out. I pointed the beam at one of the benches, startling two squirrels. They bumped into each other, then darted off in opposite directions. I should have followed one of them—I figured it might lead me to the old oak tree—but couldn't decide which one. I wandered aimlessly for several minutes not knowing where to turn next, until a full moon emerged from behind some clouds long enough to reveal a massive oak tree about fifty yards away. I reached the tree on the stroke of midnight, can of Dog-B-Gone at the ready. John Johnson—nowhere in sight. Nothing to do but lean against the tree and wait. My flashlight flickered on and off. I had to keep tapping it to get it to work.

The light went out for good. I heard a blood-curdling, high-pitched, animal-like screech, followed by a *thwack*. Then a muffled cough and footsteps fading away. Someone or something ran off. Then a lethal silence. The moon came out again and I surveyed the scene. A bloody butcher knife pinned a decidedly dead squirrel to the other side of the tree. Several miniature marzipan skulls were stuffed in its mouth and a note scrawled in red ink was snagged by its claws:

Final warning! If you value your life, BACK OFF!

24. Sector D9c?

Since Grimes would have kept his cool by that old oak tree, I kept mine. And more so. Threaten me with a butcher knife, you'll feel the brunt of my cunning, the blaze of my investigative eye, the clout of my clandestine maneuvers, the merciless fury of my resolve. Ha, ha. My ancestors laughed at butcher knives. I laugh at butcher knives...and butchered squirrels.

Grimes would have also noticed something familiar about that red ink, like I did. The writer used Freeman's Super Duper Red, I was sure of it. Surprising. Dip pen ink stores rarely carry it anymore. I tried to buy some back in Fern Creek. Grimes would have said it's unpopular because "the chemical properties of its red pigment make it unstable and short-lived." And he would have dropped the name of some scientific article he happened to have read on the subject that morning. I knew most stores now carry the more permanent Freeman's Scarlet Red instead. So if I can find a store in East Harlan that carried, or did carry, Freeman's Super Duper Red, I'd be that much closer to finding and crushing Mr. Engaging Smile and his boss, whomever he or she may be.

Hard to believe there were four dip pen ink stores in East Harlan. I thought maybe there would be one, two at the most. The first carried a partial Freeman's Super Duper ink line, stocking Scarlet Red, Ultramarine Blue and Spring Green. The owner of the second store spat when I mentioned Freeman's.

The third acted proud to carry the full line, insisting his was the only store in the East Coast to do so, but he hadn't had any stock for six months. He told me to check back often, though. I entered the fourth store with little hope.

"I need some Freeman's Super Duper Red. Do you carry it?" I asked.

"It's difficult to come by. I had one bottle. Sold it a couple of days ago."

"To a well-dressed man, sells knives, tips his hat, engaging smile, I suppose?"

"No."

"Then to whom?"

"That's confidential, as you can well understand."

I pressed him for more information. Anything to go on. He wouldn't budge.

"Buy something," he said awkwardly after a time.

"Okay, a nib. An Esterbrook Jackson Stub #442."

"Just one?"

"A box of them."

"Only one?"

"A case of them."

The shop owner opened up immediately. "The man had shifty eyes and wore filthy whites with gravy stains across the front. He kept looking back over his shoulder, and when some sirens sounded down the street, he ducked out without the ink."

"But you said you sold it?"

"He sent a young woman here about twenty minutes later to collect it. She made some excuses for what happened, paid, and picked up the ink."

"What'd she look like?"

"Hard to tell behind her sunglasses and scarf."

"Did you get her name and address?"

"That's even more confidential, seeing it was a woman."

I wasn't about to be bullied into buying another case of nibs. I needed to find another way.

"By the by," said the shop owner, "now that you've bought something, you can enter our contest. Win a case of Esterbrook Jackson Stub #442 nibs. Fill out this card. Just provide your first name and note your favorite nib, if any, though I think I can guess. Drop it in this basket."

I entered the contest. It's hard to pass up winning more nibs.

So how to find out who bought that ink? I called Wilbur, if only to keep him in the loop if I ever needed him.

"Do what Grimes and Watley would do," said Wilbur. "Get in after hours and search the place. The store must have some record of the sale. Then once you find the man, or woman, who bought that ink, slap him, or her, around a bit. Rough him, or her, up a lot. Make him, or her, squawk. See what he, or she, knows about Chambers and Butter Bar and Blackeye Pete's."

"How about I find him, or her, then you slap him, or her, around?" I said. "Put Harry on."

"I'm not one to suggest you skirt the law by busting into the ink store after midnight to check the store receipts," Harry told me, "but if you can wait until my day off, I could rig up some pulleys and wires and harnesses to a skylight and you could drop down and hover over the counter so you won't trigger any floor-level motion detectors."

"There's no skylight. No motion detectors. It's a simple mom-and-pop store without the mom."

"I'm off two weeks from Friday," said Harry. "Say the word. I'll come to East Harlan that Thursday evening. In the meantime, I'll buy the equipment."

"Put Wilbur back on."

Wilbur loved Harry's skylight pulley harness plan, so I was on my own once again.

The owner left his ink shop at 8:00 p.m. sharp, locked the door, looked left and right, seemed satisfied no one else was about, and placed the key above the doorframe. I emerged from behind a shuttered newsstand, edged over to the door, looked left and right, satisfied myself that no one else was about, and reached up for the key. No key. Where was the key? Ah ha, the old locked door/doorframe snow job. A gambit from one of my novels. Grimes used it himself in *The Mystery of the Maligned Manatee*. Throws off anyone who's watching. I tried the door. Locked. But flimsy and easy to shake open.

It's eerie how quiet a dip pen ink store can be at night. No scratching of sharp metal nibs while testing wrinkly parchment surfaces. No rapping stubborn inkwell caps with wrench or pliers edges. No hordes of boisterous customers clamoring to get their cracked dip pen nib holders repaired.

A spike stick for receipts next to the cash register held a pressed-down stack of maybe thirty to fifty receipts. Not a lot to go through—only the top three were from the last four weeks. (A mental note to self: Think twice about getting rich opening the fifth dip pen ink store in East Harlan.) And the second receipt from the top was for the bottle of Freeman's Super Duper Red, but damn, it just said *Betty* with no address. Not much help. I started to leave when I noticed a table set up with the basket of contest entries, a blindfold, and the prize case of Esterbrook nibs. The receipt search ended up a dud, but while at it, why not rig the contest so *my* entry card was picked? I would win a second case of nibs. With all those extra nibs, I could start a dip pen and ink club in Fern Creek for troubled youth. There were two contest entries in the basket including mine. I didn't want to be a pig about it. Let someone else have a chance, but it didn't take me long to increase my odds twentyfold by putting another twenty marked *Rodney* into the basket.

Huge crowd. Wall-to-wall people in the dip pen ink store.

Word had gotten out—the contest results were about to be announced. An oversize digital clock suspended over the awards table wound down to zero. The store owner called out the last few seconds. "Three, two, one." How did he read the countdown clock through his blindfold? After feeling around for, then finding, the basket of entries, the owner made a great show of mixing up the cards. He picked one. "And the winner is..."

He knew enough to insert a dramatic pause while removing the blindfold. I began to make my way to the counter.

"The winner of this fine case of nibs is...*Betty*."

Betty? The guy picked the one card in the basket that wasn't mine. Holy smoke. I didn't think to check that second card. Though it could be a stroke of luck. A chance to shake down or shake up Betty.

All eyes darted back and forth, expecting a Betty to reveal herself. "Last call for Betty. Betty, are you here? Going once. Going twice..."

Someone peeked into the shop. That Mabel woman I kept running into in the street, still with the sunglasses and scarf. Was she the one who picked up the Freeman's Super Duper Red?

"You're Betty, aren't you?" said the shop owner hopefully. He must have recognized her.

"Yeah, what's it to ya?" she answered, cracking her gum like a volley of rifle shots.

"Congratulations."

"Betty, do you need a hand carrying all those nibs?" I asked, knowing I needed to play along. Luckily, she didn't seem to recognize me from when I called her Mabel.

"They're not that heavy," she said. "Ever juggle four dinner-size orders of 'mile-high' meat loaf, mashed potatoes, and signature gravy on a serving tray? Now that's heavy."

"Have far to go?" I asked, holding out my map of East

Harlan, sector grid lines and all, and handing her a black marker. "I don't mean to pry. Curiosity's getting the best of me. I'm almost embarrassed to admit this, but I'm dying to know where you're headed next. You see, lately, I've been wondering where a woman who won lots of dip pen nibs would take them."

Time stood still as she decided what to do. She finally relented, like she had a soft spot in her heart. Though the phrase *ulterior motive* came to mind.

"Promise not to tell?" she said.

"Who on earth would I tell?"

She put a dot on my grid region D, winked at me, cracked her gum twice more, then jumped into a taxi and sped off while I tried to refold the map. I called Wilbur from a phone booth across the street. When he picked up, I could hear Harry in the background.

"You're on speakerphone," warned Wilbur. "Don't say that insulting stuff you usually say about Harry."

I filled them in about the contest results and the new lead on the possible whereabouts of at least one of the food trucks. "She gave in too easily," I said. "Like she's trying to lure me into some sort of trap."

"Where there's a trap, there's a villain to nail," said Wilbur, "but take precautions." Harry advised me to "keep my eyes peeled." Then Wilbur reinforced the safety issue by warning me to "stay on my toes." Then Harry said, "Sounds like the break you were hoping for, but watch your back."

Betty had pointed to sector D9c in the midst of East Harlan's sprawling industrial park. Warehouses, factories, garages. Plenty of hungry workers. Plenty of places to operate one or both food trucks. But how best to find them? It became obvious. Conceal my true identity, take a factory job, check out the complex from the inside.

The phone book listings were confusing, though the

central location of one company in sector D9c caught my eye—Anthill Aeronautics, possibly an ideal place to anchor my search. I dialed their number.

"This is Anthill."

"Are you hiring?"

"Can you rivet?"

"With the best of 'em. Once I shoot 'em in there, they won't wriggle out."

"That sounds good. But since it's safety first here at Anthill, let me ask you this: If the top sheet is greater than $40,000^{th}$ thickness, would you double-dimple or countersink?"

"Absolutely I would."

"Where'd you work before?"

"Harry & Sons Stabilizers, for three years—*It's nothing if it's not a Harry*. Then Wilbur Airplane Rudders, two years—*For the unexpected turns in life*. Then Nose Wheels R Us, but for only six months. I left when they ran out of nose wheels. They also didn't have a catchy slogan."

"Well, we have a great one here: *An Anthill in every cockpit*. Can you come by now? I'm itching to see what you're made of."

The taxi got me there in no time, even before I could fully psych myself up for what I expected would be my big riveting test. Anthill's manager, Hank Beeson, showed me two short sections of sheet metal, predrilled and ready for riveting; a bucket of mixed-size rivets labeled *Mixed-size Rivets*, some of which, I think for test purposes, weren't even rivets; and a tabletop filled with different types of what I guessed were riveting guns, but couldn't be sure. To be frank about it, this would be the first time I ever saw a riveting gun up close. Also, up until now, I wouldn't have known a rivet if I tripped over one.

"I'll be back in a half hour," said Beeson. "On second

thought, given all your experience, make that fifteen minutes." Beeson left.

A janitor entered the room and began to change a garbage can liner while I fiddled with one of the guns. "No. No. You're holding that all wrong," he said. "Let me show you." He set ten rivets before I knew it, then twenty more, and left.

I called down the hall after him. "Thanks, mate."

Beeson returned. "Very impressive. Some of the best riveting I've seen. Can you start tomorrow?"

Dare I set, or try to set, even a single rivet on a plane that might end up carrying me or my mother if she were still alive or any other living creature for that matter? Not in this life, or the next one. No souped-up reputation as a mystery writer or private investigator would be worth it. No food truck coconut cream pie. Though I can well recall Butter Bar's. I once needed three days' rest after one forkful. But if I can return to the here and now, could I count on that janitor coming by each time to bail me out? There was a limit to how messy I can be or how much garbage I could generate for him to pick up. And speaking of limits, my stint at Anthill was limited, so I had to work fast once I got my Anthill photo ID. I also needed a clever cover story if I were to have free rein to search the Anthill factory complex and the nearby companies.

My ID card photo was flattering, especially since it showed my best side. I was not looking directly into the camera, so it was also nice that it was more candid and casual. And it was attached to a lanyard for around your neck, so if you're holding packages you don't have to put one of them down to dig out your ID. Anxious to test it, I sniffed around a nearby Anthill security guard. "What's that smell?" I asked him outright.

Since we hadn't met before, he scanned my ID barcode and checked his laptop screen to verify my employment. I passed with flying colors.

"The smell?" I reminded him.

"It's coming from the next building. The old spice warehouse."

A spice warehouse? It didn't hurt to ask. His answer prompted a vision of two competing food trucks knocking out comfort food across the street, the distinctive aroma of frying peppers and onions masked by tens of thousands of pounds of nearby cardamom, cumin, and coriander. That would be another reason why they've been so hard for me to find. I put searching the Anthill facility on hold, centered the ID on my lanyard, grabbed a clipboard, crossed the street, and approached the first group of spice warehouse workers I saw.

25. Way Mild Chili

KUDOS TO ME FOR A STUNNING ploy. I made out like I'd been asked by Anthill to organize an East Harlan Industrial Park bowling league and three spice warehouse workers signed up on the spot: a woman sporting a two-hundred thirty-eight average and two guys with high games of ninety-six and a hundred and eight respectively. The guys also happened to own their own bowling balls. They always brought them to work, as a matter of fact. All three happily forked over five dollars for an embroidered bowling league sleeve patch—eighty percent polyester, thirty percent rayon, twenty percent cotton—ready in four to six weeks, once I placed the order.

"The patch is well worth waiting for," said the woman.

When I advised them to pick a rousing bowling team name and claim it before another company did so, they decided on 'Strike Now!' Probably won't be a management favorite.

The spice warehouse had burlap sacks of pungent spices piled everywhere in pyramid-shaped stacks. Not a food truck in sight, though I didn't expect to find one inside the building. I noticed a few workers with greasy chins tossing paper bags and cups into a garbage can.

"Where do you all get lunch around here?" I asked the bowling team members.

They all thumb-motioned to a rear door and the woman said, "Lately, out in the alleyway between us and Simpson Storage. There are two food trucks, both new in town, set up at opposite ends. Get in on the price war while they're still there.

The chili cost $2.99 three days ago, $1.50 two days ago, and 75 cents yesterday. Today they're probably giving it away. Anything to attract the most customers, showcase their specialties. I figure it's a matter of pride with the cooks."

"What do the food trucks look like?"

"The green one nearest us has all kinds of graffiti. There's a nice sign on the red and yellow one. Says something like *Butter Stick*."

"How about the cooks?"

"One's shifty-eyed. The other, we've never seen his face."

"What about the waitresses? Did you notice their names?"

"Only one had a nametag but I couldn't read it," said the woman. "She had it on upside down."

I stared at the alleyway door for a moment, mostly trying to picture Ginger's nametag smiley face turned upside-down. I'd hate it if that meant she were sad. Could my search for Butter Bar and Blackeye Pete's in East Harlan be coming to an end? Perhaps it was wishful thinking but despite tons of spices all around me, I thought I detected a faint smell of homemade buttermilk biscuits out of the oven; crisp, but not too crisp, bacon; and fried eggs over easy. Here's to Butter Bar's breakfast anytime policy. I also longed to see Ginger's nametag right-side up again. I'd even settle for it sideways. One bowl of Blackeye Pete's' sweet corn chowder, please, even if Butter Bar's cook prepared it. I took several nervous steps toward the alleyway when a voice called out from behind me. Hank Beeson. That security guard must have told him where I was.

"So there you are, Rodney," said Beeson. "Come join us. We're celebrating Anthill's 50th anniversary. We've got eight-layer, seven-layer cake with all the trimmings. Ha, ha. We always go one better here at Anthill." He smiled as he put his arm around my shoulder and firmly guided me back to Anthill. Not the best timing, but nice of him to make me feel so welcome on this, my first (and probably last) day on the job.

Anthill's anniversary party could have been a veritable gold mine of prospective bowling league team members with lots of league patches to be sold. Unfortunately, all that had to wait. And the barbecue beef sliders being passed around were hard to resist, but I had to save myself for a long-awaited food truck feast next door. Don't ask how many sliders I would have eaten, however. Okay, nine. I don't mean to imply that's near any kind of record, but I'd still say it's a lot. In any event, what a nice bunch of people and how helpful was this? Some Gary guy returned to work after being out for three months having stubbed his big toe on some misplaced airplane struts. As his co-workers welcomed him back with several rounds of *He's a Jolly Good Fellow*, I slipped out unnoticed and headed back to the spice warehouse.

Too bad Wilbur and Harry weren't there to witness the next few moments. Not one but both food trucks were about to be smoked out. There would be a proverbial feather in someone's cap and I was that someone. Even Grimes would be proud. But, on the other hand, there also had to be a 'Now what?' moment once the cooks were confronted, so I ended up delaying my impending triumph and called Wilbur.

"And if both trucks are there, what then?" he asked, echoing my latest concern. "How will you bring food truck comfort food back to our town? How will you expose the 'who's really doing the cooking' fraud we think we've uncovered? More importantly, how will you connect them to Chauncey and Maris Chambers?"

I realized then and there that I hadn't fully thought this out, but with minutes left to my lunch hour, I had no choice but to hang up on Wilbur, dash through the spice warehouse and bust open the alleyway door.

Nothing, nada, zilch. No food trucks. Just piles of end-of-meal trash to add insult to injury—soiled paper plates, crumpled napkins, and sticky soda cups—scattered everywhere by a strong wind and swirling around...around some woman's feet. Betty, in sunglasses and scarf. Holding a Styrofoam container.

"So, we meet again," she said. "One of the cooks thought you might come by and asked me to give this to you. It's his *Way Mild Chili*. A more pleasant, easy eating, and comforting dish he says there ain't."

I haven't had Blackeye Pete's' *Way Mild Chili* back home in Fern Creek, but if it's the same as Butter Bar's by no means spicy *Easy Eatin' Chili*, which I expect it would be, look out below. I was famished.

"Wait," said Betty, as she grabbed back the small plastic fork she had first given me and handed me an extra-large metal spoon instead.

I swallowed two huge spoonfuls and started a third. A sweet peppery taste greeted me at first. Then it all hit the fan. *Aghhhh*! Have your lips ever been ablaze while atomic heat blasted out your ears? Have you ever almost drowned in cascades of your own forehead sweat? Has a nuclear firebomb ever detonated in your mouth?

"Problem?" asked Betty, casually, after seeing my reaction. "The cook assured me it's the opposite of spicy hot. He handpicks the mildest of mild chilies himself. But quick, if it's burning that much, you better drink this."

She held out a glass of ice water. I drank it. The heat increased a hundredfold. Did you ever feel your eyeballs bulging out of their sockets? Were you ever sorry you're blessed with pain receptors?

"Aw, my mistake," said Betty. "I forgot that cold water spreads the burning. It's a chemistry thing. Oops, look at the time. Gotta go."

She left me all alone in the alleyway, squinting in pain, vulnerable. I had no idea where to turn. I could barely make out the sun sliding into a bank of menacing black clouds. It grew dark, and darker still. There was pelting rain, violent thunder, then quiet, then rapid footsteps behind me. I assumed Hank Beeson had come to fetch me again. Nope, not Beeson, because I saw a blurry him and two or three spice warehouse workers in front of me some distance away, looking out from the warehouse door, motioning frantically. But who was coming up behind me? I spun around. All I saw was a butcher knife gleaming high against an ominous sky. A burst of lightning bounced off its shiny blade. Heat from the chili peppers faded from consciousness. The knife began a slow-motion descent. I felt a piercing sensation, then blacked out. Peace at last.

26. Who's Whom?

NICE SIGN OVER THE POLICE headquarters entrance: *Welcome to East Harlan—You Better Watch Where the Hell You Park.* And there was a table inside loaded with complimentary doughnuts of every imaginable kind. With my mouth still sore as all get-out from the chili, I passed up grabbing two doughnuts—vanilla bean salted caramel and maple-glazed sour cream—before three patrolmen shoved me into interrogation room 4. Hank Beeson had called the cops after someone accosted me in the alleyway. At his request, they looked into my background and seemed most concerned about my professed riveting expertise. I guess they all had family members that fly occasionally.

"Ow. Easy does it," I said. "I'm recovering from some *Way Mild Chili*."

"Wow, that does sound dangerous." Two of the cops started laughing their heads off.

"And don't you know some guy stabbed me?" (Grazed actually. Almost grazed, to be truthful.)

"The doc here says you're okay," said one of the cops. "Couldn't even find a scratch."

"Now why are you in East Harlan posing as an expert riveter?" yelled a square-jawed police detective as he shined a five-hundred-watt lamp in my face. "And who's out to get you?"

I wondered why he shouted at me. I was the victim here. "Shouldn't that be 'whom's out to get you'?" I hoped that misconstruction would buy me a few moments to come up with a good story about my Anthill job. "Aren't you referring to the object of a clause?" I asked, adding fuel to the fire.

"Who?"

"Youm."

The detective called his captain over, who settled the grammar question with the simple phrase 'nominative pronoun.' He also said he heard what happened and suggested I come clean about the whole mess. No suitable story came to mind. I was afraid to reveal anything about the food trucks, so I feigned amnesia. After all, I did black out.

"Sorry, I'm drawing a blank," I said. "I don't even remember what I just told you minutes ago."

"You said someone tried to stab you," said the captain. "Well, I'll have you know, we don't stand for such shenanigans in this town."

I didn't realize that plunging a butcher knife into my heart would be a shenanigan.

"If what you claim is right," said the captain, "it was lucky for you Mr. Beeson and a bunch of spice warehouse workers happened by as they did. And lucky for you one of *whom* had his bowling ball with him. What a shot and just in time. Knocked your alleged assailant off his feet and headfirst into two heavy garbage cans with a sharp-breaking hook. Both cans went down. Made a 7-10 split. Not so easy to do. The guy never got up. Dead as a doornail. Fell on what appeared to be his own butcher knife."

They made me identify the body. An uncomfortable first for me. Inspector Grimes' first was in one of my earliest novels, *The Slippery Slab*.

"Is this the guy that tried to stab you?" said the captain.

"Dunno," I said. "My eyeballs were blurred by chili heat."

It was Mr. Engaging Smile from the elevator and the oak tree squirrel disembowelment!

"And we found this cruise ship reservation in his pocket. Leaving on the *Queen Mary 2*. In about two weeks. Anything to say about that?"

"Shuffleboard anyone?" *He works…he worked, for Maris Chambers and had planned to sail with her!*

"And we found this in his other pocket. The bottom half of a tie. What about that?"

"Won't be easy to make a knot, other than a half-Windsor." *I was right. He is…he was, Wilbur's snipper!*

"What about this?" asked the captain, holding up the butcher knife found at the scene.

"I don't know nothing, I mean, anything, didn't see anything. He came at me from behind. And just so you know, I'm giving up riveting."

"Get the heck out of here." The captain clearly had more than enough of me.

"Wait. Don't I get one free phone call?"

"That's if you were arrested and you weren't arrested, but what the hay, here you go," said the captain, handing me the telephone before leaving the room.

I figured all outgoing calls were recorded and that he'd gone next door to listen in. I had to watch what I said. But I still needed my favorite ink, so I dialed Hudson's back home. "Do you have any Freeman's Super Duper Black in stock in the economical 4.2 fluid ounce size?"

"We're just out of it," they answered.

I called Wilbur from my hotel room and told him all about the fracas in the alleyway and the snipper's final frame.

"Eh, he wasn't so tough," said Wilbur. "He took me by surprise."

"Listen, Wilbur, I've hit a dead end. I've no idea where to look next."

"For the food trucks? But you're hot on their trail. You

missed them by several minutes, maybe even seconds, and got to enjoy some free chili. It's time to rev your engine. Drop the clutch. Power shift. Pedal to the metal. Burn rubber."

They were good muscle car analogies to pump me up. Too bad I can't drive a stick shift. But why did I have the feeling that maybe Wilbur wanted me to stay in East Harlan a few days longer, that he was using my apartment for wild parties, and that Harry was storing undelivered mail sacks in my bedroom? If only there were a tiny phone in the fish tank, I could find out what was going on back home. I hung up on Wilbur. Maybe a closer look at the still unsigned agreement between me and Blackeye Pete's would help. Mabel told me there was no need for me to read the fine print, almost one hundred pages of it, and I had followed her advice. I turned on a side lamp, propped up some pillows and started to flip through the agreement when Wilbur called me back.

"No particular reason for the call," he said. "I'm merely curious, nothing else, but do you think you could really be out of tonic water and chips?"

"Turn down that dance music, Wilbur, and hang in here with me for a while. I'm looking at the agreement and after the gravy-stained signature page on top, the rest are a treatise on The Black Eyed Peas."

"That should be helpful. Anything on the other food truck as well?"

"The hip hop group, not Blackeye Pete's."

"Still could be useful."

"My point is, what's all that have to do with the agreement?"

Wilbur was silent for a moment. "Let me pose a question to you instead," he said. "What's all that have to do with the agreement?"

Harry grabbed the phone from Wilbur. He had heard what I said on speakerphone about hitting a dead end and had some kind of epiphany. "The writing's on the wall. Right before your eyes. It's clear you need to—"

"What?"

"...just—"

"What?"

"...get some great detective to help you. Like that brilliant Inspector Grimes you're always writing about, with his super-duper powers of observation and deduction. Okay, real and imaginary worlds would collide, but if anyone can help you solve the mystery of Chambers' disappearance, the whereabouts of the two food trucks, the signature gravy conundrum, how you can get Ginger to go out with you again, how best to position your Eames coffee table...it's your own literary creation, the fictional Inspector Grimes Rhymes with Crimes. Some of his genius might even rub off on you."

"Lots of *my* genius has already rubbed off on him, Harry, I created him. I appreciate the suggestion and the thought had crossed my mind earlier, not that I could really make that happen. But even if I found some way to pull that off, I would still reject it. Grimes is terrific, but I'm starting to do well enough on my own."

I didn't get into this with Harry but I had even begun thinking about ditching my *Inspector Grimes Rhymes with Crimes* mystery series and my Randall Reed pen name for some new *Rodney, P.I.* mystery series, though I'd need to come up with a good rhyming scheme for the title. Grimes could retire at the end of my current novel to spend the rest of his days planting daffodils and hanging out with Watley at the local pub. Though I'm well aware that Grimes will do what Grimes wants to do and my trying to control him is easier said than done.

"Look, Harry, I'm grateful for all that Grimes has done for me, but I do not need his help in East Harlan or Fern Creek or anywhere else at this point."

27. About a Bout

Killing time in my hotel room had its advantages. My publisher had been pleading for my manuscript and it was the most writing I'd done in one shot in more than a month.

"Hello, what?" exclaimed Inspector Grimes, standing before a vacant lot. "Our favorite apple vendor here day after day, even yesterday, then today he and his cart vanish into thin air. How am I to get along without my daily dose of England's finest apple, the Cox's Orange Pippin? Even you, Detective, know that small crops due to the stress of the local climate yield remarkable and concentrated flavors some say are reminiscent of apple combined with melon or pear, others with orange or mango."

"He must have moved his cart to a better location," said Watley.

"I think not, my good fellow. There is an unmistakable stench of foul play in the air, and on the ground as well. Note a lingering odor of rotten apples and traces of mashed apple pulp in the soil, that is, whatever is left after some birds had their way. When had you known our friend the vendor to allow such a waste of God's handiwork?" Grimes also pointed to some inconspicuous parallel ruts in the soil leading not to the street as one might expect, but to the adjacent woods.

"It appears the cart was dragged, not wheeled. How peculiar," Watley offered, beaming that he beat Grimes to the punch, a rare occurrence. "And the tracks are relatively shallow," he said, adding to his triumph, "though the dirt is soft and, by appearance, the cart heavy if memory serves, even when devoid of fruit."

"Yes, dragged, not wheeled," said Grimes. "You are learning, my friend. Well done. The wheels must have been tied off to keep from turning, but why? There are several incongruous bits of information to be sure." Grimes eyed the nearby woods. "Dragging the cart would leave a more identifiable trail, one we could find and follow, yet one would also assume there would be deeper grooves in the dirt. There must have been an attempt to sweep dirt across the tracks to make it appear the perpetrator tried to cover up his actions, but not so much as to completely obscure them. He wanted us to see those tracks. To the woods, Watley, to the woods. However, I fear we are much too late."

The two men skirted around a hand-painted Pippins poster axed to pieces and were met with a grisly scene.

"Poor fellow," said Watley, nodding toward the vendor's mutilated body, partly hidden under leaves and branches. "So what do you make of it, Inspector? Not a sign of the cart. And not much else to go on this time, even for you, I daresay."

"A mere doddle, Detective. So obviously the work of Jon Johns, carried out by Drago. Yet another attempt to distract us from pursuing them, even if temporarily. They banked on the fact that I stop to purchase an apple here each morning. You know the old saying."

"I suppose you've done it again, Inspector. But I can't see how you were able to arrive at such a conclusion, and so quickly. What did you base it on?"

Grimes handed Watley the bloody note scrawled in red ink he had found stuck by butcher knife to the dead vendor. The detective read it out loud. "You've witnessed another sterling job by Drago, for Jon Johns."

"Come on, keep up," said Inspector Grimes, urging on a lumbering Detective Watley as the two men made their way down several steep flights to a dusty storeroom in the sub-basement of the Metropolitan Police Bureau. Grimes pushed open the door of the Records Unit. "I can tell you now, Detective, the apple cart was not dragged to the woods. On the contrary, they loaded it onto a truck, drove away, and hid it somewhere. Pinpointing that 'somewhere' might prove useful."

Grimes screeched open a metal drawer and started to thumb through some tightly packed file folders.

"But the apple cart tracks lead to the woods," Watley reminded Grimes.

"I don't recall finding the cart in the woods, do you?" Grimes shot back. "Perhaps my memory is failing me. Perhaps it's time for me to retire. How about right this moment? I could spend the rest of my life planting daffodils and hanging out at the local pub. Here's my inspector's badge. You take over. Get your own bumbling assistant!"

Grimes was apparently in one of his moods. Then, recovering a bit, "Sorry old boy, but the tracks were a clever attempt at deception in theory, though poorly done. If you had your wits about you, my friend, you would have noticed that the left and right tracks in the soil were, at first, perfectly parallel as one would expect from fixed cart wheels, but they were that way only for a short distance. The tracks then drifted too close together, then too far apart. You don't have to be a wheelwright to know such disparity's a physical impossibility. Instead, the tracks were faked. This also explains why the wheels were tied off to keep from turning. The cart would be much more stable while being transported in the back of a truck."

"Brilliant deduction, Inspector."

"And killing the apple vendor, not just a diversion," said Grimes. "I have had my eye on him for some time. Do you think I liked his apples? Give me an Alkmene any day. Sharper and juicier than the Cox. The vendor worked for Jon Johns to keep tabs on me, and outlived his usefulness. Yes, here it is," Grimes noted, as he pulled a thin file folder from the cabinet drawer.

Watley read the label out loud: "G. Gilbert Holdings. G. Gilbert. That can't be...?"

"I am afraid it is," Grimes continued. "None other than Sir Giles Gilbert himself. I don't mind repeating what we already know. Gilbert's a vicious killer and con man in his own right. One of my archenemies. Confidant of Jon Johns. So Gilbert and I may meet again. I came that close to crushing him at our last encounter, but he slipped through my noose unscathed by dodging those cucumber tea sandwiches laced with Base-17. He mumbled something about a bout of indigestion."

"About a bout. An extraordinary turn of a phrase," remarked Watley. "Not much to the file, though. One enterprise listed."

An hour later, the two men stood in the midst of Gateway Industrial Park before a warehouse with a simple metal sign that said *Gilbert Affordable Storage*. "This is where we will find the apple cart. Get that door open, my good man," Grimes directed. "We don't have all day." He looked on passively as Watley struggled to drag the heavy warehouse door on some steel tracks embedded in the concrete.

"Wheels need some oiling," Watley complained weakly, trying to justify the delay.

"Then you should have brought some," Grimes responded, ever relishing a good jab at Watley. Someday he would give Watley his just due for years of exemplary service and uncompromising loyalty, but not yet. He wouldn't want such praise to go to Watley's head.

"Be careful not to get grease from the door edge on your new tweed jacket," Grimes warned. "Oh. My apologies. Too late. I aimed to tell you sooner, but while fussing with a knotted tobacco pouch string, it must have slipped my mind." Grimes smoked another pipeful, cleaned his pocket knife, and completed the morning's crossword before Watley's tussle with the warehouse door had ended, revealing a cavernous area with large, closely packed wooden crates. "Now to examine the apple cart," Grimes announced.

"You can't be certain it's here and even if it is, how would you know which crate to open?"

"Pork and parsnips, my friend. Climb to the top of the nearest crate and report what you see."

Watley struggled to do Grimes' bidding. "There's a large black arrow painted on top. It points to one of the next crates over, on the diagonal."

"Jump onto that next crate," said Grimes.

"Again an arrow. It points to a third crate. It looks like there are...let me count...fifteen crates in all, all with arrows."

Grimes noticed controls for the chain and claw mechanism suspended from the ceiling that is used to grasp and move the crates. "Steady on, my good man. I'm going to raise you high enough to afford you a marvelous global view of the entire setup."

Moments later, Watley, lift chains now secured around his waist, waited patiently for Grimes to figure out how to operate the controls. "Gilbert, you're a devil," Grimes cried out while secretly relishing even more of a challenge. Not only were the lift, rotation, and speed levers unmarked, they were covered with motor oil and difficult to grip. "Stiff upper lip, my boy, I'm about to try this first lever."

Watley's next few moments were too frightening to describe, but Grimes finally had him at the highest point in the building. Once there, Watley called out the direction of each crate's arrow as Grimes sketched the arrangement.

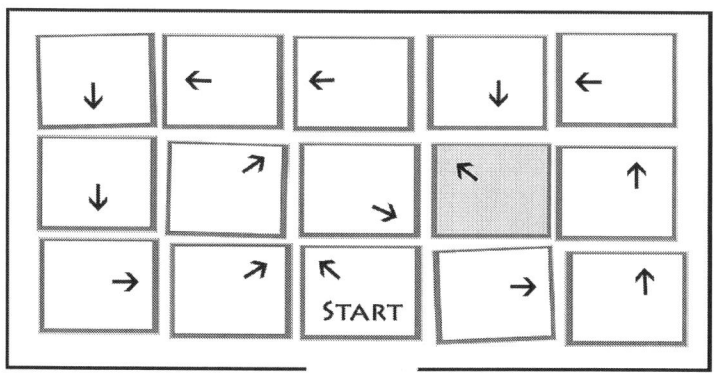

Grimes lowered his friend back atop the first crate. "Now follow the arrows as you jump from crate to crate. Call out each move. Continue until I tell you to stop."

"Stop," Grimes yelled about four minutes later. "You've reached our target."

"Congratulations, I suppose, but how...?" asked Watley, as he eased himself down to the warehouse floor.

"Come on, man. Exercise your God-given wits if you can still find some of them. I suppose even you know today's date."

Watley consulted the newspaper he carried in his side pocket, then looked back at it once again. "Why, it's the twelfth of August."

"Well done. Yes indeed, the twelfth day of the month. Starting with the first crate and moving in the direction of the arrows, the twelfth crate is the one we sought. Therein lies the missing apple cart."

"But what if we hadn't come here until tomorrow, the thirteenth? The twelfth day occurs exactly once each month."

"Are you certain about that?"

"Absolutely certain. At least I think so, but I know you're likely to somehow prove me wrong."

"Not this time, my good man. The apple cart disappeared this morning and Sir Giles is clever enough to know it would take me only several hours to arrive at its most logical hiding place."

"Well, if you are not right about this, we, I, can break open all the crates until we find the cart," said Watley, trying to give Grimes an out, ease some of the pressure.

"Not possible. Gilbert amuses himself with a warped sense of fair play. I'm certain the crate with the cart will be safe to open. But each of the others, I suspect, will be booby-trapped. Besides, failing's not an option, Detective. I have a reputation to protect. No, the twelfth crate will be opened. And it's the correct one, I assure you."

Watley ceased jousting with Grimes and began to make his way to the selected crate, carrying a crowbar he found leaning against a nearby wall, but Grimes stopped him in his tracks.

"As I told you," said Grimes, "the wrong crates are booby-trapped. You stand back. I'll take it from here."

When Grimes ripped off the first of the twelfth crate's side panels, both men could hear gas hiss violently from the crate.

"Watch out, Inspector," yelled Watley, as he ran to push his friend out of harm's way.

"Not to worry, my boy. The gas in this crate is harmless. Yet one other way Gilbert sought to amuse himself." The inspector proceeded to knock off the other three sides, revealing the missing apple cart. "Hmm. Recently painted," he said, somewhat disappointed, "a shrewd attempt to obliterate any useful clues. But there must be something, some hint as to the whereabouts of Gilbert and Johns." The inspector closed his eyes and slid his right hand lightly across one side of the cart's wooden frame, then the other.

"Inspector, shouldn't we—"

"Wait, Detective," Grimes interrupted, "I think I...yes, what's this? A hair from the brush they used to repaint the cart is partially stuck to the frame. European ox hair if I'm not mistaken, most likely part of a batch processed in a small hamlet in Bavaria four, no, six months ago. The batch was flown across the Channel and stored in a Liverpool warehouse at an average temperature of nineteen degrees centigrade for about five weeks before being sent on to one of three paintbrush manufacturers in Manchester. My educated guess would be Farrington Brushworks."

"By Jove, great find, and how telling," said Watley.

"Wrong you are, my good man. That gives us next to nothing we can use. Puts us nary a half step ahead, even less. There's got to be something else." And after another minute or two, "What do we have here, wedged between these two planks? A matchbook, printing covered over in paint, except for two letters I can barely make out. They seem to be an 'i' and an 'n'. Little to go on, but I believe it's from the…Gnawing Newt Inn. Yes, based on the distance between those two letters and the number of matches already struck, quite so."

"Now we're getting somewhere," said Watley.

"Wrong again. You yourself lent this matchbook to the apple vendor the last time we saw him."

"I warned him smoking was rotten for his health."

"Drago butchered him," Grimes bothered to remind his friend, then continued his search. "Aha. So opportunity knocks." The inspector grabbed Watley's handkerchief to lift out a torn piece of fabric.

"Sign of a struggle," Watley offered.

"Merely used to wipe the brush," corrected Grimes, now sniffing remnants of paint on the cloth. "That's strange. Some type of anti-fouling product specifically designed to coat and protect a cargo ship's superstructure. It stops slime, seaweed and barnacles from attaching to the hull. I believe this one's based on silylated acrylate polymers—coincidentally, the topic of an article I just read in the Annals of Fluids Engineering."

"Highly plausible," added Watley, though he understood not one whit.

Grimes continued, "Now why use such a specialized paint on, of all things, this apple cart?" The inspector immediately answered his own question, as he was often inclined to do. "Whoever did the work chose something near to hand, like surplus paint from a corrosive seawater-inspired face-lift. A cargo ship that's been painted dark green recently should be easy to identify. Find that ship, find…well, we'll see. Name the city's best seafood restaurant."

"The Bashful Barracuda at Canary Wharf, no doubt."

"To the Barracuda then for dinner. My treat. After which, a midnight visit to the London shipyards might be entertaining."

28. Mirror, Mirror

While waiting for Dandy Diner's jumbo, charcoal-broiled turkey burger and cornmeal-crusted onion rings, I asked the cook, "You don't happen to have a good-looking identical twin brother cook in Fern Creek, do you?"

"Yeah, he runs Butter Bar. But I wouldn't say he's good looking."

"Meet his number one customer."

"I like the sound of that."

"How's business here in East Harlan?"

"Couldn't be better."

"Even with two food trucks new in town?"

"So you know about them. Okay, I'll level with you. Get it off my chest. Business is way off. Factory workers have stopped picking up breakfast and lunch here like they used to. They're buying from the food trucks. That's okay and not okay. I'm all for helping out my brother. He started to have trouble making ends meet in Fern Creek and came here with the other truck because he heard there are too many hungry people and too few places left to eat. But I have no use for that other cook. I sense he's conning my brother. I don't even think he can cook, the dirty rat."

"What can you tell me about this rat?"

"Not much. I heard he almost got into a serious mess about three years ago. Something having to do with using the barn at his uncle's abandoned farm to store and sell bubble gum laced with THC, you know, the main ingredient in marijuana.

They couldn't pin it on him, however, even though the guy's a chemist and there were customers lined up around the barn day and night. And I know he got out of jail not too long ago. His former employer put him there."

"How do you know all this?" I asked.

"I have friends in low places."

"Where is this barn?"

"Just outside Fern Creek."

I called Wilbur from my hotel room. "Change of plans. I'm taking the afternoon bus to Fern Creek. If the food trucks are still here in East Harlan, so be it. I'll deal with them later on if I have to. I'll get back to you when I'm on the road. In the meantime, get Harry to contact every one of his mailman friends who had, or still have, a rural route and ask if they know of any abandoned farms in our area. And borrow Harry's car while you're at it. Make sure it has plenty of gas."

Good riddance to the Excelsior hotel. "Checking out," I told the lobby desk clerk, trying my best to be civil.

"What's your name again? It's Rodger, isn't it? I can't seem to find your record."

"No, Rodney."

"I expect the room was to your satisfaction."

"Couldn't have been better."

The bus jerked and banged most of the way from East Harlan. The highway department had been chopping up the roads before repaving. We ran out of gas in front of Chuck's Stop—visions of their elusive chicken pot pie began to dance before my eyes—but it had just closed for the day. As the last few customers were filing out of Chuck's, selected bits of their conversation penetrated the laminated safety glass of our bus windows: "flaky," "toothsome," "crispy." Needing a chance to get to a phone and touch base with Wilbur, I volunteered to walk down the road to a filling station we had just passed.

"Listen carefully, Wilbur. Pick me up at the bus depot around 9:00. Bring two flashlights and extra gloves."

"Okay, boss. We're busting into the Chambers mansion again? This time, I'll bring lots of chopped meat spiked with sleeping pills for that pipsqueak of a dog."

"Much bigger than that, but I'll clue you in when I see you."

I carried the gas can back to the bus. Once we got going again, three tenors in the front row sang (and I'd guess are still singing) *The Song That Never Ends*. All in all, not such an easy trip, yet I couldn't care less. Like I told Wilbur, this next move could be big.

Wilbur filled me in on the results of Harry's research. "There are three farms in the area that his mailman friends say are no longer in use. Take a look. Harry circled them on this map. None of them were owned by anyone named Black, though. He shows the last names from the postal records: Connors, Brown, and Sands."

"Take the north road out of town to this first one. Should be five, six miles. Got the flashlights?"

We drove in silence for about ten minutes until we reached the Connors farm. The main house was well lit and the fields, the little we could see of them, seemed full of late crops of some sort. "Looks lived in, wouldn't you say? I often wonder where Harry gets his information."

"Where to now?" asked Wilbur.

"The Brown farm's seven or eight miles in the opposite direction."

Once we arrived, we could hardly make out some buildings in the pitch dark, but the fact that there were no lights anywhere seemed promising. Wilbur pulled off the main road and drove about two hundred yards on a dirt road leading to the farm. We got out and approached the house, or what remained of it. Huge mounds of cinders and rubble. There had been a terrible fire some time ago. But the nearby barn appeared to be intact.

"The barn door's been nailed shut," I said. "Let's pry it open, but I want to be careful not to leave traces that we've been here."

Our flashlight beams were soon shifting back and forth over piles of hay, rusted farm tools and splintered wood barrels. Before long I heard Wilbur let out a horrific howl, followed by a shriek which may or may not have come from me. Wilbur had his flashlight trained on the cuffs of a cook's striped pants and leather clogs suspended about five feet off the ground, and he wouldn't move the light from that spot.

"Any chance some legs and shoes could be up there dangling on their own?" asked Wilbur. "Otherwise, I think there's someone hanging from the rafters, but I'm afraid to look."

"This is hard to take," said Wilbur. "First time I'm seeing a dead body."

"Second one for me after the snipper, though for Grimes, it would be too many to count."

"Recognize him?" asked Wilbur, who still hadn't looked at the victim's face.

"I'm afraid so. It's Chauncey Chambers. Although he doesn't look nearly as good as when I last saw him working Chauncey's Chow. I guess he could look a lot worse. I'm no expert, but I'd say he's been dead less than a day."

"Should we cut him down?"

"I'm still trying to figure out how best to handle this."

"Murdered, by hanging," said Wilbur.

"I'm not so sure." I went closer to the body and probed and prodded a bit, checking his hands, lifting his shirt. "Note the bruise marks on his wrists. His hands were tied for a number of days. Probably with this rope." I bent down and picked up four pieces of rope of varying lengths. "These have been cut. If his captor or captors hanged him, why not leave his wrists bound as they once were?" I took some time to survey the rest of the scene, as much as the narrow flashlight beam would allow. A six-foot ladder near the body had been knocked over and there were some empty metal plates and cups, a partially filled water bucket, and a broken mirror, all by a small hay pile near a rusty tractor motor.

"Here's what I think happened," I said. "They held Chambers captive, keeping him alive for some number of weeks chained to the tractor motor. I think those are chain marks around his waist. I don't see the chain anywhere, but we can still look for it."

"Why the chain? You said his wrists were tied with rope."

"Not at first. They left food and water and a chamber pot for him. He couldn't eat or drink or, well, um…so readily if his hands were tied. But he would be free to move around if he were chained. With a fairly long chain at that. At some point they removed the chain, tied his wrists with rope, rope that he could eventually saw through on some sharp metal edge. And they left him a large coil of rope so when he broke his bonds, he was free to hang himself."

"What? You think he committed suicide? Why would he do that?"

"He's a nationally known TV personality and public speaker. His face is synonymous with comfort food everywhere."

"So?"

"See this mirror?"

"Yeah."

I shined my flashlight on Chambers' mug. "He saw what they did to him."

PART III

29. Bloody Deceitful

Wilbur and I left Chambers in the Brown farm barn and I phoned the police as soon as I got to my apartment, describing what we had discovered. I had planned to place an anonymous call from some random phone booth, then realized that would look too suspicious if they ever found out the call came from me.

Wilbur phoned early the next morning. "What happened when you told the cops?"

"I had a tough time explaining what led us to the barn. I tried to tell them that since Chambers' food truck disappeared, I had become frantic at the notion of having had my last portion of Chambers' brown sugar ham hocks and beans, then thought I detected that glorious aroma as we were driving past the farm, so we checked it out and inadvertently came across Chambers. The cops had had Chambers' ham hocks many times so they knew where I was coming from. Then I confessed that my ham hocks story was a lot of hooey—that even I didn't buy it—and admitted that I'm a mystery writer looking for material for my next novel who got lucky."

"I found the dangling feet," Wilbur reminded me.

"The cops knew about my Inspector Grimes series and seemed satisfied, but warned me not to leave Fern Creek—they'd still be in touch. That's all I told them. I didn't spill anything about suspecting Maris Chambers and Peter I. Black, and I won't until I can personally blow the case wide open. Oh, and I had to tell them you were with me. I had already said 'us' and 'we' several times, instead of 'me.' I told them you were my trusted sidekick."

"Nice. Then you owe me a badge."

"I just *told* them you're my sidekick. I gotta go now, Wilbur. I better get some writing done. And thanks for the ink."

After I gave the fish too many flakes, I opened my lap desk. Wilbur had dropped off another small bottle of generic India ink and several new candles. I lit a candle and dipped my favorite Esterbrook nib in Wilbur's surrogate ink, but before I began to write, I took one more tour of my apartment, so glad to be back home. It never looked so good. Shame on me for thinking my close friends Wilbur and Harry would take advantage of my absence and throw wild parties in my apartment. They were even kind enough to line up dozens of empty beer and soda bottles, and stack about five squashed pizza boxes neatly along a kitchen wall ready for recycling. Saved me a lot of work. Now that's real friendship. And talking about friends, the fish were so excited to see me they swam round and round so fast a resulting waterspout splashed tank water on my stocking feet. I'm not a clean freak by any means, but I had started taking off my shoes when entering the apartment about two years ago and finally paid the price. Oh yeah, the writing.

"We'll be breathing down the necks of Johns, Drago, and Gilbert in no time," said Detective Watley, checking the bullets in his revolver for a third time, then taking aim at an unsuspecting pigeon on a nearby postbox. "After a superb meal at the Barracuda, a trip to the shipyards for a good whiff of the ocean and much more than that, I presume."

"The dinner will have to wait, my friend," said

Grimes, unfolding his copy of *The New York Times* and handing it to the detective. "Take a gander at this."

"***Study proves too many chicken livers may—***"

"Not that one. The comfort-food cook. In America."

"***Television celebrity chef Chauncey Chambers was found hanging from a Fern Creek barn rafter, a possible suicide. His food truck had mysteriously vanished when a new food truck appeared in town, though police have no evidence of foul play. Chambers' third wife, Maris, heir to Chambers' millions, was too distraught to speak to this reporter. Chambers was found by a connoisseur of Chambers' ham hocks, one Rodney (last name unavailable at press time), who has authored a series of mysteries using the pen name—***"

"Not necessary to read more at the moment," said Grimes. "And we will indeed be visiting the shipyards, but not for the reasons you expect. We sail tonight on the RMS *Castleton*. It's a rare chance to flaunt my abilities in America where the perpetrators of this crime—yes, I do see some intriguing elements of crime here—make Johns, Gilbert and Drago look like Boy Scouts. When one adds a third wife's inheritance to the alleged suicide of America's king of comfort food, one gets a deadly recipe for wrongdoing. In addition, there's the possible duplicitous actions of two other food vans."

"Why two other food vans?" asked Watley. "The article mentioned one."

"You stopped reading, didn't you? Apparently, one competitor had been there already."

"You suspect those food vans have something to do with Chambers' plight?"

"That, and something else. Something especially heinous, though at this point, more of a side issue."

"How they prepare their cod and chips, I gather?" said Watley, daring to poke fun at Grimes, who, gastronomically endowed, now seemed visibly shaken by what he was about to reveal.

"If it were only that," Grimes noted. "I don't mean to shock you, my friend, but I have reason to believe that meals offered by one food van are in fact takeaway from the other."

"I can't imagine how you've come to know that," said Watley, "but good heavens. One serving takeaway from the other. How bloody deceitful. I pity the poor victims and pray we're not too late to help others."

"It's clear we must insinuate ourselves into the entire situation before this Rodney mucks things about," said Grimes. "I'll wager he now fancies himself an amateur detective."

Meanwhile, in a seamy part of London, three pairs of sinister eyes hovered over a battered, beer-stained table.

"A small piece of news to share," said Drago. He then broke into an extended menacing laugh while repeatedly plunging his butcher knife into some defenseless pork sausages.

"Out with it!" said a quick-tempered Jon Johns, reaching for his own butcher knife, the blade three inches longer than Drago's. Johns had little patience for anyone wasting his precious time.

Sir Giles Gilbert remained calm. Let the other two kill each other, he thought. It would mean more of the hidden loot for him at this point.

Drago devoured several eviscerated chunks of

sausage, then continued. "Our stooge at the Bureau says that miserable Inspector Grimes and his flunky, Detective Watley, have booked midnight passage to America."

"So, the cowards are in retreat," said Johns. "Hastening the demise of Grimes and Watley is second only to pursuing our own delectable life of crime. Drago, what say you to an impromptu vacation in America?"

Inspector Grimes' and Detective Watley's voyage across 'The Pond' was, for the two of them, routine. A jewel theft plan laid bare on day one, a murderer apprehended and sent to the ship's brig on day two, an imposter at the Captain's dinner table unmasked day three, a card sharp in the ship's casino exposed on day four, a stowaway uncovered day five, a rival cruise line's plot to foul the ship's drinking water foiled day six, and a less than perfectly folded truffled omelet sent back to the kitchen during the last meal before docking at New York Harbor, day seven.

"A truly unremarkable ocean passage, wouldn't you say so, Inspector?" said Watley, as the two men headed for the train station and the trip to Fern Creek. "But I assume our work here in the states won't be so conventional. This suicide, inheritance, and food van case sounds most perplexing and puzzling."

"Choose one of those words or the other," Grimes chided the detective. "Let's be frugal with our adjectives. Both have the same meaning. And short of several less significant pieces of this 'perplexing puzzle' that have yet to surface, and after a modicum of additional thought, you'll be pleased to know I have already solved the mystery of the Chambers murder—I do believe it *is* murder, even if he took his own life—although I'm still anxious to watch it all play out."

"Blimey. Tell all."

"In time, my friend, in time," said Grimes. "Those unresolved issues still deserve our respect and attention. Besides, without additional clues to follow, how would we spend our days? So let's leave no stone unturned, no matter how small. Let's line up all the ducks, then knock them over one by one, even if we step on Rodney's toes as we do so."

"But you said you've already solved it."

"Right you are, my good man, but the readers haven't."

"No rush to return to England, then. Lovely. They say that late-night television is rather good in America, as is the ubiquitous comfort-food menu item *chicken in a basket*."

Almost a week had passed without much to show for it, either food-, author-, or detective-wise. My kitchen cupboard was so bare I dragged myself toward FoodMart. Walking up Beacon, I came to the empty patch of nothing where Butter Bar had been. No smells or sounds of onions and peppers frying in Cook's cast-iron skillet, no blackboard touting the day's specials in barely readable smudged chalk (though they never used a blackboard), no honey-garlic shrimp salad and bacon triple-decker to bolt down, and alas, no Ginger to flirt with. The girl without crusts and her father were just ahead of me. They looked hungry so I followed them along Beacon, then right on Sinclair until coming to...holy mackerel!...a new food truck in Fern Creek called Pea Soup. Gigantic bright green letters across its roof shouted out that enticing name, and underneath, a yellow neon sign flashed an alluring message:

Piping Hot, 24 Hours.

My eyes were glued to that message. I watched for quite some time as it blinked on and off, hypnotically, until, no, yes, can't be, changing to

We killed Chauncey Chambers.

After several seconds I looked away, then back again: *Piping Hot, 24 Hours.* Either my ravenous detective's mind played tricks on me, or that had been some cosmic revelation. In no way would I throw my suspicions about Peter I. Black out the window, but Pea Soup's cook could be Maris Chambers' accomplice. I now had no choice but to grab an open stool, not that I wouldn't have done so anyway.

Despite the presence of several customers—the girl without crusts and her father had gone on by—the cook had fallen asleep across a huge bag of green pea pods, looking guilty as sin. It should be a snap to connect him with Chambers. His henchman, the waiter, dozed against some rickety shelves behind the counter. He wore a dark green vest with light green dots, a failed attempt to divert my attention from murder to fresh peas. Odd that no telltale bits of hay from Chambers' death barn were visible on the waiter's outfit, but a recent cleaning bill tossed into his apartment desk drawer should be easy to find. How much does Maris Chambers like pea soup? Her maid was sure to know. That would mean another caper at her mansion was in the cards. And what if Pea Soup was selling Blackeye Pete's takeout, which is really Butter Bar takeout? Was ethics a thing of the past in Fern Creek? I should work on an editorial to the *Gazette*.

The waiter finally glanced in my direction. My signal to order?

"A large bowl of pea soup," I said. "Glad to see your food

truck in town. No place to get good pea soup since Chauncey Chambers and his food truck went missing." I checked for some reaction, then added, "As president of his fan club, I'm investigating his disappearance, and I know you know what happened to him." Grimes sometimes lays his cards on the table. Why couldn't I do the same?

The guy went over to talk to his cook after shaking him awake, twirled a finger around his temple, then came back and stood in front of me, glaring, arms folded.

I needed to change the subject. Keep them off balance. "How about some pea soup?"

"We don't have any," he answered.

"Sold out?"

"Never offered it. Never had it on the menu. And the cook's not one to improvise."

I grabbed a menu. "This says *Ask about our Soup of the Day*. So, what's the soup of the day?"

"It depends what day it is."

I couldn't decide if it was Monday or Tuesday so I ordered grilled cheese on rye toast to play it safe. It arrived forty seconds later. The cook did a nice job toasting the bread, but he forgot to add the cheese. "Where's the cheese?" I asked.

The waiter grabbed it back muttering something about blankety-blank complainers. Were they trying to get rid of me?

"Any specials today?" I asked.

"Again, that depends what day it is."

The other customers, after hearing my back and forth with the waiter, seemed more comfortable to speak their minds.

"Half of my burger is raw, the other half burnt. How in the world did the cook even do that?"

"The fried shrimp were never shelled."

"I'm still waiting for my minute steak."

I stepped away from the truck to look at the neon sign. Still flashing *Piping Hot, 24 Hours*. Maybe these Pea Soup guys had nothing to do with Chambers' disappearance, though one thing for certain—as a food truck, Pea Soup stinks on ice.

Harry sauntered by. "Have you tried their pea soup yet?" he asked.

"It's remarkable. Order some. Followed by their grilled cheese special of the day." Payback for when Harry...I'll pick something later, it's so hard to choose.

"I think I just lost my chance," said Harry, reacting to the surprising sight now before us. We both stood open-mouthed as a Health Department tow truck backed up to Pea Soup, shooed us and the other customers aside, hooked a chain to the rear end, and hauled it away. The cook and waiter could be seen running down the block in opposite directions with customers chasing them.

"Maybe they'll be back tomorrow," I told Harry.

"That should be Rodney's flat if our source is correct," announced Detective Watley, rechecking the address in his notepad. The two men had walked from the Fern Creek train station. "I'm looking forward to surprising the chap. Shall we call on him straight away?"

"Observe first, confront later. That's the plan," said Inspector Grimes. "We'll secure our rented rooms across the street and watch his comings and goings from there, for several days if need be. Whenever he leaves his flat, you'll follow him, anytime, day or night, torrential rain or heavy snow or blazing heat, it won't faze me in the least. A necessary next step. One way to know if he has something to hide. In my mind, everyone's suspect at first, even our amateur detective, even you, my friend."

Watley, mildly put off by the accusation, became defensive. "Everyone, eh? Given that logic, then you're suspect as well," the detective told the inspector, preparing to milk his small intellectual victory over Grimes.

"Codswallop!" Grimes responded. "I've an ironclad alibi."

"How so?"

"I was with you in England when Chambers was murdered."

"Great Scott, that's right."

At that moment, half a block down from Rodney's building, a cold-blooded killer with an even colder butcher knife slouched in a murky, midnight blue rental car that blended well with its surroundings. Perfectly camouflaged, it had graffiti on the side panels and several broken-off tree branches across the roof and hood. His binoculars focused intently on Rodney's front door. Rodney was of secondary interest to Drago, of course, merely bait to bring Grimes and Watley within striking distance.

30. Blast My Tie!

"Off you go again, Detective. Rodney just left his flat."

Watley had heard that directive from the inspector once too often and tried to convince Grimes that enough was enough. "I doubt there's more to uncover. I've shadowed Rodney for almost two days now. Our suspect's consistently inconsistent," he told Grimes. "There's little rhyme or reason to Rodney's actions."

"Rodney's suspect, but not a suspect," said Grimes.

"The fellow's dodgy, though. Yesterday morning, he first stopped at Hudson's Stationers. Gazed at the window display. He went to the post office next, then the tie shop, then a park bench by the river. Got into a row there with some lads over a rubber ball. Yesterday afternoon, a different order. The post office first, then the tie shop, park bench—no lads around this time—and Hudson's. Today, so far, it's been the tie shop, the bench, Hudson's, then the post office."

"Well done, my good man. That may prove useful. Actions often speak louder than words. I have a strong feeling Rodney knows more about the Chambers affair and the food vans than he'll let on. Looking to take all the credit, I presume. His visits to the tie shop are certainly intriguing. Perhaps our own visit is in order. I dare say you need a new tie. That hideous mustard yellow and puce specimen you insist on parading before my eyes day after day is most disconcerting."

"Hideous?"

"And I'm being kind at that, Detective. Let's just say your

tie's not my cup of tea."

"Blast my tie, Grimes!"

"One can only hope. That said, out you go once more, and as soon as you both return, it will be time for us to pay our American friend a visit."

I heard three sharp knocks while feeding the fish, followed by three more. Two gentlemen filled the peephole: one impeccably dressed in a distinctive, long grey traveling coat; one with an undignified tie. I rubbed my eyes, then pinched myself, then rubbed my eyes again. But seeing was believing. No mistake about it. I had spent years dipping dip pens in ink bringing these two to life on paper, and they were now at my very own front door, no less. All the way from England. How could this be? They were the legendary Inspector Grimes Rhymes with Crimes and his capable (?) associate, Detective Watley! I considered not opening the door, then opened it. They stared at me, I stared at them. I thought about not asking them in, then silently ushered them in.

"I trust you know who we are," said the inspector.

"How could I not?" I said, trying not to act too surprised, or defensive.

"This is most awkward," said Watley. "Shall we call you by your pen name, Randall Reed, or just Rodney?"

"Rodney's fine, I guess." Proper protocol? Who knows?

"We have heard about your involvement in the Chambers affair," said Grimes, "and have come to America to offer you our assistance."

"I'm flattered, but that's not necessary," I said, pinching myself again, then deciding I was indeed awake. "I've learned much from you over the years and assume you've also learned a little something from me. But at this point I have things well in hand, so if you'd like to return to England—"

"Then I suppose you are prepared to link Maris

Chambers to her husband's death?" said Grimes.

"Well, not yet, but I'm getting—"

"And prove that she had her husband's food van—"

"We call it a food *truck* here in America."

"That she had her husband's bright orange food truck covered in green paint," said Grimes, "then gave the truck for free to Peter I. Black, and—"

"One dollar," I corrected.

"...and show exactly what Black did for her to warrant such a gift?"

"Well, not yet," I said. I didn't question how Grimes already knew as much as I did about these matters—a fact I had already started to take for granted.

"And you've uncovered aspects of Black's background," said Grimes, "that explain his true motives for being in Fern Creek and the so-called larger scheme he is working towards?"

"We say *toward* in America, but stop, please stop," I said. "Truce. Perhaps I'm not as far along as I thought. Maybe I could..."

"Don't be afraid to say it, my friend. In many ways, you and I and Watley here are family."

"Perhaps I can use your assistance after all," I said. I couldn't help but breathe a colossal sigh of relief once I got that out.

Drago's patience had run thin. Normally unflappable, so many days stuck in a rental car in an unfamiliar town in an unfamiliar country would get to anyone. He stroked his butcher knife. "Stay calm, darling, stay calm." He already saw Watley following the American several times over the last few days, but where was that detestable Grimes, his primary target? Yet fortune smiled on our good assassin. The side-view mirror showed three men about to pass his car, two with the reprehensible aura of British law. Drago lowered the window enough to accommodate the black barrel of his favorite luger, pointing it at the small of Grimes' back. "Too easy." He laughed, then withdrew the gun. "Much too easy."

Inspector Grimes looked anxious to poke around for evidence so I took him and Detective Watley to the deserted lot where Blackeye Pete's once stood. "Unfortunately, no sign of any clues," Watley remarked, as he scanned the grounds.

"Then what do you make of this?" asked Grimes. He directed Watley to spin halfway around, lean against a lone tree, and hold his right foot up behind him. Grimes lit his pipe on a third attempt, took several gentle puffs, then a long, slow draw followed by one extended exhale. "It appears our good detective's shoe has found what could possibly be a significant piece of evidence." Grimes took his handkerchief and peeled something from Watley's shoe, holding it up for all to see.

"Why, it's discarded gum and a fragment of its wrapper," said Watley, after turning around. "Hardly something of interest."

"You're jumping to conclusions again, my good man," Grimes responded. "You forget the *Case of the Culpepper*—"

"It's PinkyPink bubble gum," I interrupted, after recognizing the wrapper colors. "It's made locally. The factory's just east of town. Blackeye Pete's' waitress, Mabel, chewed PinkyPink incessantly." I tried to hide some near tears as I remembered her starting a new piece of gum before serving me a huge hunk of Boston cream pie. The freshly baked pie had not yet been sliced and she'd given me a quarter of it, including some extra crust that had fallen off an adjacent section. Woe to the person who got that next slice.

"Mabel, yes, I expected as much," said Grimes.

"Inspector, I fail to see the logic," said Watley. "First off, how do you know I, er, my shoe, didn't pick this up elsewhere?"

"A valid point, no doubt, Detective. However—"

"Sorry to interrupt again, Inspector," I said, "but I can explain." Harry nailed it. Inspector Grimes' genius had started to rub off on me. "Detective, note the minute yellow particles, pollen from that stand of poplar trees that virtually, though inconspicuously, cover every inch of this entire lot. When the inspector removed the gum and wrapper from the sole of your shoe, there were traces of such particles in the crevices of the spot thus revealed. If the gum and wrapper were from somewhere else, that spot would have been covered, protected, before you arrived here. It would have remained free of those particles. Clearly, that's not the case. The gum, therefore, came from this lot *after* you walked around a bit. Am I right, Inspector?"

Grimes seemed too surprised to speak and could barely nod affirmatively.

"Even so, surely you don't think this is worth pursuing?" asked Watley, not sure whom to address at that point.

"On the contrary," said Grimes, picking up where I left off. And putting a small, but powerful, magnifying glass he kept in a side pocket to good use, "What if we assume that this gum wad had been chewed for mere seconds, then discarded. Recently. A laboratory analysis should then show undissolved sugar molecules, even on or near its surface. Rain would have washed away that sugar if it had been lying here over an extended period of time. We might also assume this gum belonged to Mabel. We know she likes PinkyPink, and I failed to mention the minute trace of lipstick on the wrapper fragment from the discarded gum, proving a woman the owner. Mabel had sentimental reasons to visit this empty lot. If my reasoning is correct, Mabel discarded the gum when she stopped here less than four days ago."

"It could be any woman's gum, not necessarily Mabel's," said Watley.

"A valid statement, Detective," said the inspector, "but

you should know by now how I operate. Build a straw man theory, attempt to knock it down. If we can't, then we can assume the gum and wrapper were Mabel's, and while it isn't clear yet—and I emphasize the word *yet*—that there's any connection to Chambers' death, I predict this evidence will lead us directly to one of the missing food trucks, maybe both. Now, how best to proceed? Well, we must first find the store that sold the gum. Pinpoint the date and time Mabel bought it. And learn what that vendor knows about this whole sordid business."

"But many stores in Fern Creek sell this gum," I said. Odd that Grimes would think such a search would be helpful, and even possible. Maybe I'll soon be teaching him a thing or two.

"Then you and Watley here have your work cut out for you, though it's well worth the effort," said Grimes, before explaining further. "Since Rodney's novel-in-progress must reach a respectable page length to be marketable, the longer we spend now on bubble gum, including what's likely to be your futile exercise to discover when and where this particular piece of gum was sold, the more we help Rodney's cause."

"That's much appreciated," I told Grimes.

I chose to agree with Grimes that the gum clue might prove key to solving the case, at least in part, so Watley and I spent a few hours the following day visiting candy stores, drugstores, and any other stores in town that sold PinkyPink gum, beginning with those closest to where Blackeye Pete's had operated. We found nineteen stores that carried the gum, but the exercise ended up a total bust. We had the same response from each owner.

Me or Watley, in turn: "Can you name everyone you sold PinkyPink gum to in the last three or four weeks?"

The owner: "You've got to be kidding. Now are you going to buy something, or are you just wasting my time?"

Me or Watley, in turn: "A copy of the *Chronicle*, please."

As we left the nineteenth shop carrying nineteen copies of the *Chronicle*, we ran into Inspector Grimes, out for his morning constitutional.

"Impressive stack of newspapers you have there," said Grimes, trying to suppress a smile. He was kind enough not to embarrass us further, and made no reference to the fact that I had casually placed the newspapers on the sidewalk next to us and shoved them as far away as possible with my right shoe.

"With all this talk of PinkyPink gum, I still haven't tried it," said Watley.

That reminded me of the piece Wilbur had slipped me the other night. "Here, take this one. My friend Wilbur told me it's some new flavor, *Papaya Porkchop*, which you can try but are not to talk about after you do. I'm not sure Wilbur's right about that part, though."

Watley started to unwrap the piece and pop it in his mouth when the inspector stopped him.

"Hold on, Detective. New flavors *are* supposed to be talked about. Rodney, are you sure this Wilbur had it wrong? Detective, let me see that wrapper."

Watley gave it to him.

"I've a...what's that again, Detective? A *hunch*."

"Yes, a hunch. We learned that Americanism last night watching *How the West was Won*," explained Watley. "Some ornery cowpoke jawed it to an old geezer before dry gulchin' an Eastern dude and landin' in the hoosegow. He had a 'hunch' the fella was loaded. It was the dude's gun that was loaded, not his pocketbook."

"Bravo, Detective, well portrayed," said Grimes, before getting back to the wrapper. He had his magnifying glass out again. "There is something here. It's difficult to make out, but there is a small sequence of numbers below the PinkyPink logo. I believe it says...*10-46-X*. Sounds like some sort of production code. Where did Wilbur get this gum?"

"From our mutual friend Harry, but I don't know where Harry got it. I do know he has a friend who delivers mail to PinkyPink. It's all speculation, but maybe that guy somehow got it from PinkyPink and gave some to Harry. But I now have my own straw man. Let's assume that the proviso not to talk about this gum, to keep it all confidential, is legit because in this case, 10-46-X is not a production code but a *pre*-production code. Like it's an experimental flavor."

Grimes took charge. "Rodney, any place in town we can get Mabel's and Harry's gum samples analyzed, and fast?"

"It's out of town, but we can try Redd Green, a scientist friend of Wilbur's friend's scientist friend, Henry."

"Seems like a clear choice," said Grimes. "Then I suggest postponing the rest of this discussion until we can get both samples analyzed."

I looked down. All but one of the *Chronicles* we left on the sidewalk were gone. Eighteen quarters were left in their place.

Who allowed Drago into Rodney's apartment? No one meant to. Drago walked right in because Rodney forgot to lock the door before going out with Grimes and Watley. And why did Drago act so interested in the potted philodendron in Rodney's living room? Because the houseplant's canopy of large, shiny leaves covered the remote-controlled bomb Drago assembled in the back seat of his rental car and had now hidden under the leaves. One should not be so critical of him, though. A bloke has to have something else to do when he's tired of counting how many American passersby would be considered easy marks. Incidentally, in Drago's eyes, all of them.

Drago took a second look at the plant. "Are you thirsty?" he asked it. "We wouldn't want your leaves to sag, revealing the bomb before Grimes and Watley are to be blown to bits as they sit comfortably on Rodney's couch, now would we?" But despite expressing that concern, he couldn't stop himself from pouring in some boiling water from a teapot on the stove, accidentally on purpose scalding the most tender of leaves. "You might as well get used to some real heat," he added, then watched to see if the plant winced.

Drago's attention shifted to the fish tank on the opposite side of the room. Visions of shattered glass, cascading water, and fish squirming on the wooden floor gasping for breath, filled the space. And while on the subject of little fish, Drago felt odd not to have, as yet, pictured Rodney's fiery demise in the scenario, but he knew he still had some time to work that one out. He could never disclose such a failing to Jon Johns. Johns would say Rodney might as well get his, along with Grimes and Watley. That that couldn't hurt.

One final task before leaving. Drago shifted Rodney's Eames coffee table an inch and a half to the right. "A pity to leave such depressions in the rug," he said.

My doorbell rang at 7:00 pm. A distorted Maris Chambers blocked my peephole view of the hallway. What did she want? I rushed around shutting out lights, then let her in.

"I know it's dark in here, but I can't turn on the lights," I said. "It's *Conserve Our Nation's Energy* week."

"No matter," she said. "This won't take long. As I'm sure you know, with my poor husband's demise, a great deal of money will be falling into my lap. I've decided to show how charitable and forgiving I can be, despite your fanciful accusations. To prove there are no hard feelings, I'm prepared to give you $20,000."

"For doing what?"

"For coming by my house, once, tomorrow night, to take my precious poodle out for his evening walk. When he does his business, you bag it, bring it back and hold it up to me. I'll photograph you with it, then hand you the $20,000. You go on your way promising never to look back. Simple as that."

"I'm flattered. That's a huge payoff for such a piss-poor job, but I don't deal with criminals. You're rich now, but won't be rich for long. I'll soon connect you to your husband's death."

"You're a fool to pass this up. So what if I *did* have him kidnapped and killed? You have no proof and never will."

"Ah, a confession at last."

"I said *if*, and besides, only you heard it. My word against yours. Wouldn't hold up in court."

That's when Inspector Grimes stepped out of the shadows. "Like my friend Rodney said, you're rich now, my dear, but you won't be rich for long."

31. Nasty Revolver

Inspector Grimes had never been so agitated in any of my novels. "That woman," said Grimes. "What audacity. Expect to see me and Watley in this town until she gets what's coming to her. Rodney, you were there in that barn. You saw what someone did to Chambers."

"Someone? Let's just say it took place in Black's uncle's barn. And what could be worse for a TV celebrity cook who spends his life in front of a camera to be disfigured in that way?"

"The police refused to release any of those details to the tabloids, *pending investigation*," said Grimes. "But you were an eyewitness. What happened to him?"

"It's even hard to say it."

"Expect to follow in my footsteps some day?"

"The poor man's entire mouth—lips, teeth, and tongue—was turned bright orange!"

The next day, the inspector and detective found their way to The Tie Shoppe. "My associate here requires a new tie," Grimes told Maurice, the proprietor, and having motioned his thumb toward Watley's tie, he added, "something less than half as hideous."

"That's easier done than said, I assure you, sir." Maurice glanced at Watley's tie for the longest possible amount of time without wincing. He ushered his two new customers over to his most exclusive tie display. "Not a yellow and puce combination in the lot," he said proudly, while eyeing Watley. "And may I ask how you gentlemen came to visit our most humble shop?"

"This chap recommended it," said Grimes, holding up a photo Watley had secretly taken of Rodney entering the tie shop, and now getting to the real purpose of this visit.

"Please excuse me for a minute," said Maurice. He rushed into a back room. Sounds of a telephone conversation could barely be heard. He then returned somewhat more composed.

"The man in the photo?" Grimes asked again.

"Oh...yes," Maurice acknowledged reluctantly. "He comes in day after day. He has been trying to choose between two ties: a blue paisley and a red one with silver executive stripes. When I first met him outside the shop some days ago, he said he didn't need a tie but was shopping for a friend. Now he tells me he's here for himself, that he couldn't resist the, er, 'nifty'—that's his word, not mine—promotional letter he recently received from us. In fact, he seemed so excited by it he vowed to start wearing one of my ties religiously from then on, once he decides which one to get."

"Odd that you sent such a letter to him and no one else, wouldn't you agree?" asked Grimes.

"That's not true, I sent out hundreds. To people I've met in the neighborhood."

"It irked you that he couldn't choose between the two ties," said Grimes.

"He took up too much of my time. I needed to attend to my other customers. I received a great response to my mailing."

"But you sent out just one letter. To Rodney, only Rodney," said Grimes, while Watley, used to the inspector's methods, pushed aside enough of his sport jacket to show Maurice enough of a nasty-looking revolver.

"Rodney, is that his name? As I said, there were so many letters."

"You know well enough it is. Give it to us straight," Watley demanded, now sporting a chilling pair of brass knuckles.

Grimes jumped back in in full force, grabbing Maurice roughly by the collar, an action typically performed by Watley. "You needed Rodney to choose a tie already so you could plant a bug on it, didn't you? Someone wants to find out what Rodney does or doesn't know about…shall we say…the disappearance of a comfort-food cook and the operations of a couple of food vans, er, food trucks. And why we are here to help find them. Who put you up to it?"

Maurice would not be the first pigeon to turn to putty in Grimes' hands and seconds later he broke. "It wasn't my idea, I tell you. They were making me do it. Mr. Big will send his goons to kill me if I—"

> (Is any reader surprised that some shots rang out at that moment and one lone bullet found its way through an open side window to Maurice's heart? Or at the classic screech of tires as a car pulled away?)

"Well, that's it for Maurice, and a dead end for us in more ways than one," said Watley. He helped himself to several silk ties and took a woolen one for Rodney. "So the visit isn't for naught," he explained. "But Inspector, how did you know Maurice targeted Rodney and reeled him into this shop with a singular, personalized invitation?"

"Let's say I had another hunch. My, that word is coming in handy. Oh, and there's also this, of course." Grimes unfolded a sheet of heavy white stationery and showed it to his friend. "When Maurice went to call his accomplice and you were looking at some ties, I 'borrowed' what had become the new top page of a writing pad I found on a shelf under Maurice's desk. Maurice had used the sheet above it to pen the personal advertisement to Rodney. Soot from my shoe brought impressions embedded in the soft paper to life."

"What did Maurice offer Rodney?" asked Watley.

"A free tie of his choice and a hundred dollars a week to wear it around town and tell anyone he meets where he got it. In any event, Rodney's promotional piece was clearly a one-off, with a devious ulterior motive no less. And this was no dead end. We've now learned there's a 'Mr. Big' in the picture, and my having selected the last number dialed feature on Maurice's phone should prove to be most enlightening. So with all that and everything else we have going for us, it's full-speed ahead and Bob's, no, Robert's your mother's brother."

Inspector Grimes, hiding behind spectacles, a false beard, and trilby hat, spent the rest of the morning wandering around Fern Creek on his own. He had already rummaged around Butter Bar's empty lot several times to no avail but stopped there once again.

"What'll ya have? What'll it be?" the space seemed to cry out.

Grimes whirled around. A woman with a young boy stood behind him. It was she who had spoken.

"Have you ever been to the food truck that used to be here, you know, Butter Bar?" the woman asked.

"I'm afraid I haven't had the pleasure, miss. I'm new in town. Here on business. I sell thread. Fine English thread."

"Yeah, you're English. I can tell. Butter Bar was one of two food trucks in town."

"Butter Bar's the best," said the boy. "They have the best doughnuts and the best chocolate milk."

"You bet, Corey." And addressing Grimes once again, "I'm Ginger. I worked there, as the waitress."

"What happened?"

"We had to...pull up stakes and go...elsewhere."

Grimes could see the woman fought to keep her emotions

in check and knew this could work to his advantage. "Please go on," he said, most sympathetically.

"I'd rather not talk about it anymore."

"It might do you some good."

"All I'll say is that the other food truck—Blackeye Pete's—told us they were going to a town north of here where huge crowds were lining up at this hot dog stand because there weren't enough places in that town to eat."

"This other town, East Harlan, I surmise?"

"Yeah. Hey, you're a sharp cookie. How'd you know? Cook had Butter Bar towed to East Harlan and we were going strong for a few days—East Harlan factory workers into bowling sure can put it away—but in the end it didn't work out so Cook towed Butter Bar back to Fern Creek. He now says he might have to sell it. It's in some garage a few blocks away."

"My name's Chatsworth," said Grimes. "Please tell the cook I might want to convert Butter Bar for use in my thread business if the price is right. I'd also like to find that other food truck. Having two trucks would be better than one. I could cover both sides of town at once and sell twice as much thread."

"Beats me where the other one is."

And since Grimes never passed up a chance to double-check working theories, he offered Corey some gum.

"Yay. PinkyPink. PinkyPink."

"Thank the nice man, Corey. My roommate, uh, former roommate, was also nuts about that gum."

"Was?"

"I guess she still is. But I haven't seen her for a while."

I had slipped a note under the door to Grimes' and Watley's rooms across the street, saying I had big news and asking them to meet me at Tuffy's Bar on Hanlon Boulevard as soon as they could. We could have met at my apartment, but Grimes had organized a covert meeting at a local pub in *The*

Weeping Stone Enigma with great success. Why not try my hand? We were to pretend it was a retirement party for Grimes if anyone asked. Might also be good practice if my plans for a Rodney, P.I. mystery series took shape. Before long, both men met me outside the bar and I led them inside to a back table where we could talk privately, after calling out "retirement par-tay" and giving a finger-gun "what's-up" to Tuffy, or maybe it was some guy who works for Tuffy.

We ordered celebratory beers and waited as a waitress set them down and left. Grimes started us off by recounting his earlier experience at Butter Bar's empty lot.

"You met Ginger? You saw Ginger? My Ginger?" I said, a bit too loud. Other customers started to look our way.

"She did call herself Ginger."

"What was she doing there? Where would she go from there? I'm dying to see her. I've got to find her."

"Utmost apologies, my friend. I had painted myself into a corner, giving her a false name and having pretended not to have heard of Butter Bar. So I couldn't mention you nor could I ask where she's staying without appearing to be a stalker. But let's hear your news."

I made sure Tuffy was out of earshot, then reported in hushed tones, "The lab results are in. Harry's and Mabel's gum samples are identical. It's *Papaya Porkchop*, PinkyPink code 10-46-X, for both, and Mabel's had gads of undissolved sugar as you predicted, Inspector, meaning she chewed it briefly, then tossed it. Recently."

"So they do match" said Grimes. "I expected as much. That would say—"

"...a clandestine visit to the PinkyPink factory is in order," I said, completing Grimes' thought. The tie between me and Grimes began to get spooky. "Harry's, then Wilbur's, possession of the 10-46-X gum samples can be explained away. Harry's friend delivers mail to PinkyPink. They ply him with experimental flavors—he's a trusted guinea pig of sorts. He then gave three of the samples to Harry, who gave two to Wilbur, who gave one to me. Mabel, however—"

"...has no obvious connection to the factory," said Grimes. "How would she come upon some 10-46-X unless—"

"...unless she and Peter I. Black are involved in some way with PinkyPink," I said, honing my newfound ability to match wits with the esteemed inspector. "Maybe Blackeye Pete's is selling food there."

"Aren't you forgetting something?" asked Grimes. "Wouldn't that be problematic? Haven't you concluded by now that Blackeye Pete's needs Butter Bar takeout to function?"

Grimes had me there. "Then they could be involved with PinkyPink in some other way that could give Mabel access to those gum samples. And if we can confirm that 10-46-X was just produced like Wilbur implied, that's even more proof that Mabel visited Blackeye Pete's' vacant lot in the last few days."

"Rodney, we still need to account for the fact that Mabel chewed that gum for merely seconds before discarding it," said Grimes.

I assumed that was Grimes playing devil's advocate, having already guessed the answer. "*Papaya Porkchop* is awful, it's as simple as that," I said. "Mabel tried it and spit it out. If Mabel is still around, Peter I. Black and Blackeye Pete's are likely to be nearby. Anyone interested in an after-hours tour of a gum factory tonight?"

32. 'Real' Liver

WE BORROWED HARRY'S CAR and right after midnight, Grimes, Watley, and I left the main road and pulled up in front of the lift gate blocking entry to the PinkyPink bubble gum factory.

"Curious. No guard outside to contend with," said Grimes. "Not the case in England, I assure you. I believe there is a night watchman inside, however. I did some digging myself."

"Bubble gum-related crimes are not much of an issue in Fern Creek," I said. "The night watchman's a political appointee. Detective, would you mind raising the gate?"

Watley got out and started to lift the gate out of our way. When it sprang up sharply, a small hook on the end snagged the detective's wristwatch and flung it into some bushes about fifty feet away.

"No *time* to get it now, Detective," I said. "We'll look for it on the way out. Better get going."

I turned off the headlights and drove us to the back of the factory, parking out of sight in between two dumpsters. We skulked past a maintenance truck and approached the massive building.

"Picking this lock's a cinch," Watley boasted as we reached one of the rear doors. A distinctive click preceded a "Bravo" from either me or Grimes, I don't remember who (or whom), then the three of us entered a grimy storeroom, our flashlights exposing walls covered with old advertising posters. One in particular caught my eye: *Dentists Love PinkyPink*. A dentist—I assumed the guy's a dentist given the poster title and the fact that he wore whites and stood before lots of scary dental equipment—is saying via a comic book-style speech balloon, *Nothing like a relaxing chew after a hard day's drilling.* I thought that made a lot of sense, though one would have to be a dentist who does a lot of drilling and chews PinkyPink to know if that's true.

"Let's synchronize our watches," said Grimes. "Apologies, Detective. Next time, you'll know to carry a spare. Rodney, it's twenty after midnight. The night watchman should be fast asleep by now since he came on at nine. Data collected in England in eight separate studies over the last fourteen years shows that three hours and seven minutes is the longest a person sitting on a hard wood chair in a gum factory working the graveyard shift can stay awake before dozing off. They found jaw fatigue from chewing all that freely available gum to be the determining factor. The average over all the studies was two hours, forty-six minutes if either of you are interested."

Impressive. Grimes was even more knowledgeable than I thought he'd be, but I needed to show him I was also a force to be reckoned with. "I'm not so sure about that average. I would have guessed it to be, let's say, oh, I don't know…slightly higher or even a drop lower."

The inspector considered my contribution for quite some time, which boosted my confidence. I peeked out of the room into a maze of long corridors. "Why don't we split up to cover more ground?" I said. "Detective Watley, please go left. Inspector, would you mind taking the right hallway? It's straight ahead for me. Let's find out if Blackeye Pete's has any connection to PinkyPink."

I didn't mind wandering on my own through a deserted gum factory at night. What's the worst that could have happened, I run into two or three vicious Dobermans? I think all you have to do is become the aggressor, show them who's boss, then reward them with doggy treats, assuming you have some in your pockets. Not necessarily the more expensive kind you see advertised on TV made with, quote, 'real' liver. Dogs in those ads appear to go bananas for it, though I wouldn't bet they can tell the difference. Anyway, they'll be eating out of your hand in more ways than one, and may lead you to whatever you're trying to find, or even protect you from some wanton attacker once you're in their good graces.

But what in the world was I doing in that factory, sneaking down a dark corridor, looking for who knows what? I should have been home getting a good night's sleep so I could get up early in the morning and get back to the novel I've been trying to work on. Crap. I needed to order more candles from that bee farm in Michigan, and while at it, check if they sold honey.

Have you ever had honey on waffles instead of maple syrup? We had a great old waffle maker in the house growing up. After the waffle cooked, you pulled a secret lever and some type of blades would come down and cut the waffle into bite-size squares. That's what my mother told me. I never saw it work. My sister and I invented a great waffle game. We took our waffle squares and filled some with butter—we did those first while the pieces were still hot—and some with maple syrup, the others with honey. Then we set them up like soldiers and moved them around in battle. Butter beat syrup but honey beat butter. If my piece 'killed' my sister's piece, I would get to eat her piece. Hard to top the butter men in taste, but I preferred the honey ones. Generally speaking, though, there's nothing like eating maple syrup squares followed by butter squares followed by honey squares.

I should have already admitted I dropped my flashlight a minute into my factory escapade, sending it clattering across the highly polished floor until it crashed into a metal garbage can. And that the lens shattered when my flashlight fell. The light still went on for a few seconds at a time when I shook it, but I mostly made my way in the dark.

I heard whistling. Coming from around the corner and getting progressively louder. And there were snatches of flashlight beam moving up and down and side to side, heading my way. I figured it was Watley. I couldn't picture Grimes whistling. Or else the night watchman. Talk about being on the other end of his nightstick, if he felt strong enough to swing it. I tried to duck into some room. Best to avoid any distractions. Door locked. Door locked. Panic set in, with maybe seconds to spare. Locked...locked...open! Inside just in time. Smelled like a broom closet. The whistling increased in pitch as it approached, reached a peak as it passed me, then trailed off in the opposite direction. Sort of like the Doppler effect. I peeked out. All clear, not that I could see very far.

Too bad I didn't bring a candle, which wouldn't break if it fell, though I couldn't light it without a match. Can you imagine if I found and woke the night watchman and asked him for a match? I'd thank him directly and walk off. He'd be rubbing his eyes like he's seeing things, or think he was dreaming, then go back to sleep. I saw it play out like that numerous times in TV sitcoms.

I knew it to be physically impossible but the corridor refused to end. I shook the flashlight every few steps with little to show for it until one particular shake lit up a building directory. Employee relations, 140. Mailroom, B5. Cafeteria, B7. (I made special note of that location.) Product Development, 208. Bingo. A place to check Harry and Wilbur's claims about the *Papaya Porkchop* gum. I found a staircase, went up a flight and soon came face to muzzle with a large guard dog who came muzzle to face with me. And me without any doggy treats made with 'real' liver.

"*Grrrr*," said the dog, baring a vicious set of teeth.

"Scat!" said I, as loudly yet as quietly as I could. The dog hobbled off, whimpering, head down, paws clicking and slipping on the highly polished floor. He, or she, seemed as old as Methuselah. It must have been another of those political appointments.

So where the hell was room 208? I was opposite room 282. Next, 280. At least I was heading in the right direction.

So many troubles lately, and much of it is Peter I. Black's fault. If only I could turn back the clock to before Chambers disappeared and Blackeye Pete's arrived in Fern Creek. Times were so pleasant then. My fish were ebullient, if I'm using that term correctly. I enjoyed snubbing my nose at Chauncey's Chow to indulge in comfort food at Butter Bar, like their richly caloric chicken-fried chicken livers or their slow-cooked ham bone soup. Ginger was (and still is) the apple of my pie. Peter I. Black is the reason I'm not safe at home under the covers, but in a gum factory after midnight, with vicious guard dogs lurking around every darkened corner. Blackeye Pete's. What kind of name is that for a legitimate business, if it is one? It sounds like a den of pirates. Black should be made to walk the plank. And then there's Mabel. What kind of name is that for a waitress? (Okay, now I've gone overboard.)

The corridor ended at room 210. I peeked around the corner. At last—Product Development, room 208. A sign warned *RESTRICTED AREA*. Not unexpected. But it surprised me to see a maintenance cart halfway down the other corridor and bright lights coming from one of the rooms. Someone whistled while he worked. I watched as the room lights went out, a man emerged, locked the door, and pushed the cart one room farther. He opened that door, turned on the lights, tossed keys onto his cart and went inside. I inched my way around. Room 208, locked.

I eyed the keys on his cart, then started to make my way over there. He came out again. I froze, hugging the wall in the dim corridor light. He picked up a spray can and went back inside. I broke all records making it there and back with the keys before he was any the wiser. Each key had been numbered. I opened room 208, propped my wallet between the door and the frame and returned the keys to the cart, but not until I pressed the key into the clay key mold I had in my back pocket. Wilbur had picked it up at our local spy shop. I wished Grimes had been there to see me. He would have been as impressed as all get out. So we could now make a duplicate key if we ever needed to return to room 208, and for some unknown reason I knew we would be back.

Product Development occupied a much larger space than I expected, based on the size of other rooms I had peeked into. I shook my flashlight and looked one way, then another, briefly lighting up all sorts of test tubes and beakers and beeping machines and lab coats draped over ergonomic chairs. I chanced turning on a desk lamp. A tall bank of glass-doored refrigerators with *Open Briefly—Controlled Environment* signs filled a rear wall. About fifty metal containers, all identified by production codes, were partly visible through the glass. None that I could see were labeled 10-46-X.

I shuffled through a bunch of file folders on one of the desks, then noticed a bulletin board plastered with red, green, and blue announcements. A blue one dated that morning caught my eye:

Call for focus group participants.
Evaluate PinkyPink's newest experimental flavor.
Papaya Porkchop, just three days old.

PinkyPink created *Papaya Porkchop*, code 10-46-X, three days ago, which was proof positive that Mabel had been in Fern Creek within the last three days. And where there's a Mabel…

33. Boom, BOOM!

As THE THREE OF US MADE our way to the PinkyPink factory that night, we didn't know we were being shadowed by a shadowy figure with a butcher knife three inches shorter than Jon Johns'. And as we entered the factory's rear door, we had no idea that that same person waited to follow us in. I should have pulled the door closed behind me, but the thought never entered my mind. Who else would be crazy enough to be where we were, doing what we were doing, at that hour of the night?

"This scheme of mine's a real corker," Drago mumbled to himself, while crouching beside some bushes. "I'll wait until they're inside, then come upon Watley from behind and knock him out cold. A rag soaked in this ether-type junk should do the job. Then I'll haul Watley back to the American's apartment and tie him up. And if he needs a second or third dose of this chemical stuff, he'll get it for sure. I'm not stingy—I'm a giving bloke. But some might say that I should be more careful, that Watley may overdose, that he may croak. Well, if that happens then sue me. At any rate, I've already planted the bomb in Rodney's place, or should I say, placed the bomb in Rodney's plant?"

Drago approached the factory door. "I still need to set that countdown thingamabob for five minutes, activate the remote sensor and return to my rental car to wait for Grimes and Rodney to arrive. Then as Grimes struggles to undo some extremely tight knots to free Watley, I'll trip the device from the car and a few minutes later...boom! No more Grimes! No more Watley! No more fish! Why no mention of no more Rodney? Who the devil cares about Rodney?"

Drago peeked around the partially open factory door and caught the tail end of Watley's sport jacket turning left. He entered, admired one poster in particular, dismissed thoughts of stealing it, and also turned left, following silently, keeping his distance until the right time to pounce.

I eventually came upon Grimes in the factory's garage, sitting on some cartons next to a corrugated steel door. Three PinkyPink trucks were parked on one end, with another one up on a lift. No sign of any food trucks. Grimes smoked his pipe. "So we meet again," I said. "I had to slip past the night watchman."

"Yes, the watchman," said Grimes. "And stationed at an inopportune place, at the junction of four key passages. I had to inch by him myself three or four times. He never woke up. But I don't suppose you ran into Watley? Oh well, no matter. He probably tripped and fell into an open trash chute. It wouldn't be the first time, nor the last. Nevertheless, Rodney, if you'll permit me." Grimes reached over and pulled a chain. Up rolled the steel door, screeches echoing in all directions.

"Blackeye Pete's! So it *is* here," I said. "Surprising, but not that surprising. Anything point to why it's here or what their plans are?"

"Well, the full account eludes me," said Grimes, "but I believe Black wants to keep his food truck hidden from the general public for the time being. As to why, this may shed some light on the matter." The inspector held out a note he said he found inside a red envelope taped beneath a cutlery drawer in the truck. It had a cut-and-pasted message that began *$10,000 keeps me mum.*

"So they know somebody's on to them serving Butter Bar

takeout," I said.

"That appears to be the case. Odd that the stamp on the envelope has no postmark. Who delivers mail to Blackeye Pete's?"

"Usually my friend Harry. Otherwise Edgar, if Harry's out sick, or that replacement guy if Edgar's also out sick. But it's not like Harry to pass up the free coffee he gets at Blackeye Pete's for any reason, even if he's sick, so most likely Harry delivered that envelope."

I said nothing more to Grimes about it, but now wondered if Harry could be blackmailing Blackeye Pete's behind my back. Nah, not Harry. Well, maybe Harry. Can I put anything past him? Like hampering my efforts to expose Blackeye Pete's? One could make a case. It was Harry who suggested I team up with a fictional detective, rather than working with real Fern Creek police detectives. Though that may backfire on him—the dynamic duo, Rodney and Grimes, can't be beat.

I should also ask Wilbur what he thinks about the note, though not so fast. Maybe Wilbur's in on it with Harry. They've both been acting more inept than usual, perhaps on purpose, like when they sabotaged my all-important macaroni and cheese taste test at Checkerboard Park. They also both pushed me to continue my wild-goose chase in East Harlan. I wasn't sure I could overlook that, though those five hot dog cart hot dogs made my stay in that town worthwhile.

Grimes continued. "The other open question is why someone high up in PinkyPink would agree to let them hide the food truck here. Black would need such approval. This section of the factory would be swarming with workers during the day who would be quick to raise a red flag. It does seem Black has plans to put Blackeye Pete's back in business, however. I found crumpled receipts signed by him yesterday for deliveries of paper goods and canned sodas, and the truck has been washed clean. Soap suds in inaccessible corners gave that away. As for Mabel, I found a lace handkerchief exquisitely embroidered *To Mabel from Granny* in plain sight on the truck's counter, surely a cherished gift that Mabel wouldn't leave behind, though we can't say for sure that Mabel is presently in town, and with Black."

"She has been here in the last few days," I said.

"How do you know, my friend?"

"Well, we've already shown it's likely that Mabel chewed that *Papaya Porkchop* gum."

"Quite right, and somewhat recently given those obstinate sugar molecules. But the more precise 'when' of it still eludes us."

"No more than two or three days ago," I said. I handed Grimes the focus group announcement from room 208.

"Jolly good show," said the inspector.

It still wasn't clear what Peter I. Black was up to. Could the inspector have missed something important? I searched inside the truck without result. But while circling the outside, I blurted out, involuntarily, "Eureka!" then felt I needed to explain. "A very American expression," I said. "It comes from California gold rush times."

"It's from ancient Greece," said Grimes.

"Well, I spotted something here in America. Paper under the left rear wheel. Inspector, please help me push the truck."

I put the gears into neutral. Grimes and I got behind and with a lot of difficulty managed to roll Blackeye Pete's a few feet forward, exposing several parts of a torn flyer. I picked them up and pieced them together on the hood. "This looks promising. It's about a big event in Fern Creek sponsored by PinkyPink and hosted by none other than Blackeye Pete's. Dignitaries galore. A bubble-blowing contest. In five days' time." I had a slight feeling Grimes already knew about the paper but wanted me to get the credit. "What could it all mean?" I asked.

"That remains to be seen," said Grimes, "but given that our Mr. Black is involved, something truly dreadful, I expect. It's now clear we have less time than we thought to figure it all out. Our good friend the detective will have to fend for himself. Serves him right for being so clumsy. Let's leave everything as we found it and get out of here before roosters start crowing and that night watchman awakes."

Grimes and I walked up the two steep flights to my apartment.

"We'll wait here until Watley shows up," said Grimes. "It's only a three-mile walk from the factory, so he's bound to be here shortly, unless he's still out there looking for his watch."

There was a ghastly quiet as I opened the door and a disturbing sight as we both entered the apartment. A dazed Watley had been gagged and bound to one of my dining room chairs. Grimes uttered a troubled "Hello, what?" and rushed to his friend's aide.

At that same moment, in a rental car down the street and unbeknownst to me or Grimes, an excited Drago pushed a red plastic button marked *Press and take cover*. The resulting click reassured him that in five minutes time, his work in America would end with a bang. He would then be free to ditch his rental car at the Fern Creek train station and head back to New York to board the next available flight to London.

Grimes ripped off the tape covering Watley's mouth and Watley, still groggy, was finally able to speak.

"Don't get your knickers in a twist, Inspector. I'm all right, though I'd like to meet up with the bloke who came up behind me. I'd gladly give him a bunch of fives. Last I remember, some pleasant-smelling rag covered my face."

"Halothane. It knocked you out," Grimes told his friend.

"Somebody pinched some yesterday from the town veterinarian. But we must work swiftly to free you of these ropes. We may have only moments to spare." As Grimes struggled to untie some extremely tight knots, he also glanced around the room for something, anything, out of place. "Rodney, your plant. Lift those leaves!"

"Whoa, some scary-looking device," I said, almost choking on my own words. "With a countdown clock. There's four minutes, twenty-two seconds left."

"Don't touch it," yelled Grimes. "It's a bomb and it might detonate when moved. These knots won't budge. Get me a sharp knife, and fast."

I rummaged through a few drawers. "Damn, none around. I knew I should have ordered that Super Steel-o kitchen knife set I saw on TV. Any one of the thirty-seven knives can cut through brick, they showed that on the screen, though not with all the knives, just one of them. I'm sure they were pressed for time, but the announcer implied they were all as sharp, so I guess ordinary ropes would be a breeze compared to brick. A great deal. Only five easy payments of $19.95 plus shipping and handling, but when I called them to—"

"Bottle it!" yelled Grimes, "and check the timer."

"Two minutes, forty-one seconds left."

"Then save yourself," said Grimes. "I'll try to dismantle the bomb. It's the one hope to save Watley. No chance to move him in time."

"I better warn Wilbur," I said. I ran to my workroom, grabbed my lap desk, any ink I could find and the case of Esterbrook nibs, then ran down the stairwell three steps at a time. I banged on Wilbur's door as hard as I could, yelling for him to get out. No answer. He must be at the all-night poker game at Harry's. I had no choice but to continue on. As I hit the pavement, a deafening explosion shook me and my building. Glass shot from my living room window in all directions and two fish landed at my feet, one already a goner, one still taking its last few breaths. I thought I heard fiendish laughter coming from an open window in a murky midnight blue car driving away at breakneck speed. Some dismal music coming from on high (or from an apartment across the street) heralded the final curtain call for Inspector Grimes and Detective Watley. How would I ever come to grips with that? And what would now become of my *Inspector Grimes Rhymes with Crimes* mystery series?

> *The Inspector and Detective both dead? Knowing Grimes by now, do readers really think that's the way it went down? Here's what actually happened:*

Grimes and I walked up the two steep flights to my apartment.

"We'll wait here until Watley shows up, though I'm beginning to suspect he may already be inside waiting for us," said Grimes. "Something's rotten. I can smell it."

Grimes' concern was justified as I opened the door and a disturbing sight greeted us as we entered the apartment. A dazed Watley had been gagged and bound to one of my dining room chairs. Grimes uttered a troubled "Hello, what?" and rushed to his friend's aide.

At that same moment, in a rental car down the street, an excited Drago pushed a red plastic button marked *Press and take cover*. The resulting click reassured him that in five minutes' time, his work in America would end with a bang.

Grimes removed the tape covering Watley's mouth. The detective was too groggy to speak. "We must work swiftly to free you of these ropes, my good man. We may have only moments to spare." As Grimes struggled to untie some extremely tight knots, he also glanced around the room for something, anything, out of place. "Rodney, your plant. Lift those leaves!"

"Whoa, some scary-looking device," I said, almost choking on my own words. "With a countdown clock. Four minutes, twenty-two seconds are left."

"Don't touch it," yelled Grimes. "It's a bomb and it might detonate when moved. These knots won't budge. Spread your coffee table rug on the staircase. Then slide Watley in his chair down to safety. I'll stay to dismantle the bomb. But first, get me a screwdriver."

I rummaged through a few drawers. "Damn, none here. I knew I should have ordered that apartment owner's tool kit I saw on TV: Six different screwdrivers, three were Phillips head, three ordinary slotted, or it may have been the other way around; an electronic stud finder; and a pair of safety goggles. Why they call it a *pair* I'll never know—you get one of them. Great deal, though. All that for only five easy payments of $13.69 plus shipping and handling, but when I phoned them to—"

"Bottle it!" yelled Grimes. "Get me a butter knife. Never mind, I'll get it myself."

I couldn't open my apartment door from the inside. The doorknob popped off. Wilbur had 'fixed' it a few days ago. Enough said. Our fate was now in Grimes' hands.

"Two minutes, forty-one seconds left," warned Grimes, as he gently pried open the bomb's plastic cover, exposing a mess of colored wires. "Now one minute, three seconds. It seems to me I need to disconnect one of these wires, and I'm guessing it's either the yellow or the blue. The correct one should stop the timer. The wrong one, well, we might be sorry we didn't say our goodbyes already. Rodney, which one should I disconnect?"

"The yellow?"

Grimes disconnected the blue. Me, the inspector's equal? I'm not fully there yet.

Drago grew impatient waiting in his car down the block. He knew it should have been the end of Grimes and Watley by now. "Ruddy hell. Five minutes can't take this long," he said out loud. "Blast. I bet there'll be no blast after all. Drat that Grimes." Drago turned beet red, dove for his butcher knife and the door handle in a sudden fit of rage, then thought better of it. "Maybe it *is* back to square one for me, but I'll make them pay even more. And as I now see, being blown to bits is too good for the likes of Grimes and Watley. They need to suffer." Drago drove out of town to the middle of a cornfield, slumped down in the front seat, and fell asleep.

"Drinks all around," I said, carrying in a tray of my best juice glasses filled with some nondescript red wine Harry or Wilbur gave me on my last birthday. Watley still seemed out of it so I left his glass on the tray. "Inspector, you were expecting trouble, weren't you?"

"Right you are, my friend. I had become exceedingly suspicious over the last few days each time I passed a particular rental car parked down the street. My calculations showed that every time it has been moved then reparked, the wheels were, on average, approximately two and a half feet from the curb, with the back tires two times farther away than the front. That struck me as especially odd. My conclusion? Unquestionably a driver used to having the steering wheel on the right. He cannot properly judge the distance to the curb when steering from the left like you Americans do. Someone from England was stalking someone on this block. As for who, one might put two and two together. I am now convinced Jon Johns or one of his thugs, most likely Drago, is here in America after me, and I suppose Watley as well, or he is using Watley to get at me."

Watley perked up at the mention of his name, then spaced out again. What a waste to pour him a glass of wine. Once my guests leave, I could try to get Watley's portion back in the bottle, though unless I had that funnel that Wilbur insisted he left here, which I think I returned to him, it wouldn't be easy. I wish I had Wilbur sign some sort of receipt. Live and learn.

"And how did you know a bomb was hidden in my plant?" I asked the inspector.

"A slice of pudding, my dear Rodney. Watley, bound and gagged, served as fresh bait to draw us in and keep us here for an extended period of time. The most likely scenario—an explosive reception. As I scanned the room, I noticed that the leaves on the philodendron closest to us were a gnat's whisker less hydrated compared to leaves on the opposite side of the plant, just three to five percent less, but less all the same. An insignificant difference to all but a highly trained eye, like mine, I assure you. When you last watered the plant using, I suppose, the Alice in Wonderland coffee mug you picked up at a yard sale for ninety-nine cents, some object impeded the distribution of water to the root system of leaves on one side of the plant, getting in the way as water hit that soil. The large leaves evidently blocked your view, and hence you never noticed the device. Given all the above, I was fairly certain that's where the bomb must be hidden. Rodney, it has been great fun today. I should get the detective back to his bed in our rooms across the street. So it's cheerio until the morning."

"But what about the bomber?" I asked, though I mostly wondered how Grimes knew how I got the mug.

"He bombed, and is long gone by now."

"How did you know about the mug?" I had to ask.

"When I went to get the butter knife I noticed the Alice in Wonderland mug on the counter had a few droplets of water on the inside and specks of potting soil on the rim. You had clearly used it to water your philodendron, the only plant in the room, and must have inadvertently touched the rim to the soil as you were watering. You had also never bothered to remove the price sticker from the side of the mug, the easy to remove kind used at charity sales, though the writing had faded having been through your dishwasher, I would guess, three times. One could still make out what it said, however. The mug was first priced at $2.95. Then marked down to $1.50. Add some haggling, and I expect you got it for ninety-nine cents."

"Nope. Ninety-five cents." So, other than choosing the right bomb wire to disconnect, Inspector Grimes was not all that smart.

34. Bigger Bubbles

OUT EARLY THE NEXT MORNING, despite my attempts to reverse direction, a feeling of comfort-food deprivation pulled me toward Butter Bar's empty lot. Why I needed to inflict such pain on myself, who knows? The imagined smell of onions and peppers added to my misery. I tried again to change course. No dice. Then it happened. I saw Butter Bar set up and running, with Ginger dishing out breakfast to three eager customers. Cook's back was wide as ever. I ran over, took Ginger's hand, and wanted to say something heavy on my heart, but the words weren't there.

Ginger managed a friendly, "Hello, Rodney. How've ya been?"

I sensed she was glad to see me and thank goodness she didn't call me Rodger. I grabbed the last empty stool and took it all in, including an order of Cook's breakfast sausage and fried egg sliders.

"I missed you," I said. "I missed Butter Bar. Thought you might never come back."

"Don't ask," she said. "We weren't doing well enough here, so we tried to strike it rich in some pathetic town north of here. East Harlan. Know it?"

"Not really." No way I would get into all that happened in East Harlan right then and there.

"That didn't work out," she continued, "so Cook brought Butter Bar back here to sell it—some English thread salesman wanted to buy it—but Cook changed his mind after a frightening dream. Miles and miles of English thread wound around him and Butter Bar, with long and short sewing needles poking him every which way. Cook decided to make one last go of it and here we are."

"Tell Cook I love him for that. No, you better not say it just that way." I nodded goodbye, then left, afraid I'd wake up from a dream if I sat on that stool any longer. I needed Butter Bar's return to stay real. I thought telling someone might help. I walked home and called Wilbur.

"Wilbur, it's baaack! Butter Bar's back in town. I say, Butter Bar's back. Serving up pies, hot from the oven: Dutch apple, blueberry crumb, caramel peach. After a terrific breakfast, I tasted all three. They hadn't yet cooled properly, but Ginger let me try them anyway. And it's aces to see her nametag again, and she's looking cute as ever. Wilbur, you still there? Wilbur, are you paying attention?"

"Yeah, I hear you. Nooooo. Oh crap. I can't believe the score's already ten-zip. Go on."

"Ginger told me that Cook considered selling Butter Bar to some Englishman—our own Inspector Grimes, in disguise, posing as a thread salesman—but changed his mind. The inspector expressed interest in buying the truck as a ruse to learn more about it. Wilbur?"

Utter silence. He must have accidentally hung up the phone. I redialed.

"Stay with me, Wilbur. So Butter Bar has now reopened here to try to make it work one more time. Wilbur, say something. You are listening to me, aren't you? I've been trying to tell you, Butter Bar's back."

"Lemme turn down my TV. What a lousy Badger game. I knew I shouldn't have recorded it last night. What's that you were saying? Something about buttering a bear's back?"

"Forget it."

"Rodney, wait. Don't hang up. I made a note to phone

you after I watched the game. My cop friend called me last night. A Peter I. Black served two years recently for selling PinkyPink trade secrets to Gumm Gum. Of course, Black claimed innocence."

"I thought your friend couldn't find a police record for Black. Now he found one?"

"My friend looked up the wrong name, Pedro A. Block, and I'm afraid that may have been my fault."

"Do tell."

"I may have had a huge mouthful of taffy when I called my cop friend the first time."

"May have had…?"

Inspector Grimes, on his own for a time and once again in disguise, took full command of Butter Bar's third stool later that same morning.

"Nice to see you again," said Ginger, handing him a menu. "Sorry Cook changed his mind about selling."

The girl without crusts came by with her father. He sat on the second stool next to Grimes, leaving the first stool for his daughter.

"Switch with me, Daddy," she said. "I'm scared I'll fall off the end, like my friend Audrey."

Her father did so.

Grimes ignored the menu and called to the cook, "Eggs and bacon, my good man."

"Cook will pretend he doesn't know what you want," whispered Ginger. "Flip the order. Ask for bacon and eggs. Here in America, the bacon comes first. I'm not sure why. I guess it's alphabetical."

"Alphabetical? Ordering eggs and bacon, not cricket? Well, loving a challenge as I do, then I will take up the gauntlet and revise my selection without introspection so it is spot on alphabetically for your United States of American cook. I will therefore opt for the following repast, assuming the sequence in which I state that which I desire pleases His Majesty the Cook: apple, bacon, coffee, doughnuts, eggs, figs, granola, hotcakes, jellyroll."

Most of what Grimes said flew past Ginger, but she gave the order to the cook.

The father leaned forward, looked over at Grimes, and spoke past his daughter. "Sorry, sir. I couldn't help overhearing. That was extremely well done, except you left out something that starts with the letter 'i'."

"I'm not all that hungry," Grimes responded, wondering how a smidgen of British wit would go over in Fern Creek.

"You're English, aren't you?" said the father. "First time in Fern Creek, I suppose? Allow me to introduce myself. I'm Mark Diamond, marketing director at Gumm Gum. It's a bubble gum company here in town. This is my daughter. Honey, this man came all the way from England across the great big ocean."

"Daddy, I don't want anything English. I want French toast for breakfast, without the crusts. And I want the cook to cut them off this time."

"Sweetheart, you should know by now he won't serve it that way. But I'll cut them off for you."

"So...Gumm Gum," said Grimes, seizing what might be a golden opportunity. "Serious rival to PinkyPink, I expect."

"Well, we don't like to consider ourselves—"

"I love PinkyPink," said the daughter, talking over her father. "I don't care if Daddy works for the other company. PinkyPink has the best comics on the wrapper, and makes bigger bubbles. Even my friend Audrey says so. Her big brother works there. And her parents let her have PinkyPink all the time. It's not fair. I'm not allowed to chew PinkyPink at home, or at school, or in the playground, or anywhere. Even when I say I'll hold my breath if I can't. It's not fair."

"Now, honey."

"Who runs your company?" Grimes asked the father. "I have some ideas about a possible business venture."

"Why, it's Simon Biggs, the president."

"I call him Mr. Big," added the girl without crusts, a smile lighting up her face.

"I'm stunned that Rodney hadn't even thought it significant to tell us there was a second bubble gum factory in town, given all the talk about PinkyPink," said Detective Watley, after Grimes recounted his experience at Butter Bar. "Were you surprised to discover that, Inspector?"

"I confess I was not," said Grimes. "I had known about Gumm Gum ever since our visit to The Tie Shoppe, where I noted the last phone number dialed by Maurice. I apologize for not telling you sooner, my friend, but as I am sure you know by now, there are some cards I like to keep close to the vest. I redialed the number after business hours that evening and was treated to an informative and amusing recording: *Thank chew for calling Gumm Gum Company. If you know your party's extension...*"

Watley tried his hand at moving one puzzle piece in place. "So someone at Gumm Gum directed Maurice to bug Rodney's tie, then silenced Maurice when we got too close. I suppose they could have been the ones behind the attempt to finish off Rodney in East Harlan."

"Possibly," said Grimes, "but we also know from Rodney that Wilbur's snipper had a connection to Maris Chambers, though further speculation at this point may lead us astray. Let's let the facts speak for themselves, at their pleasure. Now, a visit to Rodney is in order."

Inspector Grimes and Detective Watley showed up at my apartment at two that afternoon. Minutes later, my apartment intercom buzzed again.

"It's Harry and Wilbur," said Harry.

"It's Wilbur and Harry," said Wilbur.

Grimes had asked me to invite them over, saying he and Watley were anxious to meet my illustrious friends and get to know them. But I knew Grimes wanted to see what Harry knew about Peter I. Black.

My four guests took seats around my coffee table. "I forgot to mention it when you and Detective Watley were here last, Inspector, but it's an Eames." I knew I took a chance, half expecting Grimes to say that I was dead wrong, that in no way was it Eames, but he didn't, at least not yet. So maybe Wilbur was right for once when he first said it was an Eames. If so, chalk one up for me, and chalk one down for my generous Aunt Agnes. If not, well, that's my friend Wilbur.

"So, what kind of work do you do?" Watley asked Wilbur, to break the ice.

"I'll say what I wish I did. I've always dreamed of being an airline pilot. Flying one of those humongous 747s with the lives of hundreds and hundreds of defenseless men, women, and children in my hands. Mostly, I'd like to travel the world. Pilots travel the world, don't they?"

Grimes took out his pocket-size journal and jotted down some notes for the treatise he's writing on the mentally unstable, then turned the spotlight on Harry. "And how about you, Harry? Rodney tells me you're a mailman. Tough job. Through rain and snow and ice and mud and all that sort of rot."

"Mud?"

"I was at Blackeye Pete's' empty lot the other day. Does the ground get muddy, I mean, when you deliver their mail after a heavy rain?"

I could see Harry starting to sweat a little.

"I...haven't noticed much mud," said Harry.

"Ever speak to Blackeye Pete's' cook?" asked Grimes. "What's he like?"

"Who Black? I...don't really know him. I used to talk to the waitress instead. Her name's Mabel."

Grimes had reminded me that he and Watley have a set routine where, after a time, Watley plays bad cop. Too late to warn Harry. But even I wondered what Harry might say, especially given my suspicions about the blackmail note delivered to Blackeye Pete's.

Watley slammed down a sticky *Syrup World* magazine he had picked up from my coffee table. "Cough it up, Harry, you know much more about Black than you're letting on."

"No, I don't. Ask Wilbur, or Rodney."

"Harry, I sense you're wasting our time," said Watley, who I knew from my novels has a wonderful knack for turning red, feigning anger at will, and scaring the daylights out of anyone he's addressing.

"Easy now, Detective," said good cop Grimes, physically positioning himself between Watley and Harry. "You promised me you would never again do what you did to that last chap who wouldn't cooperate. I still don't know how you knocked out three of his back teeth on one side and three on the other, all with one punch."

"Maybe it was these," said Watley, polishing his pair of brass knuckles with Wilbur's tie, after having jerked Wilbur by his tie over to Watley's side of the coffee table.

It seemed Harry had been trying his best to hold back information from the two men, maybe to protect his interests, but he caved under the mounting pressure.

"Okay, okay," said Harry. "Blackeye Pete's' cook, Peter I. Black, worked at PinkyPink several years ago. But I just found out, I swear. A mailman friend of mine used to deliver mail at PinkyPink addressed to Black, even handing it directly to him when he needed Black's signature. Until yesterday, my friend had never mentioned Black to me by name. He just spoke about some guy high up in their product development lab working on experimental flavors. Then about a few weeks ago my friend recognized Black at his food truck, but we didn't see each other again until yesterday. That's when he told me."

"Don't think of stopping there," said Watley.

"Over the years," said Harry, "Black or some of the other guys in the lab would give my friend different gum to test, and my friend would give some to me. A few of the new flavors were okay, most were awful. If I were you, I'd refuse something called *Garlic Surprise* if you're ever offered a piece. Black worked there for about six months until he ran into some serious trouble. What he did I swear I don't know, and I think they fired him for it."

"Black was a chemist at PinkyPink," I said. "That explains the textbook I found—stood on—in his food truck."

"I don't know about any books," said Harry, who looked like he was about to lose a lot of blackmail money.

"One last question," said Grimes. "Do you know the girl without crusts?"

"Yeah, everyone does," said Harry. "What about her?"

"Her father, Mark Diamond, now at Gumm Gum. What have you heard about his background?"

"He worked for years in the Merchant Marine, some kind of signalman, or something. That's all I know."

35. Plans Go a Rye

MARK DIAMOND WOULD HAVE preferred being drawn and quartered to being summoned to the office of his boss, Simon Biggs, but go he must when called.

"Diamond, great news for you," said Biggs, talking around his cigar. "In a few days' time, Gumm Gum will have no local competitors. That other company in town, whose idiotic name even pains me to mention, will disappear in a flash after I'm through with them. Why am I telling you all this? Because I want you to run back to your office and create a new, no-holds-barred, dazzling marketing campaign for Gumm that's ready to go as soon as I give you the word. And need I say, your job depends on it. Now get out. Meeting over. I have other pressing matters to attend to. Don't you dare breathe a word of this to anyone if you value your position here at Gumm, or having any kind of job at all in this miserable town."

Diamond had absolutely no idea how to respond and could only back up, head down, out of Biggs' office.

"You look like you're in shock," Mrs. Diamond told her husband when he returned home after work.

Diamond couldn't stop pacing back and forth in the kitchen while his wife cut off the crusts of their daughter's grilled cheese sandwich. "It's Biggs. That man's reprehensible. He's cooking up something terrible, something I doubt I can be part of."

"What is it?"

"It beats me, except that he's out to destroy PinkyPink. Sure, that would make my job easier. It's a marketing director's dream to have no real competitors, but I've never balked at some fair competition. And I have good friends that work there. Who knows what this might do to our town's economy and reputation, to good old Fern Creek?"

"What the heck could he have in mind?"

"I tell you I don't know. I think he sensed my reluctance and didn't say anything more about it. One thing, though. It may have to do with something called 05-47-Y. Biggs kept looking at this slip of paper when he first asked me in, then crossed out something on it, tore it up and tossed it in his garbage can. He wasn't there when I went back a few hours later to kick around a few marketing ideas. I felt I better show lots of initiative after the way he threatened me. I had started to worry about paying our bills—sweetie's braces, piano lessons, even our mortgage, everything. Biggs and his secretary must have gone for the day. All the lights were off, his desk clear, the computers shut down. I started to leave, but then walked in to see if that paper was still in the can. It was. Maintenance hadn't come around yet. I pieced it together as best I could, read it, then tossed it back. Hard to make out the writing, but I think it said *05-47-Y*."

Their daughter peeked out from behind the dining room curtains. "05-47-Y, 05-47-Y, have another piece of pie. What does 05-47-Y mean, Daddy?"

"Never you mind, young lady," said her mother. "And I don't like you hiding there spying on us, but come eat your sandwich."

Detective Watley took a turn at Butter Bar the following day. "A cup of tea with milk and an egg salad sandwich on wholemeal bread, if you please."

"You mean whole wheat?" asked Ginger.

"Of course, pardon me, wholewheat."

"It's two separate words, not one, and no dash. But the whole…wheat has been eighty-six'd."

"Eighty…?"

"It means we haven't got any left," said Ginger.

"Then your American white bread would be fine, or German pumpernickel."

"Eighty-six'd and eighty-six'd. Give us a break. We just reopened. We're sorting out our bread deliveries. How's about rye? We got it in from Marty's. It's still warm. Right out of the oven. How's that sound?"

"Better than a kick in the teeth," said Watley.

Ginger looked confused.

"Sounds lovely," said Watley.

The girl without crusts and her father came by then for lunch.

I was worried about my fish. Anyone would be, to look at them. They used to be so happy and carefree, chasing each other around the hunk of fossilized coral, or peeking in and out of the sunken Spanish galleon on the bottom of the tank, or basking as a community under the tropical sun daylight fluorescents. Now it seemed like they were always cowering, open-eyed, behind a fake flaming ludwigia plant. They were even hesitant to come out for breakfast or dinner after I dropped in much too many flakes. I was afraid they would never be the same. And who was to blame? Drago. They must still have been shell-shocked from the other day at the prospect of being blown to bits or blasted out of a broken living room window. And it was not like my apartment was at street level. After they're no longer with me, euphemistically speaking, I'll get flying fish next time. But for now, I should wait for Drago to fall asleep in his rental car with an open sunroof, then drop in about a hundred piranha as the car fills with water during a torrential rain.

I desperately needed to collect my thoughts so I headed

to my favorite bench by the river. As soon as I sat down, a rubber ball rolled under the bench and bounced off the back of one of my shoes. Two boys came running up.

"Hey, mister, betcha you can't throw the ball all the way across the river."

"Sure I can," I said, thinking of Grimes' display of athletic prowess in *The Cricket Conflagration*, one of my earliest novels. The ball didn't even make it halfway and the strong current swept it away in a flash. I think the wind must have been against me.

A third boy reached my bench out of breath. "Aw shucks, mister, that was my ball."

That third boy looked familiar. "Aren't you delivery boy Danny's brother?" I asked.

"Yeah, and you're the guy who blocked his bike. He told me how he tricked you. Still looking for those Buffalo wings? Ha, ha, ha. And I'm telling him you owe me a ball."

"It's curious what that little girl did with her crusts," Watley told me and Grimes back at my apartment at the end of the day. The more the detective described what he saw, the more it aroused our interest.

"So let me get this straight," said Grimes. "The father cut off the crusts on his daughter's toasted sandwich, like he always offers to do. I have seen that myself. For some reason, the cook refuses to do it. I want to know why he won't, but that's another matter entirely. She ate the sandwich—well, you said that her father ended up finishing some of it—then she played with the leftover crusts on the counter in a deliberate manner, after breaking them up still further."

"Quite so," said Watley. "I sat next to her and it was hard not to notice. I couldn't look away, even though my cup of tea required some immediate attention. On one hand, I assumed it was merely a child playing. On the other, she seemed to have a serious goal in mind. She worked intently, surprisingly so, finally arriving at one particular configuration. Then she jumbled up the pieces and after some effort, placed them the same way as before. She did that over and over again. She tried in vain to get her father to notice what she created. She pulled at his shirt-sleeve, but he kept chatting up the waitress. The waitress finally swept the counter clean and that was the end of that."

"Show me exactly what the girl did with her crusts as best as you can," said Grimes.

The inspector cut eight four-inch strips from a section of cardboard and placed his pseudo crust pieces before Watley. The detective cut the eight pieces into eighteen, some larger, some smaller, moved them one way and another, then shifted them several more times until settling on one arrangement.

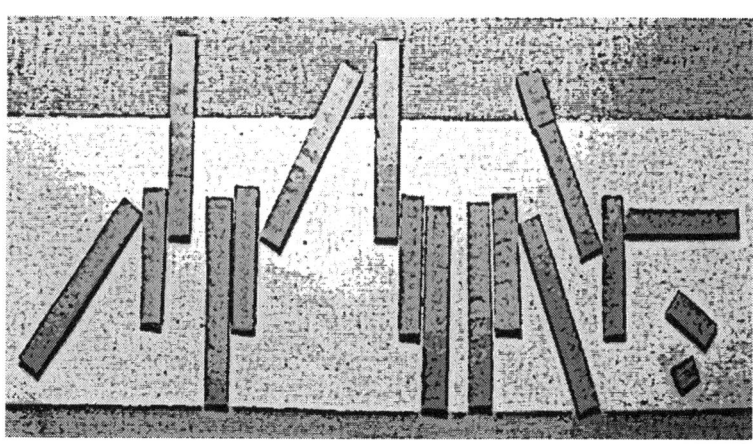

"That's it. I'm sure that's it," said Watley. "What a memory I have, even if I do say so myself. Though, again, I watched her set up the crusts the same way at least a dozen times."

I moved in for a closer look.

"Hmm," said Grimes. "I'm beginning to think we have in front of us some extremely useful information. A clue of some kind, inadvertently given to us by a young girl trying to impress her father. Something she saw or heard somewhere. We need to decode it."

The inspector lowered his eyes, seemingly deep in thought. I pictured him accessing a large cerebral database of personal knowledge.

"Detective, are you certain about those two small pieces on the right?" asked Grimes. "I do not believe they are an essential part of the setup, but let's agree that's the way the girl did it. Two toasted bread slices, eight equal crust sides to start, each broken into longer and shorter sections. She could end up with an extra piece or two...uh, only one, if my assumption is correct. Perhaps she made a small mistake there, though one of little consequence. By Jove, my good fellow, it called out to me all along. I have it and you've done it!"

"Done what?" asked Watley, still focusing on the arrangement and adjusting one of the pieces an eighth of an inch down. "What does it represent?"

Grimes mentioned a specific combination of numbers and letters, but wouldn't explain further, though that served to get my own detective juices flowing and was my chance to grab more of the lead from Grimes. So when both men concentrated again on the display, I slipped out of my apartment, not to be seen again until well into the next day.

36. Green's Green

IF WILBUR HAD BEEN OUT walking his friend's Pomeranian puppy the previous evening, he might have seen me enter Fern Creek Car Rental and drive away minutes later in a black station wagon heading east. The PinkyPink factory happened to be east of where Wilbur stood, among many other places in Fern Creek and, of course, far beyond, but Wilbur would have no reason to choose PinkyPink as my destination.

And no way Wilbur could know I hid the car between two dumpsters, approached one of the PinkyPink factory's rear doors, picked the lock using Watley's pick-and-wrench technique, and disappeared inside, not to emerge for another hour and a half. Or maybe two hours. I had forgotten my watch, though I could have used Watley's if I had stopped by the front gate and found it.

When Redd Green, owner and head chemist at H.M. Green Laboratories, arrived for work the following morning, he couldn't help but notice a black station wagon in the parking lot with someone fast asleep at the wheel. On closer inspection, the person looked remarkably like me. Green pounded on the roof, then pounded again. "Wake up. You shouldn't be here. It's private property."

With some effort, I opened one eye and rolled down the window. "I'm Rodney," I said, still somewhat woozy. "You analyzed some PinkyPink gum samples for me a few days ago, remember? My friend Wilbur's friend's scientist friend is your friend Henry and he has an urgent favor to ask."

"I'm not sure who the *he* in your sentence refers to, but if Henry's involved, how can I help?"

"I didn't get much sleep, so I'll get right to the point," I said. I reached into my jacket pocket and pulled out a handful of individually wrapped bubble gum pieces. "Mr. Green, these were found at the PinkyPink factory a few hours ago. Henry and I need them analyzed this morning. They're different from the ones I sent before, and there's not much time. Lives may hang in the balance. Every chemical in this gum must be identified and quantified, but most of all, we need to fully understand its physical properties and the implications if this gum is ever chewed by someone."

"They look innocent enough in their colorful wrappers," said Green. "But anything for Henry, my old gum, I mean, chum. Come inside. How about a cup o' joe?"

I sat in Green's office enjoying some high-octane coffee and homemade brown sugar cookies while Green left to instruct several staff members about the task at hand.

"The analysis will take some time," Green said upon returning. "But let's hear what Henry's been up to lately. It's been a while."

"With Henry, I wouldn't know where to start, but did he ever mention me to you? I write the *Inspector Grimes Rhymes with Crimes* mystery novels using my pen name, Randall Reed."

"No kidding? I have read some of them," said Green. "*The Litigious Laboratory*'s my favorite. The one where Grimes fingered an informant in a lab like ours. Amazing how Grimes knew the guy had applied two dabs of aftershave that afternoon three hours apart, rather than one dab that evening as the lab's director foolishly assumed, and that the informant's English springer spaniel was an English cocker spaniel in disguise."

"Yes, it all sounded like a dog's breakfast to the novel's

characters at first, but it turned out fine in the end."

"I'd like to meet a genius like Grimes someday," said Green.

"As a matter of fact..." I dared not finish that sentence.

Two hours later an assistant handed a detailed lab report to Green, who reviewed it carefully, then passed it to me.

"So, Henry's concerns were real, his suspicions one hundred percent justified," I said, rising abruptly. "Thanks Mr. Green. I must return to Fern Creek immediately."

Green looked unsettled as he shook my hand and told me to give my friend Wilbur's friend's scientist friend Henry his warmest regards. Actually, Green seemed sick to his stomach. "In all my days working with police forensic labs and counterintelligence units," he said, "I've never seen anything so disturbing, so wretched, and in what looks to be a candy store favorite, no less!"

Drago was down but far from out. With a failed bomb plot and a terrific nap behind him, a much more satisfying plan had now surfaced. Flyers advertising a bubble-blowing contest for state officials and sponsored by a gum company named PinkyPink were appearing all over town. His rental car window had been plastered with them, even while parked in that cornfield.

Drago gathered a handful of flyers and tossed them in the air. "It's like manna from heaven. Both Grimes and Watley are sure to be at this event," he said to himself. "They'll be in the midst of the heavy Fern Creek constable presence one would expect, given all the dignitaries. Won't Jon Johns be impressed when word gets out that I made the impossible possible, that I found a way to kill that accursed inspector right out in public. And that loathsome detective friend of Grimes will then wither away and die on his own, without his mate to protect and guide him. Now I just need to bait the hook."

Peter I. Black strolled into the PinkyPink president's office with the air of someone about to go on a long, well-paid vacation. "We've spruced up Blackeye Pete's and are now all set for PinkyPink's contest," he announced. "We are honored to be part of your event, but it's also the grand reopening of Blackeye Pete's in Fern Creek, after being away the last week or so for our annual charity event in East Harlan."

"Splendid," said the president. "Your truck's still in our garage, I take it. I'll have several cases of our best-selling gum, *PinkyPink Original*, brought to it this afternoon. Enough for the contestants and plenty for attendees, as giveaways."

"Wrong! All wrong!" said Black. "*Original* is fine for us to give out to the audience, but it's still old hat. You're missing your big chance for a major publicity splash. Instead, you need to use one of your experimental gums for the contest. I hear that one in particular has received rave reviews with test groups: *Caramel Cream*. It will create a whole new buzz for PinkyPink. Everyone will be talking about it for weeks or months to come, I guarantee it."

It was doubtful the president noticed the devil in Black's eyes.

"Marvelous idea," said the president. "Arrange it with Simpson in Product Development. You know him, don't you? I can see it now. Both state senators, our mayor, and other state and local muckety-mucks, all chewing our next blockbuster product launch, *Caramel Cream*, PinkyPink's 'new flavor of flavors.' Yes, that's how we'll advertise it."

That part went well, thought Black. He entered the lab minutes later. "Simpson, great to see you again." Black ignored Simpson's scowl. "You know Blackeye Pete's is hosting PinkyPink's big contest, right? Well, the president told me to pick up gum for the contestants, but he first wants you in his office on the double. I'll wait here until you get back."

Alone for a time, Black did what he came to do.

"The president didn't want to see me," said Simpson.

"Sorry, my mistake. I must have misunderstood. But I already got what I came for. See you around sometime. Oh, can I get a pass to get by security with this package?"

All Black had needed was the opportunity the president had just given him to put his plan to destroy PinkyPink into action.

37. Gummy Macaroni

As Wilbur and Harry and Inspector Grimes and Detective Watley and I grabbed Butter Bar's five stools, we were treated to a welcome view of Ginger's nametag and an even more welcome view of Cook's massive back. So what if the guy never turns around? Who wants him glaring at us? That would mean he wasn't leaning over his hot stove grilling sausages and peppers, or frying eggs sunny side up in lots of foamy butter, or flipping buttermilk pancake silver dollars. I had dreamed of seeing his face while sitting at the counter, but I now knew I've had that wrong all along. Let him do what he does best—comfort food. I'll do what I do best—comfort feed.

And by now I should have admitted that Cook had no part in Chauncey Chambers' disappearance and murder. Shame on me for suspecting him. He runs Butter Bar, for Pete's sake. (Not the Pete in Peter I. Black.)

"I see there are now five stools," I said to Ginger, who looked to be in great spirits. There used to be four.

"Well, once again, we're the only food truck in town," said Ginger. "Cook has this whole new, positive outlook about things. He's even talking about getting a few picnic tables and chairs at some point. Takeout is still slow, but our counter business is starting to pick up. Turn around, you'll see what I mean."

I hadn't noticed that a large crowd had begun to gather behind us and those in front seemed to be eyeing our stools. Maybe Butter Bar was finally getting the recognition it deserved. That was good for Cook and Ginger, that was both good and bad for me. I wished them well, of course, and needed them to continue dishing out comfort food. Also, the more Ginger earned, the better it would be for me after wedding bells chime, but there wasn't always enough of their country-style Polish kielbasa and fried onions to go around.

"Can we get right to it?" I asked Ginger. "Menus will not be necessary."

"Sure as shootin'. What's it gonna be? What'll ya have? What's your pleasure? Let's start with you, good lookin'."

Unfortunately, that compliment wasn't directed at me.

"The *Smoked Bacon & Chives Mac & Cheese* I've heard so much about, young lady," said Grimes.

"Likewise," said Watley.

"Ditto," I said, already picturing the glorious mouthfuls to come.

"Same for me," said Harry.

"I can't decide what to order," said Wilbur.

"The bacon will be done properly, I trust?" asked Grimes, loud enough for Cook to hear. "Crispy with pressed-out curls and drained on a double layer of lint-free kitchen towels." He didn't particularly want his bacon like that, he told me later, but used the opportunity to test a theory he has on giving advice to cooks.

"Easy on the cheese, for me," said Watley. "I have a bit of the collywobbles."

"The macaroni should be nice and gummy," noted Harry. "That's the way Mom always made it. Never liked hers much, but I got used to having it that way."

"Me too, I'm in as well," said Wilbur. "The macaroni and cheese, but I like it with twice as many chives as the cook threw in last time."

"Cook cooks it...the way he cooks it," snapped Ginger, putting my four companions on notice, then smiling at me in appreciation for not rocking the boat.

At long last, Cook nodded slightly to Ginger, who picked up and delivered five heaping, steaming portions of Cook's famous macaroni and cheese. Each plate looked and smelled better than the next, if that was even possible. The crowd behind us became more and more restless and began to push forward, knocking into our stools. I heard a small voice in back of me ask, "What's Cook makin'?" Then a louder voice answered, "Makin' bacon." An even louder voice asked, "What'd ya say Cook's makin'?" Someone else answered, "Makin' bacon." Then the entire group started a staccato chant which became much louder and stronger still. "What's Cook makin'? Makin' bacon!"

They kept going, the sound deafening. It bounced around the sides of the food truck, shaking plates, tinkling silverware. The ground began to rumble and even Ginger seemed rattled. As for Cook, who can tell? He's hard to gauge, but I doubt he had a problem with Butter Bar's newfound popularity.

"I've never known the fine folks of Fern Creek to be so unruly," I told Watley, who repeated my words to Grimes. "But can you blame them for being impatient? We're talking about Cook's special macaroni and cheese."

"Rodney, do something. Anything," said Harry, who started to fear for the safety of his order, at least what remained of it.

"Speak to them," pleaded Wilbur, hovering over his portion.

"Me, step in to soothe such a scary mob?" I protested. "You've got to be kidding." Well, with Inspector Grimes once again casting his shadow over me, I even surprised myself. I spun around, stood up on my stool—Wilbur held it steady—and gave it my all, having dug down deep enough to discover a previously hidden bit of assertiveness, though I had doubts how long this 'new me' would last. In my loudest possible voice, I said, "Quiet. Cook can't hear the sizzle." That seemed to settle them down a little, but I needed to pinpoint the source of their trouble.

"What in the world are you all so agitated about?" I asked that hungry mass of humanity.

That mass of humanity edged even closer.

"It's got to be something other than just waiting for Butter Bar's macaroni and cheese, a dish so spectacular it could launch a thousand ships, stop a charging elephant in its tracks, and satisfy a Maharajah and his entire harem. A dish with ingredients so fresh they are way before their time. Dare I even mention the homemade golden egg pasta, the mild and extra sharp country-farm cheddars, buttery heavy cream, hickory smoked bacon and vibrant green chives? So what if Cook runs out of those ingredients and your turn doesn't come today? What's the big deal?"

So much for my attempts at crowd control. That didn't work so well. They were now more riled up than before, so the five of us were even more anxious to finish.

"Not the most pleasant meal of the century," said Watley after his last forkful.

"But surely the best food we've had in America so far," added Grimes, completing Watley's thought.

When we got up, fifteen people somehow made it onto our five stools and someone in the group called to Ginger, "Fifteen orders of *Smoked Bacon & Chives Mac & Cheese*, and hurry, hurry, hurry."

"Cook will get to it when he gets to it, get it?"

"Got it."

"Good."

As the five of us strolled down Beacon Street well satisfied, I proposed we play the *Shuffle Maris off to Jail* game. "For the fun of it, let's see if each of us can mention a different piece of evidence that links Maris Chambers to Chauncey Chambers' kidnapping and death. Anyone who can't come up with something is out of the game. Harry, why don't you start? I'll go last."

"A third wife happens to inherit her murdered husband's millions?" said Harry. "Gimme a break."

"My turn," said Wilbur. "Maris faked the saffron-inked ransom note she showed Rodney at his apartment. There was no need for a real ransom note because Maris was in on it with Black. And I get credit for finding her supply of saffron and rose water hidden in her bedroom shoebox."

"I'll have a pop at her now," said Watley. "She tried to buy Rodney off with 20,000 pounds sterling, I mean, dollars, for walking her dog just the once."

"If it were pounds sterling, I might have taken it," I said. "What do you have, Inspector?"

"Mrs. Chambers booked a cruise for herself after her husband's disappearance, but *before* his fate was publicly known," said Grimes. "Rodney, you're next. Can I make it even more of a challenge? Allow me to use up two other bits of evidence that have surfaced thus far: Maris Chambers' near confession that you and I witnessed at your apartment, and hiring Cloak-a-Truck to disguise her husband's food truck, then giving it to Black for one dollar. Can you stay in the game, my friend?"

"No problem, Inspector. You're still getting to know the new Rodney. I might mention her checkbook showing three $2,000 checks made out to cash, money which she gave to Black as part of the agreement for Black to kidnap, then kill, Chambers. As it turned out, he killed himself, but Black gave him sufficient reason to do so. Or that was additional money she paid to Black in exchange for the location of her husband's remains, which would allow Chauncey to be declared dead and Maris to inherit his fortune. Neither scenario has yet been proven, so instead, let me ask Wilbur, what's on Collins between Beacon and Crown?"

"Blackeye Pete's."

"According to papers I found at Maris' house, Blackeye Pete's' one-dollar food truck sits on land owned by Chauncey Chambers."

38. Mum's Favorite

TIME WAS RUNNING OUT FOR Drago. With PinkyPink's event about to start, he still had no idea how to get at Grimes. He looked again at the flyer. Some small print at the bottom now caught his eye: *Vendors welcome.* He pinched himself hard for missing it the first time. "Love a duck. That may do nicely," he said out loud. "And I saw two or three defenseless pushcarts at the town park the other day." He reached the park in no time flat. It was mostly deserted with only one cart in sight.

"Ice cream?" asked a feeble old man from behind his ice cream cart. "Please buy some ice cream. Nobody's coming by today. Everyone's off to some gosh-darn contest and I've no way to move my cart there even though it's not that far…unless, of course…you'd move it for me."

"Oh, I'll be moving it, but first, is there anything you're out of?" asked Drago, as he looked at the faded color photos of ice cream choices plastered across the front of the cart.

"Let's see. I know I sold my last Strawberry Flake Bar the day before yesterday."

"I'll take one Strawberry Flake Bar, and make it quick."

"But I told you. None left."

"Check. You could be wrong. I need one right away."

"I already did. This morning. Sorry to disappoint, but I don't have any."

"Check again. There might be one you didn't notice, way at the bottom. Under your other bars. I had my heart set on Strawberry Flake. My dear old mum's favorite, and today's her ninety-fifth birthday, or it would have been if she hadn't been run over by a school bus on the way to help peel potatoes for starving boys and girls at the orphanage."

"Oh, I'm so sorry." The ice cream vendor became more sympathetic and eager to please. Too eager, in this case. As he leaned over his cart and reached in to move some ice cream bars out of the way, he must have felt one last thing before being knocked out cold—the heavy hinged steel freezer lid slamming down on his head. Is it surprising Drago would do such a thing? That Drago would amble off with the poor man's white jacket and hat and ice cream cart while eating a Chocolate Double Crunch Bar he didn't pay for? All that, after laying the guy down on a park bench, dousing him with liquor, and covering him with newspapers so the police would haul him off as a vagrant if he ever came out of his coma?

Before leaving the park, Drago undid the false bottom of his attaché case and perused his panoply of poisons. Some were pleasantly painful, others much more painful, still others, forget about it. "How would you like an ice-cold poisoned ice cream bar, Inspector Grimes? No, no. You're insulting me. Put away those hard-earned pennies. With all the good you do in the world, there's no charge for the likes of you. It's on the house."

PinkyPink's big day had arrived. The whole town planned to attend. A few might have been interested in which dignitary blew the biggest bubbles. Most were probably curious to see who made a bigger fool of him- or herself. I'd heard that Blackeye Pete's had reopened, set up and ready to be dead center of the action. So both food trucks were back. I didn't care at all for Peter I. Black, as one can well imagine, but it might be fun to see Mabel again, though I'd never admit that to Ginger. Nah, it wouldn't be. I was glad I told Grimes, Watley, Wilbur, and Harry that I'd meet them at the event, because out of loyalty I first wanted to stop at Butter Bar.

Ginger and Cook were going hot and heavy filling large takeout orders when I got there: urns of coffee and boxes of muffins and doughnuts. I was their only customer. Other Butter Bar 'regulars' must have already gone to the contest, even the girl without crusts and her father.

Ginger barely nodded hello. Too busy. However, without waiting for me to order, she brought me Cook's special of the day—*Glistening Ham and Cheese French Toast.* Boy, oh boy, what can I say? I didn't expect ham and cheese French toast to have all that creamy butter and buttery cream, and a river of warm maple syrup, no less. I demolished the dish, then pulled myself away, but not before suggesting Ginger come by the PinkyPink event as soon as she had a chance.

"And see Blackeye Pete's in the spotlight?" she said. "Not going to happen."

"Trust me. You won't be sorry. You'll be delighted."

Ten minutes later I made my way through the PinkyPink event crowd toward a Blackeye Pete's no doubt besieged by dozens of customers clamoring to buy coffee and muffins and doughnuts. Actually, Butter Bar's coffee and muffins and doughnuts, if the truth be told. Grimes and Watley joined me on the way.

"A refreshing ice cream bar, gents?" said an ice cream vendor in a too-tight fitting, white jacket to the three of us as we were passing his cart. "I have a few left. All the same flavor."

"Not for me," I said.

"I'll take one," said Watley, "whatever it is." And to Grimes, "How about you, my friend? It's my treat, old boy."

"Thank you, but no thank you," said Grimes.

"Tut-tut, that's unacceptable," said the vendor. "Besides, if it's for a friend, then it's buy one, get one free, for the friend, that is. That's my credo."

"You can't pass that up," said Watley.

Grimes relented, but not just to be sociable. The transaction completed, he walked briskly over to a plainclothes policeman he had met earlier and engaged him in a brief but animated conversation.

"My friend should be right back," Watley told the vendor. "I expect he wants to treat that gentleman to some of your ice cream."

Grimes and the other man approached the cart. "Arrest this vendor," said Grimes. "The charge, poison ice cream."

"Bilge!" said the vendor, now wide-eyed. "This man's a nutter."

"Then take a bite yourself," said Grimes, holding out his ice cream bar. "Your reputation for using poisons, *Mister* Drago, precedes you."

As Drago grabbed his butcher knife from the freezer and lunged at Grimes, two shots rang out. The first knocked the knife high in the air. The second sent it flying safely into some bushes about fifty feet away. Cow Boy Brantley had come to our rescue, beating the policeman to the punch. Brantley blew across the two barrels, holstered his pearl-handled pistols, glanced at me, and walked off.

"He's some Westerns writer dude I met at Blackeye Pete's," I told the group.

"How did you finger me?" said Drago to Grimes, trying to buy time, hoping to find a way out, making no reference to his knife attack. "You've never set eyes on me. And I did well to hide my accent."

"Your *gents* got me thinking and your use of the 12th century Middle English word *credo* might have given you away, but your very British *tut-tut* sealed your fate."

"To the clink with him," said Watley to two uniformed Fern Creek policemen who had joined the group. They started to haul Drago off to jail with the now melting evidence.

"Wait a moment," said Grimes. "I've changed my mind

and decided not to press charges, provided this man is put on a late flight to London, tonight."

"That's against protocol, given the ice cream and knife and all," said one of the policemen, "but if it's for you, Inspector."

Without a doubt, Drago was relieved, but still defiant. "You're much too soft for your own good, Grrrr...imes," he said, eyes now blazing with anger. "But rest assured, there'll be nothing but bad times for you and your pathetic pal here when we meet again on our home turf."

"I'm looking forward to it, Drago, I assure you. I always appreciate a good dose of competition. I hope there's no hard feelings about the handcuffs, my friend."

"You're a dead man walking," warned Drago. If glares could kill, Grimes would indeed have been a dead man.

"Yes, I know. You and your London hoodlums, Jon Johns and Sir Giles Gilbert, will keep trying to do me in. I'll counter cleverly, as usual. Frustrate all of you to no end. Nothing excites me and delights me more. Also, that keeps more options open for Rodney as he writes about us. Constables, be so kind as to arrange for a stretch limo to drive this man to the New York airport and a private agent to see him safely aboard his flight, all at my expense, of course."

Drago emitted some unintelligible sound.

"Oh, and by the way, Drago," said Grimes, "send my regards to Jon Johns and Sir Giles—"

"...and offer them this gum with our compliments," I interrupted, handing Drago four pieces of gum from the batch I had brought to Redd Green's lab for analysis. "There's a piece for you and an extra one there as well."

Had Drago noticed my subtle wink to Grimes and Watley?

The contest was about to start. Bands were playing,

children were getting their faces painted, balloons were lost in the air currents, and the mayor of Fern Creek scrambled onto a makeshift podium to take the microphone.

(*Screech, squawk, squeal, tap tap.*) "Is this thing on?" said the mayor under his breath. "Damn. It's not on yet. Can't those good-for-nothing town workers, who should be thrown out on their lazy asses, do anything right for once?"

"The mic's been on all along," yelled someone in the back of the crowd. "We've been able to hear you, loud and clear."

"Well, um, I see, ha, ha, okay." The mayor cleared his throat. "Good people of Fern Creek, what a great day for our town. A shout-out to our invaluable town workers for helping to make all this possible. They always come through in a pinch. Prepare to be treated to something special—a bubble-blowing contest with all of your favorite state senators, congressmen and committee chairs as contestants, and I can tell you, they are participating only for charitable purposes."

Two or three people in the huge crowd applauded.

"It has nothing at all to do with the fact that the winner can expect to garner lots of great media coverage before next month's election," said the mayor.

While the mayor managed to get in a heartfelt thank you to everyone imaginable, I could see some of those politicians out making the rounds, shaking hands, kissing babies, passing out cigars to the men in the crowd. I hoped they didn't get the latter two mixed up.

Wilbur and Harry showed up and I pulled them, Grimes, and Watley aside. "Try not to visibly react to what I'm about to tell you," I said, "but there's a serious issue with the gum planned for use by the contestants."

"What's the problem?" asked Wilbur.

"Are they using that awful-tasting porkchop gum?" asked Harry.

"No, they're not," I said, "but it's something much worse.

When I ran out on the inspector and detective the other night, I made my way to the PinkyPink Product Development lab and managed to get my hands on the same gum to be used in the contest. It has since been analyzed by Redd Green at H.M. Green Laboratories. Apologies for going behind your back, Inspector. I wanted to tackle this on my own."

"Not to worry. Your initiative impresses me and I trust Mr. Green was able to help."

I took some papers from the envelope I had with me. They were marked *Highly Confidential*. "It's Green's report on those samples. Six pages of scientific jargon, charts and graphs, but one paragraph in particular says it all. Harry, will you do the honors? But quietly, please."

Harry cleared his throat and began to read using a stage whisper he said he learned in high school, but he had to strain to see the small print. "Can I borrow someone's reading glasses? I need a pair that's +2.75, though +2.50 might do."

An impatient Grimes grabbed the pages and read the final paragraph of the Executive Summary to us. The first three words were in bold caps and the last three were underlined for additional emphasis. *"**WARNING! CAUTION! DANGER!** Do not chew under any circumstances. After ten minutes, not only are the most revolting and abrasive flavors released, but chemicals in this gum will turn lips, teeth, and tongue <u>bright orange</u>. <u>Permanently</u>!"*

"Well, I'll be jiggered," said Watley. "That's what happened to Chauncey Chambers."

"This confirms my suspicions that this is no run-of-the-mill contest," said Grimes.

Wilbur and Harry stopped unwrapping the gum that they had swiped from the contestants' table.

"Rodney, you need to rush up there and halt the contest," Harry said frantically, eyeing the mayor's microphone about ten steps away. "I deliver mail to some of those politicians. I do favors for them, they do favors for me. I'm about to see years of work going down the drain."

"Patience, Harry," I said, placing a firm hand on Harry's shoulder. "Let's wait and see what happens. It should be interesting."

Surprising that Grimes himself seemed so unconcerned that the contestants could be disfigured for life. "Well, they *are* politicians," he conceded.

The mayor continued. "So without further ado, let me give it over to the president of the PinkyPink Gum Corporation, which is sponsoring this event." (*Applause. Applause.*)

"Hello, Fern Creek," yelled the president, trying to get the crowd more stirred up than they already were. "Thank you, Mayor. I won't mention that you yourself are up for re-election next month and as we all know, you've been doing a heck of a job. Also, we owe a huge debt of gratitude to Blackeye Pete's for hosting us. I'm sure you've enjoyed one of their muffins or doughnuts today, but have you checked out their signature gravy? Take home a jar or two tonight, I certainly will. Now what do you say? Is it time to get on with the contest?"

"Yesssss," roared the townspeople.

"Then let the fun begin. Charity is what PinkyPink's all about, so I'm pleased to announce that a year's supply of PinkyPink gum will be donated in the winner's name to the Shady Brook Home for the Aged. That's a generous supply: six pieces per resident, per day. Is it sugarless you might ask? Not on your life. Need I tell you again, it's PinkyPink. Never sugarless. Loved by children and dentists alike."

The president ranted on for a while longer, then explained the contest rules and introduced the participants.

"I would now ask Blackeye Pete's to close shop until after the contest, but enough preliminaries," he continued, "except to say that today the contestants will be chewing one of

PinkyPink's most anticipated, experimental flavors, *Caramel Cream*. Be sure to look for it in the weeks to come wherever fine bubble gum is sold. So now...contestants take your places. Unwrap your gum, and...hold on a moment."

"This is gonna be good," said Peter I. Black.

"I'm afraid to watch," said Mabel. "We can still put a stop to it. Confess what we've done. Really, what you've done."

"Not on your life. I've put too much into this. Getting in bed with Maris Chambers—you know, babe, I don't mean that literally—got me the food truck. A dead-on perfect ticket back to Fern Creek. A way to stay close enough to exact a vicious revenge on PinkyPink. A chance to stick it to that blasted bubble gum company for canning me, and after I had given them all that I had."

"So let me get this straight," said Mabel. "You're out to destroy PinkyPink even though they were right to fire you, and then expect to collect some huge payoff from their competition? You have to admit you were selling PinkyPink trade secrets to Gumm Gum."

"Yeah, but those PinkyPink clowns didn't have any real proof, and even if they did, they should have given me a second chance. Me, the best research scientist they ever employed. Didn't I develop winning flavors that put them on the bubble gum map? Of course, PinkyPink knows nothing of the one ghastly gum I developed in secret in case they found me out. A gum which I hid in their product development lab. A gum I will now use to destroy them. A gum that disfigures, not delights. A gum that could well be called *Worse Than Murder*. They'll rue the day they let me go. They'll—"

"Calm down," said Mabel. "You're acting crazy. You're scaring me."

"Listen. Either you're with me or you're not. I've waited too long to get back at those lowlifes at PinkyPink and their rotten politician friends who railroaded me straight to the penitentiary to further their careers. And there's all that cash at stake. I won't get the second half from PinkyPink for this event, but there's the huge payoff from Gumm Gum. Besides, there's nothing to worry about. I have no doubt we'll be in the clear. An unfortunate mistake. That's what we can say. I don't even work there anymore. Current staff must have mismarked the batch. I brought only what they told me to bring to the contest: the *Caramel Cream*. Yeah, that's right."

"Before I start the contest," said the PinkyPink president, "I have an announcement. But first, let me ask: Should we let these wonderful politicians have all the fun?"

"Nooooo," said the crowd.

"Should we let more good people of Fern Creek join the contest?"

"Yesssss."

"Then here we go." The president called up a group that had been waiting behind the podium. "Ladies and gentlemen, please welcome some surprise contestants. First, a big hand for these three darling representatives of the Fern Creek Girl Scouts." The mayor checked some papers. "Hmm. Oh, well. I'll have their names for you later. Then we have Hiram Williams, pastor of the Fern Creek Fellowship. He's eighty-five and quite a gum-loving sport. Next, here's Fern Creek High School teacher of the year and former beauty queen, Ms. Ann Saunders. And last but certainly not least, eight-year-old Timmy Truman, who made international headlines after falling in a well and living on rainwater and edible moss for six days." (*Applause, Applause.*) "Okay. Contestants take your places. All set? Unwrap your gum, and...chew!"

"Yikes, Rodney, isn't that second Girl Scout the girl without crusts?" asked Wilbur. "She's waving to someone over there in the crowd."

"Hi, Daddy," yelled the girl without crusts. "Wish me luck."

"And that teacher looks pregnant," said Wilbur. "I think I'm having a panic attack."

"Like I said, Wilbur, let's see what happens."

Mabel nudged Black. "C'mon. We have to stop it now."

"Pipe down, woman. Think of the money. And what do you want from me? It's not my fault those other contestants entered at the last minute." Too bad Mabel couldn't read Black's thoughts at that moment, namely, *No way in hell I'll ever split my huge payoff with the likes of her.*

Mabel felt faint, but resigned herself to accept the wicked plan that had already been put in motion. Trying to picture a stunning diamond on her ring finger certainly helped.

Eight minutes into the contest, Black nudged Mabel and pointed to the mustachioed contestant at the end of the line. "Remember when that guy, Senator What's-His-Face, stopped by Blackeye Pete's for lunch and complained that my *Way Mild Chili* had too much cumin and not enough cayenne? What in the world did he want from me? Butter Bar's cook made it. It was their *Easy Eatin' Chili*. Well, any second now the chemicals will kick in and he'll get his."

The senator suddenly had the most frightful expression on his face.

39. A True Hero

THE BUBBLE-BLOWING CONTEST took fifteen minutes. Except for the state senator on the end who had lost a filling, the contestants were all into it and seemed to enjoy the gum.

"Fabulous flavor," said the teacher.

"I'm now hooked on *Caramel Cream*," admitted the pastor.

"*Caramel Cream* is dreamy," said the girl without crusts. The two other Girl Scouts nodded in agreement.

"Better than chewing moss," said little Timmy.

To the delight of the audience, the other state senator's bushy beard and his huge contest-winning bubble became one. The congresswoman representing Fern Creek had a bubble that continued to expand to such a scary extent—size no longer mattered, the contest whistle had already blown—that the Fern Creek fire department had to be called in just in case. The mayor, not officially one of the contestants, burst his bubble so close to the microphone that it caused a pop so loud it woke up each and every sleeping baby in the crowd. The president of PinkyPink acted delirious with joy. "We have big plans now to go national," he told some reporters, "with our new *Caramel Cream* bubble gum leading the way."

Peter I. Black had turned red as a beet, then white as a sheet. "What the hell happened?"

Mabel glared at Black. "I'll tell you what happened. Nothing happened. We expected Armageddon, we got Disney.

What are we supposed to do now? What am *I* supposed to do now? You said you had the tons of money from Gumm Gum already 'in the bag.' Well, the bag has a huge hole in it. I'm out of here. Take your food truck and shove it!"

"This has to be a bad dream," said Black. "I...I formulated that gum myself. I tested it rigorously. You saw firsthand what the formula did when I tried it out on Chauncey Chambers. I packed the samples myself and brought them here. You know that gum is horrific. This should have been the end of PinkyPink and the dawn of a hellish future for those politicians." Black didn't realize that Mabel no longer listened.

I walked up to Peter I. Black, motioned over Grimes and the same policemen who had cuffed Drago, and suggested the police draw their guns. I felt so in control. No need for any Cow Boy Brantleys this time.

Meanwhile, Mabel became pale as a ghost and started to mumble something about Black.

"Shut up, Mabel," said Black.

"What was that, Mabel?" I said. "Say it so we all can hear it."

"I watched as...watched as Peter I. Black tore open two small plastic bags and dumped white and orange powders into Chauncey Chambers' water bucket in an abandoned barn while Chambers slept. He wanted to check that Chambers' mouth would turn orange—a test way too successful. If there are still some of those chemicals left on the water bucket, they'll match those in that vile gum he tried to bring to the contest. I even think I know where he hides more of that powdered stuff. And please forgive me. I'm so ashamed. I went along with all of it. Blinded by his promises."

Black lunged at Mabel but Watley knocked him back.

"Arrest this man," I said. "The charge, for starters, is attempted brazen discoloration. With the murder of Chauncey

Chambers soon to follow."

I thought Black might implicate Maris Chambers in her husband's murder on the spot, but he had apparently spent too much time in the slammer to know it was best to keep his trap shut.

"Whoa, what's going on here?" said the president of PinkyPink, who came running over. "Don't cuff that man. The town owes him a vote of thanks for helping to make a great event even greater."

I told the president what Black had intended to do, then showed him the H.M. Green lab report's Executive Summary.

"Cuff that man," said the president. "And why is he still standing here? Get that animal out of my sight."

Black and Drago were hauled away in the same paddy wagon and it sounded like a fight broke out inside. I supposed Drago needed to let off lots of steam. What a beating. What a bashing. What a commotion. What a crying shame if someone by the name of Peter I. Black got pummeled.

I hadn't noticed but Ginger had been standing off to the side. She was still wearing her nametag. I never loved seeing it more than I did just then. And wow, did she look great. I wanted to tell her, though I didn't dare tell her in front of everyone. But I did anyway.

"Ginger, you're cute as hell, I mean...cute as a button."

"Oh, Rodney," she said. "I saw what happened with the contest and Peter I. Black, and, well, here's a kiss for our town's hero."

Boy, was I embarrassed, but in a good way. And excited. If she thought that much of me, wait until I tell her I write the *Inspector Grimes Rhymes with Crimes* mystery novels. Though how would I explain Grimes' and Watley's presence in Fern Creek? I sometimes didn't believe it myself. Weren't they figments of my imagination?

"It's a red-letter day for Fern Creek," I told the group

once I put those other thoughts aside. "In the end, the contest went off without a hitch, except for an arrest here and there."

"All's shipshape and Bristol fashion," observed Watley. "And I would say the Inspector here had a wee bit to do with it as well. Proud as always to be associated with you, Inspector."

"Hear, hear," I said.

"I'm not one to blow my own horn, but thanks, my dear friends," said Grimes, "though I would raise the flag even higher for Rodney, whose powers of observation and deduction have come a long way."

"Three cheers for Rodney," said everyone, Ginger the loudest of them all. She even came over and kissed me again. Then she held my hand.

"But it turned out to be a false alarm," said Harry. "In the end, the contest gum was fine."

"So it was," said Grimes.

"How come?" asked Wilbur.

"Don't keep us in suspense," Harry pleaded.

"I suppose some recap is in order," said Grimes. "Rodney can fill us in on the part he played, but as for me, I must admit I owe much of my own success in this venture to someone not yet acknowledged. Actually, the least likely person to be key to foiling Black's vendetta against PinkyPink."

"Least likely? Black's vendetta? But who?" asked Wilbur. "I assume you're not speaking about me or Harry. Is it Ginger? Mabel? Maurice from The Tie Shoppe? Or is it me or Harry?"

Wilbur scrutinized Harry. Harry squinted at Wilbur.

"Not even close," said Grimes. "While Maurice did play an important part, giving me the first connection to Gumm Gum, it's neither he nor the others you've mentioned. One of the true heroes of this story was most certainly..." Grimes hesitated for effect.

"Tell us already, please," said Wilbur.

"A contestant."

"Which one?" asked Harry. "A state senator working undercover?"

"Not quite. It's the girl without crusts," said Grimes.

"But she's only a little girl," said Harry.

"How in the world was she of help?" asked Wilbur.

"I'll start by saying I had the great honor to spend considerable time in the Queen's navy—Britain's Royal Marines Signal Division, to be exact," said Grimes. "So when the girl without crusts organized her crusts on the Butter Bar counter the way she did, as so accurately reported by our good detective here, I recognized immediately that she used those crusts to mimic a system taught to her by someone with experience in maritime communications. In other words, she used...flag semaphore. She must have learned it from her father, who has a background in the U.S. Merchant Marine, according to you, Harry. A crucial slice of information indeed, Harry."

"Always glad to do my part," said Harry.

"Yes, flag semaphore," said Grimes, "but she substituted crusts in place of flags and poles. Consider this chart I worked up last night, which approximates the way her crusts were arranged."

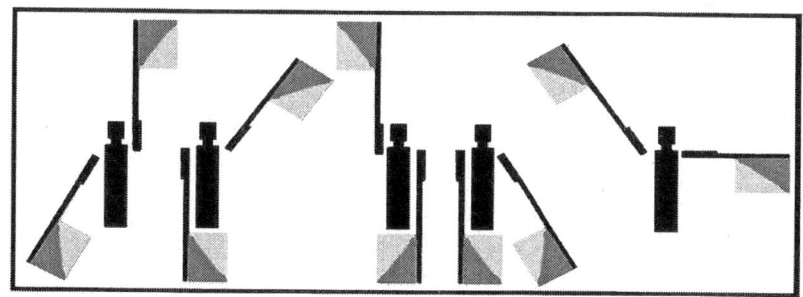

"Does it really say something?" asked Harry.

"There can be several ways to read it," said Grimes. "Most of the visual signals in flag semaphore can represent either a letter or a number. A particular intermediate signal is first used to indicate that numbers will follow, with a different one used before letters. The girl omitted those pointers, but one interpretation, the one I adopted, is that it reads *0 5 4 7 Y*."

"And...?" said Wilbur.

Watley, Wilbur, Harry, Ginger, and the PinkyPink president were on tenterhooks.

"Try grouping that as 05 dash 47 dash Y. Does 05-47-Y sound familiar?" asked Grimes.

"Not specifically, but I do recognize the format," said the PinkyPink president, choosing to listen rather than speak further.

Harry seemed clueless. Wilbur consulted Harry as if they were TV game show partners in an isolation booth. Ginger had been too far out of the loop to hazard a guess, but I intended to spend lots of intimate time with her explaining, in exquisite detail, the ins and outs of what occurred. Finally, I blurted out the answer for them—it had been apparent from the time the inspector mentioned 05-47-Y back at my apartment. "It's the same configuration as PinkyPink experimental gum production codes. For example, Wilbur, you yourself gave me some 10-46-X, *Papaya Porkchop*, to try."

"Shhh. Yeah, I did, but wasn't supposed to," said Wilbur, glancing at the PinkyPink president.

"Now where could the girl without crusts have heard such a thing?" asked Grimes. "Not from Wilbur. Surely not from her friends on the street. It must have been at home. She must have overheard her father say it recently, and he works for...for what company?"

"PinkyPink's rival, Gumm Gum," said Harry, racking up some more points.

The PinkyPink president stood there with his mouth open.

"Can I count on your votes next month?" said the mayor, sticking his nose into our group before moving on.

"It's my turn now, Inspector," I said. "You're right, Harry, Gumm Gum. Now why would the girl's father, while at home, mention a particular PinkyPink production code, either to someone on the phone or to his wife, a day or two before the PinkyPink contest takes place? I assumed it was because that batch of experimental gum had some critical role to play in the events to come, one yet to be revealed, so I broke into PinkyPink at night. I had to pass the night watchman several times—not a problem, fast asleep as usual. Sorry, Mr. President, I'm sure he's a good man otherwise."

"Hmmf."

"I found a box in their product development lab marked 05-47-Y, well hidden among other test batches."

"Which gum is that again?" asked Wilbur. "If that's Black's really bad gum, can you just call it the 'really bad gum' from now on? It would make your explanation easier to follow."

"That's a great suggestion, Wilbur," I said. "From now on, code 05-47-Y will be known as the really bad gum. So even before seeing any lab report, I began to have stronger suspicions about the 05-4...er, the really bad gum, that it might have some truly villainous role in the contest, especially when considering what Harry told us about Peter I. Black's stormy relationship with PinkyPink."

"Always like to do my part," Harry repeated.

"Black, that slimeball," said the PinkyPink president. "To think I trusted him. Next time, it's Butter Bar all the way."

"Wise choice, sir," I said, then continued. "In addition to taking samples of the really bad gum to bring to H.M. Green for analysis, to be safe, I decided to swap some other experimental gum with the remaining really bad gum pieces still at the factory. I came across focus group reports showing that a gum with working name *Caramel Cream* had been the resounding favorite, which made it the prime candidate for use in the contest. I found the supply of *Caramel Cream*."

"This is getting hard to follow," said Wilbur.

"I'm afraid it gets harder still. Luckily, all pieces of gum in the PinkyPink lab have a reusable coded wrapper. I removed the wrappers from Black's really bad gum. I unwrapped the same number of *Caramel Cream* pieces, rewrapped them with the really bad gum wrappers and put them in the box marked with the really bad gum production code."

"Wait a sec, Rodney," said Harry, "let's make sure Wilbur has this straight. I bet he's having visions of good gums, bad gums, wrappers, unwrappers, and production codes swirling every which way. Isn't this right? You filled Black's box of really bad gum with *Caramel Cream* pieces wrapped as...disguised as...the really bad gum."

"That's what Rodney just said," added Wilbur. "Maybe you're the one who's confused, Harry. I understand perfectly. It's the old switcheroo."

"You're both right, but let me go on. So then I dumped the real really bad gum behind some heavy file cabinets to preserve it as future evidence. The story gets even better. It was a double switcheroo, to appropriate your term, Wilbur."

"No problem," said Wilbur.

"As we know," I said, "the real *Caramel Cream* was used in the contest. Only one way that could have happened. Black entered the lab to retrieve his really bad gum just before the contest."

"That was *after* you went there, Rodney," said Grimes.

"Correct, Inspector. Black also needed to disguise his really bad gum. He somehow knew that *Caramel Cream* would be the gum the president would want to use in the contest. He unwrapped enough of the *Caramel Cream*, discarding the rest. He rewrapped what he thought to be his really bad gum with those *Caramel Cream* wrappers, and dumped them into the empty *Caramel Cream* box. That's the gum he brought to the contest. The bottom line: The box marked *Caramel Cream* now contained *Caramel Cream*, not the really bad gum wrapped as *Caramel Cream*, as Black assumed."

"Wouldn't Black have noticed that the gum he was bringing to the contest wasn't his really bad gum?" asked Watley.

"Apparently, all the PinkyPink gums look the same," said Grimes. "Only some chemical components differ."

Wilbur and Harry opened the contest gum they had swiped from the contestants' table and this time popped it into their mouths.

"I don't know how I can thank you all," said the PinkyPink president, beside himself with gratitude. "We would have been ruined if Black's plan worked, and I don't want to picture what it would have done to the contestants. There were three little girls and a pregnant woman and a boy, for God's sake. Horrible."

"Both the Inspector and I had suspected Black all along," I said, "but Black needed to think his plan was still in place. That's why I didn't raise any alarms before the contest, especially since I felt confident any real danger had already been averted. I watched him carefully when the contestants first began to chew the gum. If I was correct, in ten minutes he'd be expecting a really bad gum disaster—bright orange mouths, screams of outrage, disfigured dignitaries, a media free-for-all, the ruination of PinkyPink for sponsoring the event—and when none of that happened, his face gave it all away. That's when I summoned the police and called for his arrest. He was too broken to protest. At some point I expect he'll confess and finger the head of Gumm Gum, Simon Biggs, in the plan to destroy PinkyPink. There's insufficient evidence today against Biggs, but there will be soon enough."

"I've got it," said Watley.

"Got what?" asked Grimes.

"Simon Biggs is the 'Mr. Big' that Maurice mentioned."

"I think even Wilbur and Harry would be ahead of you on that one," said Grimes. "But yes, my friend, I'm sure you're right. Biggs was the muscle behind the plot to destroy his competitor, PinkyPink, and he had the perfect accomplice in Peter I. Black, given Black's obsession for revenge. We still don't know whether Maris Chambers or Simon Biggs was behind the attempts to remove Rodney from the picture in East Harlan. Rodney had eaten at Butter Bar and Blackeye Pete's so often that I'm sure Simon Biggs feared Rodney would soon realize that Blackeye Pete's' food was Butter Bar takeout and spill the beans. That would have ended Black's and Biggs' plan against PinkyPink, at least for the time being. Of course, Maris Chambers had even more reason to stop Rodney, who could stand between her and her husband's millions. And that's still something that needs to be dealt with."

"Their despicable plot was foiled," I said, "thanks, once again, to the best police officer in the whole wide world, the one and only, highly celebrated, often imitated but never duplicated, Inspector Grimes Rhymes with Crimes!"

Ginger shot me a questioning look when she heard that familiar line. Something I'll have to deal with later.

"But it couldn't have happened without the persistence and cunning of Fern Creek's very own, Rodney, P.I.," said Grimes.

I wondered if Grimes knew that ditching a mystery series about him and starting one featuring me was on my mind. I never mentioned it to anyone. He's scary. "All in a few days' work," I said. "Wilbur, what's that you have in that bag?"

"Five jars of Blackeye Pete's Signature Gravy. The mayor said it's great. I was lucky to get the last five. There's one for each of us, except you, Mr. President, and you, Ginger, but I'm confident, Ginger, that Rodney will pour you all the gravy you want."

"Bet it tastes like Butter Bar's," said the rest of us in unison.

Epilogue

I'LL START WITH A CONCERN. My fish are still traumatized from Drago's bomb attempt and I haven't the slightest idea what to do about it.

Next, a confession. I'll feel much better to get it out of the way. I have yet to help my neighbor repair the gizmo that had come loose from her doohickey. Her house guests came and went as expected and she ended up embarrassed, as I thought she'd be, but it still needs to be fixed. I should have bought the three-jaw chuck and topside creeper the sales guy at Dodson's Hardware suggested, but I figured he was conning me. I need to be more trusting. I might go back to Dodson's later today. I'll think about it.

I'm pleased to report that I finally got up the courage to ask Ginger to marry me. I don't know if finding out I'm the author of the *Inspector Grimes Rhymes with Crimes* mystery series helped, but I don't think it hurt. Except she now calls me Randall instead of Rodney. Sitting with her in the playground while she was watching her nephew Corey, I threw some PinkyPink bubble gum to a far corner and told Corey to fetch it. Then I put my arm around Ginger—not just along the edge of the bench as I've done in the past—and gave her a squeeze. Then I kissed her on her cheek and behind her ear and got on one knee and popped the question. I'll keep her answer private, but wonder if anyone knows a good place to buy an engagement ring. I should have bought the ring *before* I asked her, but I'll know for next time, though I hope there won't be a next time. I could also use some guidance on how far I can go asking her to wear her nametag whenever we're together. As I've said before, I like seeing it, especially at Butter Bar when there's a heaping plate of Southern fried chicken and mushroom cream gravy before me. And it may be hard to believe, but Butter Bar's cook and I are becoming close friends. He's already looked directly at me several times and let me poke around behind the counter, and he even spoke to me once saying, "No one flips eggs that way, you jerk."

Harry went back to delivering mail. Well, I shouldn't say he 'went back,' he never stopped. I have the feeling some get-rich-quick scheme of his didn't pan out. Harry insists he didn't try to blackmail Blackeye Pete's, so it remains to be seen who did. As for Wilbur, while I haven't yet discovered what he does for a living, I did find out that he's close to finishing that crossword puzzle he started, but he says there are still two or three clues he needs to ask me about.

Mabel turned state's evidence against Peter I. Black in exchange for a suspended sentence. She no longer waitresses and now eats grilled salami on seeded rye bread at Butter Bar once or twice a week—that's no baloney. And guess what? She and Ginger found out they really are sisters, separated at birth. (Actually they're not, but it was a nice thought, wasn't it?) Betty bought a new pair of sunglasses and a scarf at a glitzy boutique in East Harlan and continues to baffle anyone she meets as to her real identity.

Peter I. Black ratted out Simon Biggs: *He put me up to it. He was the one who wanted to destroy PinkyPink.* Not the whole truth, but it did serve a purpose. They put Biggs away for five years. Black is serving time for his part in the PinkyPink affair. His lawyer got him a reduced sentence because the tainted gum never made it to the contest, but he awaits trial for the murder of Chauncey Chambers. That should be an open-and-shut case.

I hesitate to report that Maris Chambers slipped through our clutches for the time being. She left on the *Queen Mary 2* heading for London. In spite of all the circumstantial evidence, we had no way to stop her at present, but with me, Rodney, P.I., on her trail, she'll get hers in the end. I'll work with the Fern Creek police to build the case against her for when she returns, and if she's slow to return, I'll track her down, to the ends of the earth if necessary. I might even ask Inspector Grimes to come along, to give the dear fellow something to do.

And what about the girl without crusts and her crusts? There's a new sign at Butter Bar for all concerned: *Don't like crusts? Want them removed? Don't hesitate to ask.* What else could Cook do? The girl's a Fern Creek celebrity. Best of all, her father now works for PinkyPink. She can chew their gum whenever she wants.

One more thing. As Grimes' and Watley's ship left its pier—I traveled with them to New York to see them off—the Inspector leaned over an upper-deck railing and called out to me: *Take good care of your coffee table. It is indeed a priceless example of vintage Eames.* It's hard to top that.

Oh, sorry, there's still one more thing. When Hudson's phoned me to say they now stock the ink I asked about, I got the itch to get back to the novel I had been working on. They sent over two cases, so I have no more excuses for slacking off, unless I can come up with a good one. It felt great to dip my favorite dip pen in Freeman's Super Duper Black, light a candle, and start writing again.

Inspector Grimes and Detective Watley had an unexceptional voyage back to England. Grimes deflected a curare-dipped blowgun dart speeding toward a rich widow on day one; blocked an attempt to smuggle priceless U.S. gold double eagles in a box of chocolate coins on day two (kudos to a gluttonous

Watley for chipping a tooth at the right moment); identified which one of the two hundred and thirty-seven identical first-class sugar bowls was mistakenly filled with salt by a careless pantry maid on day three; forced a skeptical captain on day four to veer the cruise ship six degrees to the right before swinging five degrees to the left, thus narrowly avoiding two lost and possibly armed naval mines floating in that evening's dense fog bank; thwarted plans to kidnap the ten-year-old sole heir to the Zipwell Oven Cleaner fortune on day five; and embarrassed the reigning world shuffleboard champion by a score of 75 to minus 20, minutes before docking in Southampton day six.

Deepest apologies for including the above passage. Knowing Grimes by now, readers could have assumed he'd do all that I've noted, even more.

Whoops, my dip pen is about to drip. I better touch it back to paper.

Deportation's a bit of all right, thought Drago, sitting in the middle seat of the InterContinental Airlines 747's 23rd row heading to London. He had nicked some cash from the wallet of the natty businessman fast asleep on his left, and nabbed the German chocolate cake from the food tray of the unfortunate bonehead on his right, who had gone to the restroom.

"Pardon, toots, but I could murder a cup of tea," he told the stewardess, who fought to maintain her composure. He had already almost pinched her you-know-what (she couldn't be sure) when squeezing by her in the aisle a while ago, and he kept pushing his call button asking for a Guinness, even after being told several times that they had only American beer on board. Drago could put on the charm if he needed to, though that was not one of those times.

Yes, all was brilliant at the moment, safe at 37,000 feet from the wrath of Jon Johns and Sir Giles Gilbert, but Drago knew it wouldn't last. They insisted on picking him up in one week's time at the train station near Gilbert's country estate in Hampshire, and he knew they were none too happy about his miserable failure in America. He never should have used his one call to clue Johns in from the Fern Creek police station. Much better to slip back into England and lie low for a few months. The call caught Johns in a foul temper, though he was always in a foul temper.

"You worthless piece of crud," said Johns at the time. "You blithering idiot. I knew I should have handled it myself. Grimes and Watley were yours for the taking."

Drago now regretted passing up the easy shot at Grimes from his rental car when he had the chance. And he knew it would be hard to stand up to Johns and Gilbert without his favorite butcher knife backing him up. Drago and his knife had worked together for many years and it was a sad moment when some crazed American cowboy blasted it out of his hands.

One might say it's ironic, but Drago found no comfort sitting between Johns and Gilbert in the Blenheim carpeted, plush full-grain leather rear compartment of Gilbert's Rolls-Royce. Did they still need his services, or had he now become expendable? And it surprised him to see a stylish woman with killer curves sitting in the seat opposite them. Perhaps Johns and Gilbert wouldn't act against him with her around.

"Permit me to introduce Ms. Maris Chambers," said Gilbert. "She's come into an extraordinary amount of money recently and we've been having a splendid time painting the town red."

Could Drago find some way to make amends? Absentmindedly, he reached into his coat pocket. He had forgotten all about the four pieces of PinkyPink gum that Rodney slipped him before the Fern Creek police carted him away from the contest. He unwrapped one for himself.

"Have a piece of gum, Ms. Chambers? How about you, Sir Giles? A piece of gum, Jon?"

Signature Food Truck Recipes

Butter Bar's
Glistening Ham & Cheese French Toast

Blackeye Pete's'
Hot Buttered Buttermilk Biscuits

Pea Soup's
Veggie-Gel Surprise

Butter Bar's
Glistening Ham & Cheese French Toast

Ginger: Cook will bust a gut if he finds out I slipped you the recipe. Hey, wait a minute. I thought you didn't know your way around a kitchen.

Rodney: That was the old me. And worry not. Cook's recipe will be safe with me, and about a million future readers. Besides, I'm gonna change it up a bit.

Ginger: All right, then. Here it is.

[Word to the wise: Stand way back when serving. Your guests will flip their lids.]

1. Prepare some pancake batter dry mix whether you expected to or not for a French toast recipe: a half cup of whole wheat flour, a third cup of rolled oats, a quarter cup of unprocessed bran, a half teaspoon of baking powder, and a quarter teaspoon of baking soda. Stay on your toes. I haven't been to your house so I don't know what's in your pantry. The baking powder and baking soda in my pantry are in the same type of can, which can lead to errors. If only I had the more usual baking soda in a box. I'll be sure to get that kind next time but the problem is my current can of baking soda doesn't expire until, let's see...well, I'll be. It expired over a year ago. It still seems to work okay. I guess. I've been using it as toothpaste recently and haven't had a serious cavity to speak of. And this same can of 'expired' baking soda also helped me attack a badly burned pan, after I failed to follow the cardinal rule of my

apartment—never leave chopped shallots sautéing over a high flame to pick up, listen to, curse at, then slam down, one of those political robocalls.

For each guest:

2. Mix lots of light cream with two beaten eggs, preferably from hens fed on dried whole corn and grain. Butter Bar's cook keeps such hens out back. Maybe you do too. That's what Ginger told me but when I went behind their food truck, I didn't see any hens, unless they were all under the truck. There weren't even any loose feathers blowing across the ground, although it wasn't at all windy. Or maybe it had been windy earlier that day and they all blew away—the feathers, not the hens. However, if there were feathers that blew away, one could still ask, "Then where are the hens?" Stir in a heaping tablespoon of dry mix.

3. Cut two thick slices of country semolina loaf. Soak well in the above mixture, then refrigerate for one hour. I'm not sure if it's best to turn them over at the halfway mark. I haven't tested the recipe both ways to compare. Wilbur said he did, but I don't believe him. If you try it both ways, let me know if it makes a difference, though that information is likely to be lost to the general readership because I doubt an update to this book will ever be published.

4. Warm plates in the oven.

5. Melt some butter with hazelnut oil in a large cast-iron skillet and fry the bread slices until crispy and crusty on each side. Remove from the skillet.

6. Add a healthy handful of thin-sliced, hickory-smoked

Southern ham to the hot skillet. Heat until soft and steamy, not browned, so the ham stays nice and tender.

7. Don't shilly-shally. Build a sandwich willy-nilly. No skimping on the filling. Pile the ham and lots of mild cheddar and sweet Muenster cheese onto one bread slice. Cover with the second slice.

8. Refry the sandwich in the hot skillet on one side, your choice, weighing it down with whatever's handy that you don't mind ruining, like that hideous bowl your aunt gave you. Turn once and fry on the other side until the cheese starts to rumble.

9. If your guests are hovering over the stove like Wilbur and Harry do at my place, create a diversion in the opposite end of the kitchen. Tossing something gooey on a far wall sometimes works. Secretly glaze both sides of the French toast sandwich with extra butter when your guests turn their heads.

10. Serve immediately with warm maple syrup. Optional: Don't let on that the plates are hot. Ha, ha. Leave it to Harry to suggest that part.

Blackeye Pete's' *Hot Buttered Buttermilk Biscuits*

Mabel: Not bad, huh? Tell everyone you got them here.
Rodney: They look and smell like Butter Bar's biscuits.
Mabel: Well, there's plenty more where these came from. I hope.

[Word to the wise: Triple the recipe shown below, at least. You'll be sorry if you don't.]

1. Line a big blue bowl with a large red-checkered table napkin. Place it out of sight to reduce pre-biscuit anticipation.

2. Keep one-half of a one-pound block of butter well chilled. Let the other half soften at room temperature, which shouldn't take long if it's summer and your central air is on the blink. If that's the case, call my brother-in-law at Reconditioned Conditioners. Mention my name for a ten percent discount. Don't mention it for twenty percent. He and I had a falling out which I would like to mend someday. He was and still is totally in the wrong, but I guess I could be the bigger person and meet him partway.

3. Preheat a baking stone in a 450-degree oven, not a damn degree higher or lower. (Only messing with you.)

4. Assemble the dry ingredients. Hint: Letting your guests feel like they're part of the process makes for a more

congenial group. It also saves valuable time. Mostly, it saves time. All it really does is save time. So ask them to bring dry ingredients from home as follows:

    Guest A—Two cups of unbleached, all-purpose flour.
    Guest B—One tablespoon of baking powder.
    Guest C—Three-quarters of a teaspoon salt.
    Guest D—One-quarter teaspoon of baking soda.

5. Sift the dry ingredients. Quickly cut in one-third cup (five tablespoons plus one teaspoon) of chilled butter until the mixture resembles coarse, stone-ground cornmeal. Don't overmix. This means you. Boo! I thought I'd throw that last word out there. It's getting close to Halloween as I'm writing this.

Work in about one cup of buttermilk. Scoop the somewhat sticky dough onto a floured surface. Toss it this way and that, sprinkling all sides sparingly with additional flour as needed to facilitate handling. Wipe your hands on your pants or dress.

6. Press out multiple two-inch wide rounds with a two-inch round floured and chilled cookie cutter from a one-inch high rectangular mound of gently worked dough. Practice saying the previous sentence without taking an extra breath.

7. Assemble two-tiered biscuits-to-be by placing one cut round over another. You won't regret doing so. There's nothing like the shiny, doughy (in a good way) center of a two-tiered biscuit. You'll know what I mean when you pull one apart later on. Drop each onto the heated baking stone.

8. Bake about twelve minutes until light golden brown unless you like them underdone with mushy middles or

overdone and hard as a rock.

9. Temper some jam, just in case.

10. Fill a small-tipped pastry bag with softened butter.

11. Pipe butter into each and every hot biscuit tier. Don't hold back. Not sure you did one? Hit it again. Heap biscuits high in your serving bowl. Hide with folded napkin corners temporarily. With your best sullen face, tell your guests the biscuit baking session was an utter failure. Then surprise them.

12. Important: Try to convince guests not to overdo. There'll be more for you.

Pea Soup's
Veggie-Gel Surprise

    Harry: They're out of business. How did you get the recipe and why share it with your readers?
    Rodney: Who wants to know?
    Harry: The Bad Food Police. I hear they're gunning for you.

    [Caution: The Pea Soup food truck received minus two and a half stars on opening day from the *Fern Creek Gazette* and closed the next day. The rating should have been lower, but it was chilly outside and the name, *Pea Soup*, so inviting.]

    1. Open two large or five small cans of mixed vegetables, any brand will be fine provided carrots, green beans, peas, corn, and lima beans are included. Dented cans are desirable since they're less expensive, but if any have scary expanding tops, I would strongly consider not using them if I were you. If you can't decide, I've found a coin flip to be helpful.

    2. Drain the vegetables, reserving an ample amount of packing liquid for later use, though not for this recipe. Spread the vegetables across a large surface. Pea Soup uses their countertop. Your kitchen or dining room table should do nicely.

    3. Separate the vegetables into piles by color, being careful not to squash any. You should have a nice gray orange, gray green, gray yellow, and gray off-white assortment.

4. Prepare unflavored gelatin in a large pot. Soften the gelatin by sprinkling two packets over one cup of canned beef broth. Stir over low heat until dissolved. Remove from heat and mix in fourteen ounces of beef broth and a splash of Madeira wine. Note: Two large cans of broth typically equal twenty-eight ounces and you need only twenty-two. Good luck dealing with that problem.

5. Divide the gelatin equally into five small pots and keep each at a low simmer until required. Don't overheat. Move each pot on and off the edge of the flame as needed. If you have four burners, be creative. I would suggest rotating the pots clockwise, others insist counter-clockwise would be best, but whichever direction you choose, there should be four pots on and one pot off the heat at any given time. Some lively music might help timing such action as long as it's not too lively.

6. Here's the exciting part, so stand up and take notice. Plan ahead. Each vegetable will get its own layer. You decide the order, but remember that a pleasing color arrangement will delight the eye and tempt the palate. Hint: Pea Soup's cook does peas first, then corn, then lima beans, then carrots, then green beans. If asked, I would switch the lima beans and carrots, but that's me.

7. Optional: Want to go the extra mile? Choose two of the five vegetable layers to stand out and shine. Stir a teaspoon or two of full-fat, light, or low-fat mayonnaise into the gelatin portions reserved for those layers, then stop and visualize the end result: three semitransparent vegetable layers will alternate with two creamy-white mayonnaise ones. What more can I say?

8. Allow one of the five portions of gelatin to cool slightly, then pour into a large aluminum mold or ceramic bowl. Gently

and lovingly incorporate one of the vegetable piles into the gelatin by hand if possible, otherwise a wooden spoon will work fine. Chill for maybe ten minutes or so. Repeat with the remaining four portions, building one chilled vegetable layer over another. Which vegetable will your guests see on top? First in, last out, so choose carefully. The order will be reversed when the mold is inverted.

9. Chill the completed mold.

10. To unmold and serve: Lower the bowl part way into a sink of fairly warm water. If it's soapy dish water—I wouldn't be surprised if you're still soaking the five dirty pots—be careful not to let any soap flow across the surface of the mold. When loosened, invert onto any handy surface temporarily, then shift onto a well-scrubbed table top, and finally, move to a lettuce-covered serving platter, ideally one with edges decorated with multi-colored dots, diamonds or squares. Pea Soup's cook prefers dots. He says they "celebrate the small vegetable asteroids suspended in a galaxy of gelatin."

11. That's it. You're done. Great job. Brace for a storm of accolades.

Bonus Recipes

Fern Creek School of Appliance Repair's
Double Dutch Chocolate Pudding

Rodney's
Smoked Bacon & Chives Mac & Cheese

Fern Creek School of Appliance Repair's
Double Dutch Chocolate Pudding

Rodney: Is that the whole recipe? There isn't much to write about.

School security guard: Then try to make it more complicated than it needs to be.

Rodney: Great idea. I'll also pad it as best I can. You know, with lots of extraneous verbiage.

[Word to the wise: Mishandling cornstarch often leads to a lumpy end result, but don't be overly concerned. Lumps can be avoided by proper use of a vitreous enameled or stainless steel double-boiler. Besides, there's no cornstarch in this recipe. I stand corrected. There *is* cornstarch in the recipe.]

1. Clean your kitchen from top to bottom, taking special care to sweep out annoying crumbs under the front edge of the stove that you and I both know are there. Some find an old toothbrush to be useful. Others, a wooden or metal twelve-inch ruler. I tried using an eighteen-inch ruler once, but I wouldn't recommend it. The ruler kept getting stuck on what I guessed was a gash in the old vinyl tiles under the stove. That said, the sooner you complete this task, the sooner the pudding's on the table.

2. Prepare chocolate extract: Mix four ounces of vodka, two ounces of water, and three tablespoons of Dutched cocoa nibs. Cover tightly and let sit for six to eight weeks in a cool,

dark place, stirring twice a day. Six to eight weeks! Okay, next time I'll make this item 1.

3. Prepare vanilla extract: Split three vanilla beans. Place in a jar. Cover with about one cup of vodka. Seal tightly and mature for a full ten weeks in a cool, dark place. A full ten weeks? This really should be item 1.

4. Four weeks in advance of pudding day, prepare chocolate liqueur. Combine four teaspoons of chocolate extract, one teaspoon of vanilla extract, one cup of vodka and one-third cup of sugar syrup. Cover. Age for one month in a cool, dark place. Make sure your next home or apartment has plenty of cool, dark places. For example, at least three are needed for this recipe alone. Mix well before using.

5. On pudding day, adopt a strong sense of urgency. Gather ingredients in a jiffy: three cups of heavy cream (not ultra-pasteurized), three cups of whole milk, one sliced and scraped vanilla bean, one and a half tablespoons of cornstarch (I told you so), one cup of sugar, four whole eggs plus one additional yolk, three ounces of chocolate liqueur, one and a half tablespoons of vanilla extract, one and a half pounds of semisweet Dutched chocolate broken into small pieces, and five tablespoons of butter.

6. Whisk together the sugar, eggs, cornstarch, chocolate liqueur, and vanilla extract. Set aside, but not too close to the counter or table edge. If it falls and that was the last of the chocolate liqueur and one or both of the extracts, you could be back to recipe item 2 and/or 3 and/or 4. Who's going to tell your guests they may have to hang around your kitchen for another ten to fourteen weeks waiting for the next batch of pudding?

7. Slowly warm the whole milk, heavy cream, and the sliced and scraped vanilla bean. Bring to a simmer and hold it there for several minutes, stirring occasionally.

8. Temper the sugar/egg mixture by blending in small amounts of the warm milk/cream, then pour the entire sugar/egg mixture into the rest of the simmering milk/cream. Reduce the heat further—no one wants scrambled eggs at this time. Stir, stir, stir the eggs, gently on the stove. Allow the mixture to thicken for a few carefully monitored minutes.

9. Remove the vanilla bean if you can find it, although it's bound to show up at some point. Swirl in the semisweet chocolate pieces until melted. Add the butter to finish. Firmly grip a large wooden spoon and stir in one direction, then the other, until your patience gives out and your craving for pudding peaks.

10. Fill five ramekins of the same pattern, or five different patterns, or some the same, some different. It doesn't matter one way or the other. Assuming there are five guests, serve all five ramekins. If there are four guests, serve four ramekins, being sure to cover and refrigerate the fifth. Three guests, serve three ramekins, etc. Consider yourself to be a 'guest' when making such a determination.

11. The pudding can be offered to one's guests warm or chilled.

[So you say your pudding turned out lumpy? What a shame. Next time be sure to question why a recipe first makes a point to caution about needing a double-boiler when working with cornstarch, then fails to make it a key part of the process.]

Rodney's
Smoked Bacon & Chives Mac & Cheese

Ginger: Isn't this really Butter Bar's *Smoked Bacon & Chives Mac & Cheese* recipe?

Rodney: No way. Check the parts about oven temperature and chives.

Ginger: I already did. It seems like you're still taking credit for someone else's recipe.

Rodney: Then Cook can sue me. Although, if you'll go out with me tonight…

[Word to the wise: Buck the system. Swim against the tide. March to the beat of a different drummer. Go with *egg* pasta in your mac and cheese for the added richness, and make it fresh egg pasta at that, even though everyone else except me and Butter Bar's cook thinks fresh pasta is too fragile for mac and cheese. Well, they haven't tasted Cook's, I mean, my, recipe, have they?]

1. Bring six quarts of water to a rolling boil in a ten-quart pot. If you're in a hurry, cover the pot. If you're not in a hurry, cover the pot.

2. Shred two cups of mild white cheddar. Cube two cups of extra sharp yellow cheddar (half-inch cubes). Chop one small white onion. Ready six slices of hickory-smoked bacon, two of which are a half-inch thick. Find your salt and pepper, and your

nutmeg, which is in your cabinet somewhere. Set all aside, then take a break. You deserve it.

3. Once recovered, preheat the oven to 176.6667 degrees Celsius. Here's the first way our recipes differ. Butter Bar's cook states the oven temperature as 350 degrees Fahrenheit.

4. Okay, who doesn't like dealing with butter and cream? Just saying those two words together plays havoc with my comfort-food senses. Melt four tablespoons of sweet butter in an eight-quart pot over moderate heat. Stir in one tablespoon of bacon fat reserved from a previous breakfast. Add two tablespoons of chopped onion and cook for a minute or so until translucent. Reduce the heat and add five tablespoons of wheat flour all at once, stirring constantly until the mixture is pale blond. Do not let it brown. Slowly whisk in two cups of chilled light cream. Keep stirring. Bring to a boil over medium heat until thickened, then simmer for a few more minutes, having added one-half teaspoon of salt, one-quarter teaspoon of white pepper, one-quarter teaspoon of nutmeg, and (surprise, surprise, a reason to read ahead next time) one cup of warm homemade chicken broth. Add the shredded mild white cheddar and blend until melted.

5. Fry the two half-inch thick bacon slices until cooked but still soft. Drain and cut into cubes. Add to the cream and cheese mixture.

6. Return to the six quarts of boiling water. Sorry to state this so crudely but dump in one and a half pounds of elbow-shaped fresh egg pasta. If I ever test this recipe myself—I haven't yet, but still might someday—I would take the easy way out and use store-bought elbow-shaped fresh egg pasta, even though I've never seen it sold in stores. Of course, one can

always make their own fresh egg pasta. I'm sure Butter Bar's cook makes his own fresh egg pasta, elbow-shaped no less. I could try to get him to publish at least that part of his mac and cheese recipe, but that could distract from my recipe and be counterproductive.

7. Don't overcook the pasta like Harry's mother would. Find a way to keep Harry's mother out of the kitchen if she happens to be visiting. Throwing pasta at her may work. Pasta is done when it sticks to Harry's mother.

8. (Note: I promised Wilbur I would mention his mother somewhere in the recipe, especially if I mention Harry's mother, so this place is as good as any. Actually, I've now mentioned Wilbur's mother so that takes care of that.) Gently fold the fragile fresh egg pasta into the cheese and bacon mixture, then pour all into a six-quart casserole dish. Stud with the cubes of extra sharp yellow cheddar. Bake for thirty minutes or so until the surface is a bubbling golden brown.

9. When the mac and cheese is nearly ready, fry the remaining four slices of bacon until done to a turn, seal with foil and keep warm in the oven.

10. Remove the casserole from the oven and shower with scissor-snipped chives swiped from your neighbor's garden. Here's the second way our recipes differ. Butter Bar's cook uses chives from his *own* garden.

11. Crisscross the casserole with the four bacon slices. Serve immediately, if not sooner.

"Worse Than Murder: Criminally caloric!"

– *Fern Creek Chronicle*

"Mac and cheese to die for!"

– *Fern Creek Gazette*

About the Author

FRED ARONSON paints, cooks, and writes humorous culinary novels. He worked for twenty-eight years directing the international activities program of a scientific computer society based in New York, traveling throughout Europe and Asia with a sketchbook, journal, and guide to local food specialties never far from his side. *Bistro A* was his first novel.

Fred is the author of the Inspector Grimes Rhymes with Crimes parodies of mystery novels. *Worse Than Murder—A Food Truck Mystery* is the first in that series.

Fred is a member of Mystery Writers of America.

Made in the USA
Middletown, DE
17 August 2021